GRAVITY GAMES

ISBN 978-0-9937548-3-8

GRAVITY GAMES

John Matsui

A Nathan Sherlock Foodie Thriller
Book 1

Editor
David Dauphinee

Contributors
Food Descriptions / Recipes
Jill Wilcox

Wine selections
Christie Pollard

ACKNOWLEDGEMENTS

David and Jan Dauphinee's shared love of the written word helped set me on a course where there was no turning back once I started writing fiction.

Jill Wilcox's knack for elevating humble ingredients to achieve delectable results refined appreciation of folks like me for new dining experiences. Jill contributed most of the non-fictitious food descriptions and provided the recipes at the back of this work.

I want to thank Christie Pollard, Sommelier In Training, for pairing wines and other beverages with Jill's recipes and food descriptions.

I owe a continuing debt to sci-fi author A.H. Richards. His wise counsel and master craftsmanship with words gave me seven league boots for my journey as a writer.

All my love and affection to my beautiful and talented daughters Jacqueline and Mary Ellen for their continuing love and support.

And last but certainly not least, to Judy for her steadfast belief in me and for her phenomenal culinary skills that forever ruined me for fast food and put my palate and my head in a space where I could imagine someone like Nathan Sherlock.

TO MY PARENTS.
NO GREATER GIFT EXISTS THAN THE LOVE, VALUES AND LOVE
OF READING THEY BESTOWED ON THEIR CHILDREN.

CONTENTS

CONTENTS

THE NOSE KNOWS

Sunday, May 11, 2014

NATHAN SHERLOCK WELCOMED the chill of Toronto's tardy spring.

His sinuses craved a cold, cleansing reset before the aromatic assault of cabbage, onion, paprika, and all things fried waiting in cousin Johnny's house.

Exhale through the mouth. Inhale, yoga-style, through the nose.

The typical tickles and tweaks announced the frosty rush, then . . .

Ping!

Nathan's eyes popped wide.

Ping! Ping!

The unremarkable-looking 27-year-old the world knows as 'Nate the Nose' lost his practised happy-to-see-you face and nearly his balance.

The wind carried something, something not typical of this white-bread suburban neighbourhood.

Aroma-bearing molecules flowed into Nathan's nostrils and splashed Shoemaker-Levy style into mucus pools.

He steadied himself against his Mercedes sports coupe.

The newly wedded compounds announced their bonding in a chemical chatter.

Nathan half gagged, not from the scent, but from familiar memories now forming a line.

The molecular buzz found an audience. Olfactory receptors without equal converted the announcement to electrical pulses that targeted a specialized brain cluster in the prefrontal cortex.

Nathan's innards thrummed. His mind whirled like a gyroscope.

The neuron pack spliced the news with images stored in sister brain cells.

No, no no, not now!

Nathan's sensory processor ignored his internal pleas, coughing out the answer to an unasked question:

Murder, definitely the scent of murder.

...

Five minutes earlier, Ana Gottschuk's eyes fell on her most precious possession.

The diamond-encrusted pendant fanned white sparks like a star topping the squat, Christmas-tree heap of cash and jewelry on her kitchen table.

That's odd.

Given a few seconds, the 66-year-old widow might have solved the mystery. Before her watch stuttered *TICK*, a bullet punched a hole behind her left ear, ending her puzzling and her breathing forever.

The finger on the trigger belonged to Pete Brooster, AKA Charlie Richman, AKA Jeffery Jackson, and 20 more pseudonyms he'd created over the years.

To ensure Mrs. Gottschuk was among the departed, Pete used the dishtowel-wrapped revolver to pump two more *thirty-eight specials* into her chest and stomach.

"It's not my fault. You weren't supposed to be back for two more days," Pete said to the lifeless body.

A twinge of regret hit him. In the weeks Pete posed as her handyman Charlie, Mrs. Gottschuk pampered him like a son, not that he knew what that felt like. His real mother, even when she was off the booze, wasn't into pampering.

Mrs. Gottschuk had a soft spot for the workman. Charlie was the name of the only child that she and her late husband Herbie had been blessed with, as short as that time had been. Charlie Gottschuk died of childhood leukemia.

During their shared lunches, she showed Charlie photos of her Charlie and of her late husband Herbie. She also showed him the pendant, an anniversary gift from Herbie after Charlie's death.

"It cost twice as much as our car."

Pete shook the memories. He focused on his checklist.

Put loot in toolbox. Check. Get rid of anything that links the real Pete to Mrs.

Gottschuk or her handyman Charlie Richman. Check. Mop up fingerprints. Check. Leave when the coast is clear.

Pete congratulated himself. *The plan's perfect.*

Life has a way of messing with perfection, Pete discovered. A peek through the curtains revealed a dozen people lining up at the entrance next door. More guests arrived in the ensuing minutes.

Must be a party. A bit trickier exiting the house unnoticed but, on the upside, more bodies will confuse witnesses about who was in the neighbourhood.

The street cleared, finally. Pete had a hand on the doorknob when a throaty baritone signalled an exotic car's approach. A Mercedes supercar stopped across from Mrs. Gottschuk's home.

Nervous fingers tapped like a speed typist as Pete watched a gull-wing door rise slowly, for its driver. The stranger stood but didn't move from the sportster. He leaned on it as if hit by a dizzy spell.

Pete's impatience morphed to concern.

Why's that guy just standing there? And why's he staring right at this house?

· · ·

For an instant, Nathan tried to ignore it, wanted to ignore it. A couple dozen steps, a mere twist of a filigreed brass door knob and wave after wave of the airborne emissaries of Norwegian Tilsit, cabbage rolls, and thin merlot will muddle the nasal topography.

But it won't mask the memory, the piercing stench, nor his duty. Nathan detected not only murder, but very recent murder, perhaps murder in progress.

By his analysis, no more than six minutes had passed since gunpowder-impelled death splashed the scent of fresh gastric juices, uncoagulated blood, and undecayed brain matter into the house.

A high-efficiency furnace inhaled the fatal perfumes before exhaling them via the house next-door's pink-trimmed vent straight into Nathan's nostrils.

· · ·

5

The guy's eyes are boring into the house like he has X-Ray vision, Pete said to Charlie.

When something really disturbed him, Pete had a conversation with himself, not the usual weighing of pros and cons, but a real point-counterpoint debate that often got heated. In this case, he used his pseudo-self, Charlie, as a sounding board.

Don't worry, just some rich guy with an expensive Benz, Charlie assured.

Pete wasn't as certain.

But why does he keep staring right here like he can see us. And who's he calling on his cell phone without so much as blinking?

For the first time in years, Pete panicked. His face flushed. Sweat soaked his shirt. He hoped Charlie didn't notice.

At last, the stranger walked toward the blue-trimmed house but didn't remove his eyes from Mrs. Gottschuk's home. When he reached the entrance, he gave one last, hard glance, turned the knob and stepped over the threshold.

Good, he's inside.

Pete's sigh whooshed the plume of fear from his body. He checked the snaps on his treasure-laden toolbox and prepared to bolt out the door.

But wait . . . what's this? The guy is now standing at the side window and is still staring right at this house. What's going on?

Calm down, calm down. He's probably watching for a friend, said Charlie.

Pete's nerves were starting to settle when a police siren let loose with a short 'Whoop-Whoop' followed by ribbons of blue-red-white light flashing through the windows. The cruiser pulled into Mrs. Gottschuk's driveway. An acidic serpent's tongue licked up Pete's throat. He felt faint.

You have a contingency plan for this, said Charlie. *They don't call you Pete the perfectionist for nothing.*

Pete grabbed the loot and scooted to the basement securing himself, Charlie, and their booty behind a false wall at the back of a closet, built during the renovations.

. . .

Nathan found the circumstance disturbing but not strange. By literally smelling death, his life intersected with police starting at age 14. On his way home from school, his nose detected, and he dutifully reported, a woman's death.

It was a homicide. Detectives grilled the youngster mercilessly, not buying for a second that he could smell a body that was scarcely cold. His youthful age, a class full of witnesses attesting to his whereabouts when the murder occurred, and an eyewitness who saw him approach the house, won his release.

That didn't stop a flat-faced Detective Briggs, he of an even flatter wit and an aura of sweat and Budweiser, from thrusting a thick finger at him.

"I'm on to you wise-ass. You're not telling me everything. I'll be watching you."

After weeks of investigation, police deduced whodunnit. Two years passed before they found the murder victim's boyfriend holed up in a vacation shack in Ft. Meyers, Florida and charged him with murder. Many more months passed to work out his extradition to Canada.

Nathan might have led police 'bloodhound style' to the Greyhound terminal before the perp hopped on a bus to the sunny south. The teenager determined that action would buy him a lifetime under the magnifying glass of Det. Budweiser or worse.

The experience taught Nathan to be wary. He had an obligation to do the right thing, but he needed a system to keep life normal. He arrived at a three-step process:

1. Will the body be found soon? If yes, do nothing.
2. Was death by natural causes? If yes, do nothing for a few days.
3. Is death or murder in progress? If yes, call Bonnie.

—

[2]

THE SPY GAME

NATHAN HIT THE SPEED DIAL for Bonnie Nakagowa, his business partner and confidante.

"Type 3 - murder for sure, 1016 Acacia Place. No time for a note. Call 911 from a phone booth a few blocks from your house. Say you heard a scream and a gunshot and then hang up."

"I'll use that Radio Shack thingy to disguise my voice, Where are you?"

"I'm right here next door. I can't leave. People would notice a $200k super-car leaving the neighbourhood."

"Isn't that why you have the Ford Focus?"

"Johnny and my brothers demanded I bring THE CAR. They read about it via Instagram. This has to happen fast. We'll talk tomorrow."

With that, Nathan ended the call and entered the house, showering himself in its Niagara of Eastern European aromas.

He smiled at but begged off conversations with the other guests, parking himself at a window with a clear view of the house next door.

Within minutes, an ear-piercing 'Whoop-Whoop,' accompanied by red, blue and white strobes slashing into the house, cut short cousin Johnny's karaoke songfest.

Guests papered the windows like moths, each trying for a glimpse of the action. By the time an ambulance arrived, half the party was outside. Despite the unseasonably frigid temperatures when the third squad car showed, every guest but one had joined the street throng, smart phones capturing the drama for Twitter and YouTube.

Johnny burst into the house with an excited message.

"Hey Nate, get out here. Some cop wants to ask you some questions."

Before Nathan could protest, Johnny was gone. The house's lone occupant complied but slowly. He ambled to a chair where he'd tossed his overcoat, an elegant, hand-tailored, navy herringbone and slipped it on, taking time to enjoy the rich scent of the fine Australian wool.

His thumb slid across the natural roughness of one of the hand-carved bone disks that served as buttons. A gentle sniff confirmed – ram horn.

"The tailor was nothing if not consistent."

With glacial quickness, he shook out the twists in his navy lambskin driving gloves. As he wiggled each finger snuggly home, the front door opened with a bang.

Framed in the entrance stood a barrel-chested figure in a cheap trenchcoat that reeked of cigarettes and bore the scent and stains of a Matisse masterpiece, coffee and cheeseburger drippings as its preferred media.

"CSIS Intelligence Officer Frank Flynn. I want to ask you some questions."

The gruff agent flashed his credentials long enough for Nathan to see a blurred photo and script.

"Why me? I didn't see anything," Nathan said truthfully. "And CSIS, the Canadian Security Intelligence Service? What's Canada's spy agency doing here? Do we have a nest of terrorists next door?"

"You were the last to arrive, about the same time the call came in."

"I'm not sure about that. There are a lot of people at the party. It's my cousin Johnny's 30th birthday."

"That's your Mercedes-Benz isn't it? That's the SLS AMG GT Final Edition coupe, gull wing doors, 6.2-liters, seven-speeds? Makes you a bit hard to miss."

"Yes agent, er, officer, it is, but I don't think I can help your investigation."

"I haven't explained the circumstances. You may have seen more than you think."

"To tell you the truth, my mind was a million miles away. I've got an important business deal going on, and that's all I was thinking about. I didn't notice a thing."

"Ain't you interested in what's going on? You haven't asked me what happened next door. Maybe because you already know."

"I don't need to ask. I presume that because there's an ambulance and a bunch of squad cars that someone got hurt and not likely in an accident. What

I can't figure out is what a CSIS investigator has to do with it."

"I'm asking the questions. What's a high-flyer like you staying in here unless you're hiding something?"

"It's been a long morning and I hadn't eaten anything so I was just getting myself some food. As you mentioned, I was the last to arrive."

"You're that famous food and wine guy. I saw a program where you ate at the world's great restaurants. I've heard you eat in palaces with kings and queens. You're telling me you couldn't resist filling your face with kobassa, crackers and cheese from the local Zippy Market? It doesn't take Nate the Nose to figure out that something smells fishy here."

"Aunt Lucy made the kobassa. Her side of the family is Ukrainian. Wars have been waged for less than insulting her kobassa," Nathan said.

Agent Cheeseburger was about to make another point when a striking blonde stepped from behind his broad back. Her appearance was sudden and graceful like a dancer moving in choreographed perfection. The suddenness snatched Nathan's breath, or was it something else?

Normally, Nathan couldn't be surprised. His nose alerted him well before anyone came near. This was different. The most prominent scents hitting Nathan were his own. He could smell his pheromones lighting up like a barbecue with burners on full.

"FBI Special Agent Rebecca Jordan, assigned to the U.S.-Canada joint anti-terrorism task force," she said, extending a slender wrist that smelled of peaches and cream, exactly complementing her amazing natural scent.

Special Agent. Wow, is she ever special, Nathan thought as his lizard brain took control, firing messages to all parts of his body, readying them for their most important primordial purpose – reproduction.

She was stunning to the eye but to the nose . . . ? She perfumed the air in a peerless pheromonal pitch. Nathan stared at her speechless. His mouth dropped open. His tongue hung limply. He panted like a lovesick puppy dog. It was love at first sniff.

Everything that his nose detected and his eyes absorbed added to his enchantment. He took hold of her hand and numbly started shaking it. Its delicate, smooth and white-as porcelain appearance proved a deceptive cover for the strength of her grip. Primal instinct all but caused him to bay at the moon. He swallowed hard and summoned his courage.

"Hi, Nate Sherlock at your service."

Why the hell did I say, 'At your service?' he thought as a static-like prickling danced all about him. His skin flooded rouge and warm, especially around the loins.

Agent Cheeseburger jumped in.

"Special Agent Jordan, I was just asking Mr. Nose here why he wasn't nosy about what happened to the neighbour lady and he comes up with the lame answer that he was hungry. Mr. $300 a plate needs a cabbage roll."

Nathan's response was instantaneous and instinctive.

"You're treading on thin ice. Aunt Lucy made the cabbage rolls, too. Besides, I saw nothing. I never met the lady, nor do I have a clue who attacked her. That's the truth."

"I believe that you saw nothing."

Special Agent Jordan's voice was the sweetest Nathan had ever heard.

"That's a relief."

The words fell from his mouth but, otherwise, her spell held him mesmerized and paralyzed. Those gorgeous blue eyes pulled at him like ocean waves. He welcomed the sensation. He started to tip toward her. He shook his head to regain clarity and his footing.

"Now can you get Investigator whatshisname out of my face."

"Not just yet." Special Agent Jordan replied carefully, enunciating one word at a time as if they weren't sentence brethren.

"You've told the truth but you've been far from honest with us. Start by telling us what happened to Mrs. Gottschuk – that's the victim's name. We want you to help us catch the killer or we'll book you as an accessory."

"I don't understand."

Nathan couldn't make sense of Jordan's statement or comprehend the contrast between her aggressive demeanor and her physical charms, which continued to play on him, all promising nirvana.

"Oh, please drop the charade. You know what I'm saying, and we know, that you know, what we're saying."

Through the deep love fog, Nathan managed to remember the need to protect himself, keep the world from learning about his abilities. He needed Bonnie.

"I want my call."

"Certainly, but if it's to Ms Bonnie Nakagowa, Mr. Nose, I'm happy to say we have her in our car," Agent Cheeseburger said with a reviling smugness.

"We can invite her to join us."

At that, the gruff agent left the house and returned moments later with Bonnie in tow.

"Nate. Can I call you Nate?" purred Special Agent Jordan, much more tenderly, as she leaned close to Nathan's blushing face as Bonnie approached.

Despite the clear threat Jordan represented, Nathan remained intoxicated by her in every way.

"We've been monitoring you for some time and the abilities you've shown the world barely scratch the surface of what you can do. We have also seen the role Ms Nakagowa has played in helping provide cover for you."

—

3

THE SIDEKICK

BONNIE NAKAGOWA'S EYES bored into Nathan as she approached.

"You're a strange dude, but no way you're a murderer."

It was late May, 2000 when both Nathan and Bonnie were 14. Police grilled him for almost two hours after the teen reported the woman's death.

Bonnie had come forward as Nathan's alibi. She told police that he had been in class all day and when he left, she had him in sight the entire time because they share much of the same route home from school.

When police finished interviewing Bonnie, she lingered outside the police station for another hour until Nathan emerged. She pounced on him before he cleared the last step of the police station.

"What's your secret? You headed right for that dead lady's door like a fish being reeled in. It wasn't directly on your normal route home . . . uhh, I didn't say that to the police."

Nathan looked at his tiny rescuer. All of five feet and skinny as a bean pole, she looked like she was 10 with straight black hair as she peered through Harry Potter glasses. But she smelled great.

He looked hard at her but shook his head and headed home. *There's no way I can trust her with my secret. I can't trust anyone,* he thought. And that was that.

Nathan lived in constant fear of people discovering the full extent of his ability. The term *people* included his parents and siblings. His weird olfactory powers made life easier a hundred times a week in a hundred different ways. But deep down, his special ability isolated him and scared him. If he feared it, how would others react? If they knew, they'd see him differently, view him with suspicion, and make him more of an outsider.

The first time Nathan became aware of his super sense of smell came a few days after his eighth birthday. He awoke with a start to powerful scents flowing like a river from his parents' bedroom that caused his head to swim. Scared and bewildered, he burst through their door, struggled upstream through the flood of aromas, and screamed as ghost-like odours flew from their naked bodies. Thus James and Janice Sherlock's passion that night came to a shocking and inglorious end.

His siblings heard the commotion. They jammed through the open doorway. The elder Sherlocks, trying to appear as composed as possible while scrambling for covers, muttered something about their youngest having a nightmare and shooed the lot of them out.

Nathan began to protest but 17-year-old Eric tucked his brother under his arm, football-style, and bolted from the bedroom like a fullback toward the goal line. Eric went straight to Nathan's room with 15-year-old Jimmy and 14-year-old Sara in hot pursuit.

"These smells . . . I didn't . . . dad was on top of mom . . . mom was making horrible noises."

"Oh brother!" exclaimed Eric, his eyes rolling to the heavens. "Don't you ever, ever do that again."

"Yeah Nate, are you ever in trouble." It was brother number two Jimmy playing echo boy.

"C'mon guys," said Sara. "He's so little. He doesn't get it."

"Get what?"

"We'll tell you tomorrow. It's . . . well it's just too complicated tonight," Sara said while bidding Nate a good what's-left-of-the-night and ushering her elder brothers out of the room.

Nathan didn't have a good night. How was it possible? His bed, stationed on the centreline of a scent superhighway, left him alone and terrified as bumper-to-bumper, olfactory phantoms rolled over him till dawn and beyond.

The next day, Nathan's parents provided an awkward explanation of the human need for sexual intimacy, filled with scientific terms that Nathan didn't understand. It was impossible to connect his father's words with what his nose had perceived. His father talked about what Nathan saw but, in the dark, Nathan's eyes recorded nothing that he remembered. What haunted him were the odours, and neither James nor Janice Sherlock said a word about that.

Nathan's mind continued to be thrashed by last night's horrifying and unending parade of perfumes. Worse, the powerful aromas from the kitchen, the furniture, the fireplace, even his own clothing, kept coming in unending lines from everywhere.

His father ended his long-winded, red-faced dissertation with, "Do you have any questions?"

"How do you stop those smells?"

"That's just part of it." James Sherlock was not quite certain he answered his youngest son's question but desperation drove him to terminate the discussion.

After that day, Nathan kept things to himself no matter what wafted his way during the day or night. He soon realized that he smelled things in a much more profound way than before. No one else seemed able to detect what he could. He set a task to track down every strange scent he encountered. If he knew the scent and its source, he wouldn't fear it.

With help from his siblings, he later understood what his parents were doing. A trip to the library filled in a few more blanks about the different types of human body odours.

James and Janice Sherlock weren't totally unaware that something was amiss with their youngest son. The family's physician, Dr. Joe Hardy, ran the usual tests, which showed nothing unusual. Under questioning, Nathan admitted he possessed an extraordinary sense of smell.

"What do you smell? When can you smell things?"

"Everything. All of the time."

"What can you smell now?"

"I smell the alcohol on your desk." He pointed to a stack of sealed packets. "I smell saliva, blood and mucus coming from the waste basket. I can smell the peppermint Lifesavers in your pocket."

Nathan sensed 80, maybe more than 100, other odours including his mother's lipstick and nail polish and the three kinds of leather from each of the adult's shoes but stopped there not wanting to be a 'smarty pants' as Eric put it.

Dr. Hardy reached into his pocket and, amazed, pulled out a half package of peppermint Lifesavers.

"Now do any of these smells bother you?"

"At first, I was afraid, but now I can just smell them."

"Do any smells bother you a lot or make you sick . . . like from the toilet or vomit?"

"No. I just smell them."

With that, Dr. Hardy shrugged.

"He's just got one hell of a sniffer. Most people who can smell like that suffer from something called hyperosmia. Difficulties arise when the condition stops them from having a normal life. In Nate's case, this doesn't seem to be a problem. I wouldn't worry about it. Give me a call if anything changes."

...

Six years later consumed in his thoughts and the scents around him, Nathan left the schoolyard as Terry Overholt sauntered by. Terry, the hulking all-star guard on the senior football team, was no star in kindness, or in the thinking department.

Several university scouts had their eye on the huge lineman but they questioned whether they should keep watching. A rumour persisted that poor grades would block his graduation from high school. Terry thought he'd solved his exam woes by scrawling the answers on his forearm.

Terry was no better a cheat than he was a student. His sweaty arm smudged the ink so much, he failed the exam. One more failure and his year and chance for a football scholarship were over. He had been in a foul mood non-stop for two days when Nathan encountered him.

"You'd better get to a bathroom," Nathan recommended helpfully. The words came out of his mouth before he realized he'd uttered them.

"What did you say?"

"Uh, nuthin'. Just muttering to myself."

Whether it was the sour milk he had at breakfast, or a touch of stomach flu, Terry was experiencing a slight leakage problem and didn't need some squirt to point it out.

"Bullshit, I'm going to smack you so hard, you won't get up till tomorrow."

Terry swung a wrecking ball of a fist toward Nathan's left temple. An instant and an inch from contact, slim fingers intercepted the massive fist and used Terry's own force to create a wider arc.

The amended trajectory directed massive knuckles to punch only air, causing the lineman's huge, off-balance body to follow. For a mere moment, Terry enjoyed the weightless euphoria of an astronaut slowly somersaulting in space. Then gravity reasserted authority. The football star came down hard on his back with a huge grunt accompanied by the low bass vibrato of a thick

16

liquid erupting.

Nathan watched, amazed, as Terry jumped to his feet and made a soggy, bow-legged dash toward home.

He shifted his eyes right to see Bonnie smiling at him, the same Bonnie whose statement three weeks earlier pried him from Detective beer and sweat's clutches.

"You're a moron. Why would you egg him on?" Bonnie shook her head and sighed as if explaining consequences to a two-year-old with a flamethrower.

"It just, just came out. But what happened, how did you . . ."

"Uki Otoshi – floating throw. Boy, when he hit the ground, he really shit himself."

"How . . ."

"My family runs the judo school."

"Uh, thanks. You seem to be saving me all of the time."

"Looks like you need saving. I think you should tell me why you need so much saving."

"No, I . . ."

"At the least, you owe me a soda."

Despite his reservations, an hour later, Bonnie had the full story. Nathan felt at ease with her. Her scent was comforting. He knew he could trust her.

"So what do you smell now?"

"Where do I start? The coffee's burnt. The apple pie has about two more day's shelf life. I wouldn't use the ketchup on the table. The grease for the fries needs changing. They use vinegar to wipe the tables and Mr. Clean on the floors. You showered this morning with Dial soap and shampooed with Herbal Essences. You didn't use an antiperspirant and you don't need to anyway.

"That Mustang idling in front is burning oil - Valvoline 10w-30. The guy at the end of the counter is really tense. A big business deal, I think. He should be using deodorant. I can keep going."

"Oh, go on. Herbal Essences, okay, but Valvoline? And 10w-30?"

"My dad uses Valvoline 10w-30. That one's easy. The rest took some prep. What I smell I remember – forever. When I began to understand what I could do, I started purposely sniffing everything I laid my hands on, partly out of curiosity and partly out of fear. When I was young, unknown odours made me nervous. Once I smell something or somebody, I never forget the smell. It's sort of an eidetic memory for scents."

"I-dead-ic?" She pronounced the word slowly, her face scrunched up.

"I do a lot of reading to figure out my condition. An eidetic memory is what they call a photographic memory when you have it for real. You remember everything you see. Well, for me, what I smell, I never forget."

"And it's a complete secret?"

"My family appreciates that I have a really good sense of smell, but they don't have any idea of my full abilities. That's the way I want to keep it. You have to promise never to tell anyone."

"Scout's honour, swear on my ancestral burial grounds."

"This is no joke. I'm a freak. No one can find out."

"You're not a freak. You're like some kind of super hero."

"A super hero that needs a girl to save him every month or so."

"Let's just say I'm your sidekick. Every super hero needs a sidekick."

Nathan rolled his eyes and gave a cautious, "OK, you're my sidekick" but inside he was smiling.

Bonnie whooped. "Just call me Bonnie, Girl Wonder, sidekick to the Nabob of the Nose, the Sultan of Smell, yeah baby! Proboscis Power."

"One more of those and you're off the team." Nathan gave a mock scowl that dissolved into a grin. It wasn't the awful alliterations. It was his relief at finally having a confidante.

—

4

BIG ED

Monday, May 12, 2014

BIG ED HENDRY SAT in his Chicago office happier than he could have imagined.

What was that term? Chortle, yes chortle. I'm literally chortling with glee.

Chubby ripples cascaded along his over-sized frame every time the image came to mind, which was every second minute or so.

How many people could describe finding themselves in such a wondrous mood that they chortle with glee, he asked himself.

Not many.

But how many know a secret like I do?

Damn few.

How many know what to do with that secret?

He took a short pause for another round of chortling before applying himself to the answer.

Just me, myself and I.

And to think that only one month ago, I was afraid all was lost.

The thousands of deals and transactions that the business tycoon methodically stacked one atop the other to reach the apex of wealth and power seemed to be a house of cards, ready to topple without him having anything to say about it.

Imagine that, Big Ed powerless.

Since his 18th birthday, he'd been the one in control and *[chortle]* he definitely was back in command today.

His mind flipped to a month ago, Friday, April 11, 2014.

On that day, his eyes scanned a note for the sixth time as dread gnawed at him like a fast-moving cancer.

The oil magnate's meaty fist shook in anger, so much so that he had trouble continuing to focus on the single page he held in his now bloodless hand.

The paper summarized a computer simulation run by his Chief Financial Officer Rick Summers. The document projected a drop in the share value of Empire Exploration & Energy from its April 11 value of $140.21 to $13.44 before the end of May. That was the good news. In June, it would be reduced to a penny stock.

"When did you last verify this data?"

Big Ed's moods always intimidated Summers.

"This morning. See the date and time at the bottom, April 11, 9:22 a.m.?"

Bulldog eyes darted to the date and then back to the numbers. Looking up from the note, Big Ed's face filled with rage and menace.

"This has to be a joke. And if it is, I'm not laughing."

Hendry, the domineering chairman of Empire Exploration & Energy (NYSE Listing: EExE) was used to setting the market. Now this insignificant slip of paper forecast that shares of the third largest oil, gas and electrical company on planet Earth would plummet – lose more than than 90% of their worth in less than 50 days.

Most important to Big Ed, his vast fortune had the same fate in store.

"I ran the numbers three times." The words came out like coughs, all crackled and chipped from a voicebox fanned dry by fear.

"The minute news of the technology gets out, we'll lose a half trillion dollars in market value. After that, share prices will be in free fall. How far prices will drop is anyone's guess."

Hendry laced his fingers and placed them over the top of his bald, greasy head – a pose he took whenever he tried to work out a complex deal. After a moment, he glared at Summers with poisonous eyes.

"Things like this don't happen to Big Ed. You know why? Because Big Ed doesn't let it happen. How many people know about it?"

"Not many, perhaps a half dozen besides our informant. But there is ..."

"Good," Big Ed bellowed, cutting Summers off. "Buy their silence. Once that's done, buy the technology. We'll bury it so deep nobody will ever know it existed."

Summers dreaded what he had to tell his volatile boss next. Avoiding the task now, however, would mean infinitely more pain later.

"I'm afraid it might not be possible to put a lid on this technology. The researcher, Dr. Plank, has disappeared. So have all his notes and key equipment. We don't know who or how many have access to the technology."

The accountant held his breath.

"If you looked up the word intimidation in the dictionary, you'd see a picture of Big Ed," Summers confided to a colleague. "With him, it's not *my way or the highway*, it's *my way or I'll bury you under the highway*."

Big Ed wasn't just rich. He was really rich. His wealth put him in the top 100 in the world. He loved being in the 100. But that horrid sheet of paper loomed like the Grim Reaper's scythe, ready to cut him down. The words and squiggles predicted Big Ed would not be in the top 100 any more. In fact, he might not be rich by his standards.

Throughout his life whenever he perceived danger, Big Ed plotted his way out of it. And this was the threat of all threats. He faced tough times and rough circumstances before and he always found a way to get the inside track. He flipped open his scheduling calendar and looked at a name and phone number he had scrawled three days earlier.

That name, number and a brief conversation now took on much greater importance. Was this the lever needed to get the inside track again? If so, that meant he'd have the knowledge and the power, not just to keep all his money, but to become the richest man on Earth.

Summers, who was expecting this to be a very, very bad day, was shocked to see the scowl melt and remold into a fiendish smile over that Churchillian chin.

—

5

THE PROTECTOR

BONNIE SCRUTINIZED special agent Jordan. It was loathe at first sight.

The way the agent slinked around Nathan appalled her. She couldn't believe that his eyes went goo-goo over this leggy, six-feet-in-heels Amazon.

Geez. Nate's nose usually makes him a superb judge of character. This bitch is as phony as her plastic boobs.

Bonnie's thoughts headed to even darker places, places beyond the boundaries of Nathan's protector.

Normally, thoughts like that would telegraph scents to Nathan and he'd look for additional clues from Bonnie. That was her job and more than just her job. This occasion was different. For the first time since she first introduced herself to him, Nathan ignored her entirely. He only had eyes and a nose for Special Agent Jordan.

He needs to get centred again, she thought. He needs to get his fabulous brain and super nose working together like he's always done. After all, it's always been Nathan who had the dream. It's always been Nathan who had an exact understanding of where he and I were headed.

While he was mostly easy-going, Nathan's stubbornness could hurt him when, as he insisted, "I know what I know." His precise nasal analysis of the elements of food and drink, and how they blended together, meant he could spot discordant elements in comestibles as easily as a symphony conductor hears a sour note, a note played too loud or too soft, or one that missed its timing.

That proved a problem. When Nathan pointed out the flaws in their dishes, all those executive chefs, in turn, pointed toward the exit.

When Bonnie got Nathan's call and he offered to make her his personal manager and a partner in his celebrity food business, Bonnie hesitated. She feared she could lose her most important personal relationship if the enterprise failed.

After working side by side for the past three years, Bonnie and Nathan's friendship grew as the business flourished. She and Nathan's ideas, work ethic and style meshed so well, Nate the Nose became to great food what Gucci is to fashion.

While not part of any written agreement, her role dating back to their high school days also remained intact – Nathan's protector.

Protector Bonnie now emerged. She inserted her body as a wedge, creating space between the statuesque blonde and Nathan.

"What is this all about? If you know that much about us, you're aware we've been helping the police in secret. Nate's major sponsors aren't too keen having their upscale food and wine product lines linked with grisly murders."

Jordan ignored Bonnie and leaned close to Nathan. Her sky blue eyes filled his vision. Her scent dominated his thoughts.

"We need your special talents to help your country and mine but, first, let's help the local police solve Mrs. Gottschuk's murder."

Then, as an after-thought, she turned to Bonnie: "We'll leave your friend's name out of it."

Somewhere in the edge of his consciousness, Nathan heard faint voices.

"Earth to Nathan."

It was Bonnie's voice so small and far away.

He realized Jordan asked a question but what was it? One by one, the time-delayed words spilled their individual meanings. He reconstructed the sentence and managed a coherent reply.

"I think you can wind things up quickly. The killer never left the house. All scents related to the crime came from the furnace vent. No door had been opened by the time I got there, and I kept constant watch from a window until the police arrived. I'd guess that if you haven't caught the guy, it's someone who is familiar with the house and knows where to hide."

Agent Cheeseburger pressed a speed dial key on his cell phone.

"Our CI thinks the perp's still there. He says there must be a secret place where the murderer is hiding."

Ten minutes later, the gruff agent's phone rang.

"You've got him? That's great."

Clicking off his cell, the rumpled CSIS officer explained how the search unfolded. "Turns out he was a contractor and he was hiding in a secret panel that he built at the back of a basement closet to stash things he stole. He must come back for the loot and didn't expect the lady to be home. So thanks to you Nate, the boys in blue got their man."

Nathan acknowledged the thanks with a smile as Flynn continued.

"Turns out the guy is a whacko. When they applied the cuffs, he started babbling something about Pete not being as smart as he thought he was, and then he told somebody named Charlie to shut up. He really got into it with himself. Creepy, like two guys inside the one head."

"And that's why the world of food is so much more appealing," said Bonnie.

Flynn didn't hear or purposely ignored the remarks. He continued his tale.

"At first, the cops had to look really close at the hidden compartment. The way he was talkin', they thought there might be two guys. They're searchin' for other houses this guy's worked at, find out what else he may be involved in. This could be a homerun for the local constabulary."

Jordan stood well within Nathan's personal space, pressing her body and agenda forward.

"We need your help with a much bigger problem. Your special abilities can prevent millions of deaths. Will you help?"

Nathan turned to Bonnie.

"We've got to help. Isn't this what we've being doing all these years?"

"Okay, but how long will this take?" Bonnie looked at Flynn, then Jordan and then Flynn again. "We need to make a lot of calls to cancel Nathan's appointments."

"Already done," said Flynn. "We got your agenda from Let's Eat and the TV studio. We told them you're on government business."

Bonnie gave the two agents her nastiest version of an evil eye.

"I get this warm tingly feeling when people ask for your help and wait with bated breath for your answer."

Bonnie tipped her head toward the gathering of friends and relatives.

"And you forgot to notify a few others who will be less understanding."

Nathan groaned.

With the agents in tow, Nathan apologized to his siblings, cousin Johnny and especially Aunt Lucy for his early departure. Three years of tight schedules taught him to be creative when circumstance forced a celebrity snub of family.

He asked Aunt Lucy to pack a doggy bag and planted a wet one on her cheek. A minute later she returned with a bulging package.

"It's the size of a small mattress," Bonnie said with a smirk.

"Best cabbage rolls, best petahe (perogies) in the world," Nathan declared loudly, adding a wink to Aunt Lucy.

As for the boys, their frowns inverted when Nathan offered them the Mercedes for a week.

"Don't forget, it only takes super," he said as he walked outside with the boys trailing.

Cousin Johnny and brothers, Eric and Jimmy, focused on the supercar's electronic key like Retrievers eying a T-bone. Nathan lobbed the fob toward big brother Eric whose fingers grasped only air as Jimmy intercepted the black plastic nub emblazoned with its familiar silver tri-point.

A hand signal to his already Mercedes-bound girlfriend and a smooth under gull-wing transition, placed Jimmy at the finish before anyone else set a toe at the starting line.

"I'll drop the car off at your place at noon tomorrow, Eriiiiiiccccccc," Jimmy hollered in his best Doppler effect voice as he engaged all 583 of the supercar's ponies.

"But it was my birthday."

Johnny's complaint had purpose and was possibly fulfilled.

"When/if Jimmy brings the car back, you'll get your turn. Otherwise . . . ?" Eric shrugged and headed back to the house.

"And your favourite sister doesn't get a mention?" Sara's eyes zeroed in on Nathan as the other family members and friends wisely disappeared.

"Girls are smarter than guys. How about a couple weeks at my villa in Tuscany?"

"Okay, I'll take that bribe if you throw in the Alpha while I'm there with my entourage."

"Done! Peace in the family, more elusive than peace in the Mid-East."

"Is your family always like this?"

Bonnie's question, delivered with a devilish smile, was rhetorical. She'd been a virtual member of the family for a decade. Nonetheless, Nathan responded.

"No, they're usually infinitely worse."

"Time to go." Flynn opened the passenger door of a shiny black Chevy

Suburban for Nathan and Bonnie.

Ducking her head only slightly to enter the huge SUV, Bonnie couldn't hold back. "Isn't this a cliché? All the agents in the secret government agencies on TV drive around in black Suburbans. Don't you think it's a dead give-away that you're spies?"

"We're not spies. I'm an intelligence officer and Special Agent Jordan is, well, an agent."

"If it walks like a duck . . ." said Bonnie.

—

[6]

QUANTICO

THE AGENTS DROVE from the subdivision, made consecutive lefts onto arterial roads, connected to Highway 427 South and then headed eastward on the Gardiner Expressway, exiting at Billy Bishop Airport. A private, seven-passenger jet awaited them.

"CSIS owns a Learjet?" Bonnie gasped with a stiff, I'm-a-taxpayer pose.

"The Joint Anti-Terrorism Task Force leases a Learjet," Flynn corrected. "It's a small team covering nearly eight million square miles. I'd say it's a good investment. Besides it has a great bar."

The agents waved at a customs official and, within minutes, the jet screamed its sharp ascent into the blue before leveling off at 40,000 feet.

The jet, indeed, had a great bar. Bonnie and Nathan shared a bottle of Meursault to wash down Aunt Lucy's delights. Agent Cheeseburger agreed he may have been hasty trashing her kitchen skills as he downed his fifth cabbage roll, third potato pancake, and reached for yet another treat.

"We shouldn't let the stuff go to waste," Flynn mumbled helpfully through perogie-packed cheeks.

An hour and quarter into the flight, the Learjet began its descent to Turner Field at Quantico, VA. Another agent in a black Suburban met them at the airstrip and transported the foursome to the FBI offices where they were ushered inside, past the security desk, without the usual credential-checking formalities.

The corridors featured museum-quality displays of memorable FBI moments from their G-man heydays on the tail of Dillinger, Capone and Bonnie and Clyde to more modern episodes as official avenging angel in pursuit of

27

the Unabomber and the last of the Hollywood-style Mafia bosses, John Gotti.

The displays featured newspaper clippings, photos, medals, badges and weapons such as handguns, shotguns and one museum-quality Tommy Gun.

Bonnie's eye held onto a showcase that related the story of the FBI's bust of the notorious Black Sky Ring. She remembered reading newspaper reports about it during the early days of Internet e-commerce. The criminal enterprise ushered in modern e-retail, e-distribution and e-booking processes for its inventory of drugs, weapons and hit-men. Among the assortment of firearms and other lethal weapons, was a huge machete.

"I'll bet that was never used to cut sugar cane," she said with a theatrical gulp. "It's a bit like a movie set in here, but for real."

The sight of the massive blade started Jordan's mind reeling back the years but she refused to go there. One day, I might tell them a story about that machete, but that day is not today.

She looked at Nathan and Bonnie until she had their attention. "We needed to get you here to meet the rest of our team."

Her hand pointed the way toward a form-follows-function, fish-tank conference room.

Nathan looked at her quizzically. "Team?"

"Take a seat. Our superiors will be joining us in a moment." Jordan answered with the first smile since Nathan laid eyes on her. The effect was devastating.

Nathan's thoughts jerked back to reality as the intensity of conflicting aromas hit him in the nose.

His mental list sorted Axe hair gel, Axe Body Wash, M&B black shoe cream, and expensive new leather on one side. On the other came whiffs of Old Spice After Shave, dried sweat on hopsack and a slight pinch from the union of lye and fat – cheap, no name soap.

All of this was spread over the background of formaldehyde-oozing furniture, the aroma of Agent Cheeseburger's cabbage roll lunch, Bonnie's wonderful scent and the heart-attack inducing, sensual aura emanating from Special Agent Jordan.

Hair gel and shoe cream walked into the room and introduced himself as CSIS Superintendent Beauchemin, a 6-feet, 3, cool drink of water. He looked to be 40 years old with a practised Dirty Harry, make-my-day glint in his eyes. He had the air and packaged aura of the guy in charge.

Next to Beauchemin was sweat-stained hopsack jacket. He introduced himself as Assistant Director Jimmy DeRoach, Counter Terrorism Division, FBI National Security Branch. His open smile and extended hand provided a civilized polish to what Nathan understood was a straight-shooter but one you'd be a fool to cross.

At 5-feet, 10 and approaching 50 years of age, DeRoach maintained the broad, athletic body and smooth movements of the college fullback he was 30 years ago. As one of the top operatives for national security, DeRoach's mind must be equally hard and agile, Nathan thought.

Nathan gave the thick, powerful hand a shake and repeated the process with Beauchemin's soft, manicured paw. He looked to Bonnie to take her turn. Her arms were crossed with hands firmly parked in her armpits and an immense scowl creasing her face. He could sense four different and dark emotions emitting from her, all jockeying for lead position.

"Monsieur Sherlock, how good of you to come to help us."

"Goodness has nothing to do with it." Bonnie's terse remark and bile-filled glare surprised the newcomers.

Beauchemin broke the awkward silence.

"Ah yes Mademoiselle Nakagowa. I hope you won't give us any bad press reports."

What a goof, Bonnie thought, adding aloud: "Researching my background is a waste of taxpayers' money. I haven't been a reporter for years and, if I were, I doubt Canada's illustrious spy agency and the FBI would worry about criticism from a small town daily."

"We are getting off on the wrong foot. We brought you here because we need you. The people of Canada and the United States need you, Nathan. May I call you Nathan?"

Nathan nods his consent.

Beauchemin turned to Bonnie and asked, "And may I call you Bonnie?"

"If I can call you Super or Soup," she came back sarcastically.

"You can call me Richard (Ree-chard) or if you prefer Superintendent Beauchemin."

"Is that okay, Mademoiselle Nakagowa . . . ?"

"Okay, just call me Bonnie."

"Ah yes, Bonnie. That's a good name, especially in French."

"We all took French in high school. It's not even a joke. What do you want?"

"Forgive me for my feeble attempt at humour. I'm trying to create a lighter atmosphere to help us begin working as a team."

"Excuse me Monsieur Superintendent, Ree-chard, but my boss here is a $10-million a year spokesperson for Let's Eat Inc. and makes another $5 million as a guest on food shows and for public appearances. I don't think he and I are going to be working with your team."

"It's a big sacrifice but your country, the entire planet really needs you." Jordan spoke in a soft, imploring voice and gently touched Nathan's elbow, sending a cybernetic shiver from his nose to his toes. He started to slip sideways from his chair.

Jordan's right hand grasped Nathan's left elbow while her left slid across his chest to anchor his opposite shoulder. Her face was so close to his that they could feel each other's breath.

"We'll work around your schedule."

"I guess it wouldn't hurt to hear what they have to say," he said.

Bonnie's stone face stopped him from continuing.

DeRoach figured it was time to step in.

"Let's cut the crap." He spoke directly to Bonnie. "We've got a huge terrorism threat and we need your boy to help save thousands, maybe millions of lives. Is that okay with you?"

Bonnie relaxed her frown and bounced her chin twice.

"You've heard of Al-Qaeda," DeRoach said. "It gained global attention when it destroyed the Twin Towers on 9/11 but it's only one of hundreds of terrorist organizations around the world.

"Most people think of terrorism as a kind of global conspiracy. When President George Bush, the second one, declared a war on terrorism, most people thought that we were going to war in some traditional sense. It's not true. Most terrorists are part of a small bunch of people who get whipped into hating a government or some group and are willing to die to hurt them."

"That's right," Agent Cheeseburger said. "The more we try to crush 'em, the more we come up empty handed. There is no organization. There is nobody who's really in charge. Our whole approach, where we try to take down an organization, has been a total failure."

"How is it possible that Nathan can help?" Bonnie flung up her arms in exasperation. "Even if it were possible to define a terrorist scent, he can't be going all over the world trying to sniff them out. Besides, when it comes to explosives, aren't specially trained dogs pretty good at it?"

"We've drawn a blank. We have some evidence but our systems do not have the capabilities to collect or analyze the data effectively," Jordan said.

"That's why we need you, Nathan. You can help us make a positive identification of the kidnappers. You can find things we've missed in our evidence gathering. We can match the clues you find with what we already know."

"Kidnappers? I think you'd better start at the beginning," Bonnie said.

Motioning to everyone to take a seat, Flynn reached into a huge wheeled briefcase and retrieved a half dozen fat folders and a laptop computer.

"Okay, I guess that's my cue since I was the first of us involved. It all started a few months ago with a relatively unknown egghead – a physicist named Gustav Plank."

The rumpled agent opened the first folder, extracting an 8 x 10 glossy print of a guy Nathan thought looked like the caricature of a crazy scientist – skinny, wild hair, thick, black-framed glasses and dressed in a lab coat.

Bonnie couldn't contain her laughter. "He doesn't look very scary to me. He looks like a cross between the uncle everybody in the family tolerates and the all-night pharmacist down the street."

"Looks that way, but the reality is, he may be the most dangerous man alive."

—

7

GRAVITY SUCKS

FLYNN PULLED A SHEAF of stapled sheets from a folder and tossed a package to each person at the table. The papers listed the major events in Dr. Plank's life from birth to disappearance.

He was born Gustav Horst Plank in a suburb of Frankfurt, Germany, the only child of Horst and Gudrun Plank, factory workers. An excellent student, particularly in mathematics, he went on to study physics at the University of Bonn, where he would graduate with his PhD. In 1988, he emigrated to Canada, took a research position in the physics department at the University of Toronto. On March 2, the university issued him a notice that his services would be terminated at the end of term.

The records showed no wife, no girlfriends, no political affiliations, and no memberships beyond professional scientific groups and the Blockbuster Video Club. He usually rented old German-language movies.

"So at the end of May, he was supposed to be gone. I'll bet he wasn't happy about that," Bonnie said.

"No, he wasn't happy at all. He fell victim to the academic rule: 'Publish or perish'," Flynn replied.

Nathan looked a bit closer at Flynn. He comes off as a brainless lout and then fires off statements like 'publish or perish.' Nathan also puzzled over Agent Cheeseburger's placement as a key member of a joint anti-terrorism task force. Is he doing some sort of weird adaptation on the bumbling TV detective Columbo, a Sherlock Holmes in an imbecile's coat?

"Now I'm no scientist. You're gonna have a lot of questions that I can't answer. Let me get through it and we can sort everything out at the end."

Flynn looked to the group and everyone nodded.

"So, this Plank labours in obscurity for years working on something called the weak nuclear force. I can't tell you exactly what this is other than regurgitating the physics gobbly-gook Prof. Coleman, the dean of science, gave to me. Here goes. In all the universe, there are only four pure forces and they create all the other forces we see: No 1, electromagnetism; No 2, gravity; No 3, the strong nuclear force; and No 4, the weak nuclear force.

"So this Plank guy works on weak nuclear for years and years and never comes up with anything original enough to publish. The weak nuclear, if I'm reading my Cliff Notes right, has something to do with the force that causes the heavier elements and isotopes to decay or, in reverse, lighter elements to form heavier elements. That's how scientists can tell how old things are by how much the Carbon 14 in any material has decayed. In reverse, it lights up the sun when hydrogen atoms fuse to make helium.

"The powers-that-be at U of T think he and his research are a waste of space so they gas him – give him notice that at the end of term he's to be laid off. That's when he surprises everybody by unveiling a secret area of research he's been working on. I guess Plank decided this might save his job. So, he starts showing a couple colleagues what he's found out and a tight group in the scientific community starts getting excited. It's clear from what he's describing that this could be weaponized."

"So he's discovered something about the weak nuclear force?" Nathan asked.

"We've already weaponized the weak nuclear force. It's called the atom bomb. This time, it's not about that at all. Prof. Coleman thinks Plank's work with the weak nuclear force opened some doors to understanding one of the other forces – gravity."

"Gravity?" said Nathan. "What could possibly be dangerous about gravity unless, of course, you're on the edge of a cliff."

"I'm gettin' to it. Give me a minute. I've got to do this in order."

Nathan caught Flynn's look of frustration and responded with a silent, body-gestured apology.

"According to my notes, gravity differs from the other three forces because of three things. Number one, it is the weakest of the three forces by a lot. You need something the size of a planet before you start noticing the effects. Number two, there are no distance limitations. You could be a million miles from Earth but its gravity still pulls at you, but weakly. Number three, we've only experienced gravity acting one way – it sucks, meaning it attracts objects to each other."

Flynn straightened the papers, scanned the top page and stabbed his finger on a line.

"It says here that all of the other forces have a positive side – they attract – and they all have a negative force – they repel. But gravity isn't like that in our experience. It is always positive. It always attracts and never repels."

The rumpled agent paused, seemed to wait for some thoughts to fall into place and resumed without referring to the notes.

"Everything that has mass exerts a gravitational pull. But you and I don't sense we're being pulled together because, despite all the cabbage rolls I ate on the plane, I don't have enough mass to create a gravitational field strong enough for you to notice. The Earth is massive enough to make us stick to it.

"Scientists have puzzled over this for decades, according to Coleman. They don't understand how gravity can only be positive. Many have come to the conclusion that gravity isn't always positive and that it can be positive or negative, but not on planet Earth. The theory goes that somewhere in the universe, conditions exist to allow gravity to be negative. What Plank has done is create those conditions on Earth."

Pulling a DVD from the portfolio, Flynn inserted it into his laptop computer.

"This is a video of one of Plank's demonstrations. I got this from Prof. Coleman. Watch and listen."

The computer screen revealed an all-too close view of thick-lensed glasses wrapped around a thin face that was half-obscured by an unruly sweep of hair. It was the man in the photo that the group had seen a minute earlier.

With his head tilted into the camera's view, the scientist addressed the camera. "This is Professor Gustav H. Plank. In a few moments, my guest will arrive and I will be conducting the 14th physical test of properties of materials subjected to the NGR pulser."

"NGR pulser?" Bonnie said.

Flynn paused the recording.

"NGR stands for Negative Gravity Reconfiguration. Dr. Coleman said his best guess is that Plank's device fires a pulse that reconfigures the gravitational orientation of material at the sub-atomic level. Can I go on?"

Everyone nodded. Flynn pressed play.

—

8

DR. PLANK'S RECIPE

THE RECORDED EVENT happened almost five weeks earlier during a demonstration attended by the University of Toronto's Dean of Science, Professor Neil Coleman.

Professor Gustav Plank, in a new white lab coat, greeted his tweed-suited boss with a warm smile.

"Perfect timing. Thank you for making room for me in your busy schedule. I promise that you will not be disappointed. I dare say this moment may be remembered in history."

Coleman was experiencing too much stress to display his calm administrator face. Knots bunched like malformed macramé in his neck and shoulders. An acidic tidal bore stabbed at his stomach.

Plank motioned to a solitary chair before a video monitor. "Please take a seat."

The younger scientist scurried around positioning cameras and mikes and adjusting equipment.

"It's important to record every step — for posterity and science," Plank said while a licked palm made yet another attempt to wrestle a hirsute promontory into submission.

"Watch the monitor. It will give you a better view."

The screen filled with Plank's grinning image. The scientist's face disappeared behind a sheet of paper printed in large letters.

NGR Properties
Demonstration Number 14
Tuesday, April 1st, 2014
After a three count, a hand flipped away the title page. The lens revealed

more words on the next sheet.

Location, Physics Laboratory 105B

University of Toronto

The third page added the final credits.

Presiding scientist: Dr. Gustav H. Plank

Observer: Professor Neil Coleman

Dean Faculty of Science

The final paper dropped from sight providing a too-close view of Plank's upper face and horn-rimmed bifocals. An off-screen mouth spoke in a slow monotone.

"This is the 14th test of the properties of materials I have subjected to Negative Gravity Reconfiguration. For the purposes of this demonstration, I will demonstrate the effects of the NG reconfiguration only. A detailed explanation of the physics and a break down of the technologies and equipment employed will be saved for another day."

More sounds of shuffling were heard off screen, followed by a *click*. The monitor switched to a split screen view with the larger window showing an airtight, glass-walled tank with two hermetically sealed gloves fixed into its side. The smaller, inset screen captured Plank's face.

"To prevent outside influences contaminating the experiment and to guard against any subject materials escaping, I am employing an isolation glove-box. You will be able to follow the actions and reactions of the materials as I manipulate them."

Straightening his thick-lensed glasses, Plank pushed his hands into the gloves and used now-clumsy fingers to grasp a pair of Lucite tongs fixed in a holder at the bottom of the isolation box.

"I am now inserting my hands into the isolation glove box."

The video camera followed disembodied hands as they slipped into the side of the box, bringing the flattened gloves to wiggling fingers life.

"I am now picking up the plastic tweezers. It is very important that the tweezers contain no metal when we are dealing with metallic subject materials."

The pinchers opened and closed in practice a few times before descending toward one of four miniscule flakes of what appeared to be a shiny metal at the bottom of the tank, each in its own numbered petri dish. The tweezers latched onto the shard designated No. 1.

"In today's demonstration, all the numbered subject materials are pure aluminum approximately 0.5 cm by 0.5 cm with a thickness of 0.0003625 cm, about one quarter that of household aluminum foil. I will use the camera's foot control to zoom in to give you better detail."

The tweezers rotated the flimsy foil for a close-up view before Plank returned the sample to its dish.

"I will now show you 'NGR Sample A' which holds the host properties. It is pure aluminum, approximately one cm by one cm with a thickness of 0.2 cm. Its mass is about 1,000 times greater than that of the numbered samples."

The tongs moved to an inverted petri dish with a small 'NGR Sample A' label affixed to its edge. A small aluminum token sat in the centre of the dish.

Plank used the tweezers to grasp the disk. The camera moved in for a tighter view of the metallic object. It's about the width and thickness of a man's shirt button.

When the physicist places the aluminum slug back in the petri dish at the top of the tank, it stays in place defying gravity.

"I will now show that all of the numbered samples have the gravitational properties that one would expect."

The scientist moved flake No. 1 to the mid-point of the tank and then eased the tension on the transparent tongs.

The scrap of aluminum fluttered to the floor of the tank. Plank replaced it in its petri dish and repeated the process with samples No. 2, 3, and 4. Each performed precisely the same drifting to the bottom of the isolation box before Plank placed each back in its respective dish.

"Now look to the top of the tank again. You may have wondered why the aluminum sample did not fall like the others. I have reconfigured this sample for negative gravity. It is not glued to the dish or held there in any way other than negative gravity. I will demonstrate."

As Plank spoke, the pinchers grasped the metallic button and brought it close to the floor of the isolation box. When the tweezers released, the aluminum disk shot straight to the top of the tank and remained there.

Plank repeated the movement, grabbing the disk, lowering it and releasing it. Again it sailed to the roof of the isolation box.

"What you have witnessed is the effect of gravity on NGR Sample A. However, this is not the gravity we are used to. With great effort and over many months, I have been able to reorient the gravitational field of Sample A to negative. Instead of being attracted to the Earth's mass, it is repelled by it. In my laboratory, I have been able to uncover many characteristics of matter at the sub-atomic level. Through careful manipulation of those characteristics, I have been able to reverse the polarity of gravity within specific objects. As startling as that is, the next step in my experimentation provided results that took me completely by surprise."

The pinchers again traveled to the aluminum flake designated as Sample No. 1, grasped it and brought it into contact with NGR Sample A, the button-sized wafer at the top of the isolation box. The tweezers descended with their metallic burden to the mid-point of the tank.

"Now watch closely."

The tongs opened. This time Sample No. 1 flew to the top of the box. Plank regrasped the flake, lowered it and, again, the metallic scrap fell up.

"I was startled to learn that the effects of negative gravity can be passed on through contact with a similar material, just as a magnet can magnetize a piece of iron that previously had no magnetic properties."

The camera captured Plank's sheathed hand as it manipulated tweezers to secure Sample No. 1 from the top of the box and lowered it once more. This time, Sample No. 1 was held an inch from Sample No. 2.

"Now for the really interesting part."

One by one, Sample No. 1 bumped against the other three shiny specks. The instant the metallic shaving tagged flakes No. 2, No. 3, and No. 4, each shot straight to the top of the tank and hugged it tightly.

Plank relaxed his grip on the tweezers and flake No. 1 wiggled free and joined its brothers at the top of the box. He pinched each of the high-flying sparkling slivers and, in turn, pulled them down to the middle of the enclosure. Upon release, each flake flew upward.

The tweezers moved once more to the button sized disk at the top of the box. Plank brought the aluminum disk into contact with a metal spoon on the bottom of the enclosure. Nothing happened. Next, he touched a piece of paper confetti with the disk. No movement. A tiny fragment of plastic was the next target. Again, nothing happened. "What you have witnessed is the change in the gravitational polarity of the small metal specks from positive to negative, thereby reversing the effects of gravity from a pulling force to a pushing force," Plank said.

"The spoon, unlike the small specks of aluminum, has a greater mass than the disk and therefore is unaffected. The other materials, while having a smaller mass than the transfer medium, were too dissimilar in composition from the medium to effect a transfer of the gravitation reversal properties."

The image on the screen switched back to the scientist's face.

"This concludes Demonstration No. 14. Each sample accepted the new properties upon contact. Date of demonstration, Tuesday, April 1. The time is now 2:50 p.m. Total elapsed time, 37 minutes."

Plank uncurled his stooped 40-year-old frame as much as he could and gave another pat down on his uneven sheaf of hair. He gave an apprehensive grin, motioning to the isolation glove box.

"There you have it. I need some more laboratory time over the next six months and, perhaps, a full-time assistant."

"Very impressive. But surely you realize that it's not as easy as all that. We need third-party researchers to replicate your experiments and, frankly, they can't do it the way you did. This area of research comes as a complete surprise to all of us. You've cut too many corners. Your security measures are not close to what they should be, considering the potential impacts that you've described to me."

Dr. Coleman spoke in a gentle voice, choosing each word carefully in an attempt to soften the message to the volatile Plank.

"And unfortunately, Gustav, we both know you've run out of time," the older man said, his voice trailing off almost to a whisper. After a pause he added, "I'm sure there are other universities and research institutes that will gladly bring you on once you can verify your data to their satisfaction."

A raging red face and a hate-filled glare instantly replaced the physicist's hopeful smile.

"You colossal ass."

Plank paired his rant with a physical outburst, slamming both fists repeatedly against the laboratory box, a move that caused Dr. Coleman to blanche.

"Easy, easy Gustav. Please, you, you don't want to damage the box," the dean stammered.

Panic jacked Coleman's eyes wide as his gaze shifted between the angry scientist's face and fists, which continued their assault on the isolation box.

"You are loathsome, ignorant. You're no scientist. You're a bureaucrat. The entire faculty is a bunch of gnat-brained sycophants, not an original idea among the lot of you. This is . . . is the scientific breakthrough of all time and you say, 'Sorry, you've run out of time?' You and all of my esteemed peers can go hang yourselves from your snobby academic towers. You'll all look ridiculous when I win the Nobel Prize and I tell the world of your stupidity."

...

Flynn clicked on the controls in the computer window and froze the video.

"Questions?"

"So, the spoon was heavier and bulkier than the piece of aluminum and that meant its gravity didn't change. For the smaller bits of aluminum, they were smaller or the same size and that meant their gravity orientation was changed, right?" asked Nathan.

"That's the way I understand it."

"And the other things, the little pieces of paper and plastic, they didn't switch to negative gravity because they weren't aluminum?" Nathan twitched his nose when he posed the question, his body's reflexive attempt to gather more information. It found no additional data to solve the mystery this time.

"The way the dean explained it to me, they had to be close to each other on the table magazine."

"Table magazine?" Nathan asked.

"Yeah, I think. Professor Coleman mentioned that as long as the elements were close enough on the table magazine .... wait let me look at my notes. Oh, it's the periodical ... uh periodic table. As long as the elements had the same properties up and down the periodic table they could transfer the negative gravity properties. So in this experiment, the aluminum could infect the other bits of aluminum.

"There was one other thing. The mass of the material doing the infecting had to be greater than what was being infected. Otherwise, it wouldn't take. As long as you had those two things, you could keep repeating the effect."

Nathan didn't buy the dumb cop routine. Flynn played the stupid card too often. He couldn't yet see the CSIS agent's angle. There was time. He had to learn more about negative gravity.

"Let me puzzle this out," Nathan said. "A negative gravity nail can't launch the Eiffel Tower into space. You need something at least the size of the Eiffel Tower."

"That's the way I understand it."

"But he touched one piece of aluminum after another and they all got the negative gravity treatment," said Bonnie. "I'm thinking that one nail could pass on its negative charge to an entire box of nails, one nail at a time. Eventually, you could have enough nails to match the mass of the Eiffel Tower. Yikes! It would be, 'Climb aboard the Eiffel Tower. Next stop Mars'."

"Or deep space," said Flynn. "Mars has gravity, too."

Nathan cast an inward smile. *If this guy's trying to play dumb, he should be a lot more consistent.*

Curiosity now outweighed Bonnie's animosity. "Does the stuff it works on have to be metal?"

"That I do know. It works with anything – compounds that are not pure elements – as long as whatever material gets its gravity changed to negative, contacts material that substantially matches its profile. In theory a piece of granite could change a piece of granite as long as all the component elements are the same. In practice it might have to be worked around a bit."

Bonnie's hands formed a frame that held an imaginary periodic table. She pointed to an invisible square and then described the other invisible squares above and below it. "So if you take silver, it will infect copper and possibly gold and nickel but not sulfur."

"I'm no expert but I believe that's right."

"What about organic stuff like wood? Can you float people?"

"That I don't know. I suspect you'd need Plank to answer that one."

"Okay, I think I've got the technical side covered but what about the threat? Who the hell would want to steal this technology?"

"Foreign governments, terrorists both foreign and domestic, specific industries, and even organized crime," DeRoach chimed in. "Unlike nuclear weapons, terrorists wouldn't need sophisticated technology or stealth. They'd just need a small sample, the head of a pin, and keep growing it to reach weaponized size."

That remark caught Bonnie's interest. "What the heck do you mean by weaponized size?"

Flynn rolled up his sleeves and started to get animated.

"Let's take your nail / Eiffel Tower example. You get a dump truck and strap in to the ground. Then you give it the negative gravity treatment and fill it with huge rocks. The rocks are enough to keep it on the ground without the straps.

"Then you drive toward the White House. When you get near, you trigger the truck's dumping mechanism, a little, so you lose some of the rocks. The truck becomes airborne and has momentum toward your target. When you're up a few thousand feet, you dump the rest of the load. From that height, provided your aim is right, goodbye White House.

"We couldn't shoot it down without the boulders crashing down on its target. The terrorist can keep riding the truck into space or jump out with a parachute. It's a lot easier than hijacking a jetliner or trying to build an atom bomb. It's be easy to hijack an entire fleet of dump trucks. In theory, they can do the same thing with almost anything. It would be absolutely unstoppable."

"I get that, but you also mentioned foreign governments, industry and organized crime. What's their interest?" asked Bonnie.

"That's where I take over," said Jordan.

"My job is to stay a step ahead of anyone who might use the technology as a weapon. The possibilities for its use and misuse are endless. For instance, the mob reverses the gravity of the lead plates in a diving belt. They wrap the belt around someone, living or dead. The solution to the problem is out of this world, literally."

—

9

CLEOPATRA RISES

BIG ED SMILED LUSTFULLY at the notation in his leather-bound personal calendar.

Yes, Cleopatra is back.

When she first called, he dismissed her message as another gold digger from his past trying to con him.

When his own high-level sources related the same story and seemed to know less than she did, he seized the opportunity.

But what's her angle?

Money of course. It's always money.

Money, they say, is the source of all evil. Big Ed begged to differ. He knew money is the source of everything.

The billionaire was accomplished at many things but it all came down to his expertise with money: What it would buy; how it influenced; how to make people stampede to it; how to make people run when they thought they'd lose it. It was this singular understanding that all things revolved around money that made Big Ed so powerful.

He also employed a tactic used to great effect by politicians, mobster bosses and billionaires before him – staying one step from the action. It gave him that all-important plausible deniability.

The task of direct action fell to Richard B. Summers.

Summers was the Chief Financial Officer of EExE Holding, Big Ed's mother company that controlled the largest single stake in EExE, one of the world's premier multi-national oil and resources corporations.

To an outsider, the lofty title made Summers look like a mover and shaker.

In reality, he felt nothing like the successful businessman he ought to be. He made a grave mistake as a young chartered accountant when he hitched his wagon to the Big Ed caravan, believing Hendry's rise to riches would mellow the man.

Two decades later, he realized how wrong he had been. Hendry was every bit as evil, possibly more so than his younger version. Despite Summers' official position, Hendry used him more like a personal secretary than financial counsel.

Summers' office in the EExE Holdings headquarters in Chicago was, well, not an office. His desk, in the anteroom of the large room Hendry occupied, positioned the frail accountant to be available at all times.

Why had Summers remained with Big Ed all these years? That's a question Summers had asked himself on almost a daily basis for more than 15 years, ever since Hélène Augustine walked out of his life.

Hendry's official biography tells of a high school dropout who started work in the oil fields and through hard work, perseverance and uncanny business acumen rose to become the most influential man in the oil and gas industry and among the richest men in the world.

It was the epitome of the American dream, a rags-to-extreme-riches story. That's the official story. In real life, Hendry didn't have business smarts so much as a silver tongue, the ability to play one adversary against another, and a psychopath's lack of conscience when it came to engineering his path to riches with fraud and lies, regardless of the cost to anyone else.

After his parents died in a suspicious fire that destroyed the family's Chicago home, 18-year-old Hendry pressured his sole remaining relative, a maiden aunt, to introduce him to the two rich widows she lived with as their full-time caregiver.

Over a period of five years of weekly visits, gushing compliments, and running errands as a surrogate nephew, he persuaded them, as their financial advisor, to give him carte blanche to execute their stock trades without a signature on every deal.

"See, this was Manifest Gas yesterday," he explained, flashing a series of graphs that showed Manifest's Everest-like spike. "If I we bought the shares here at $40 in the morning," he said, pointing to a narrow plateau on the chart, "we could have flipped them out in the afternoon at $43. But we have to act really quick, quick like only I can. You might have had a 7.5% return in a single day. What are you getting for your bonds, 2% a year?"

Once he had the sisters' signatures, he spent the next two years investing heavily in oil projects he had in play. Some of the projects made tremendous returns, but backdated trades showed Hendry as the owner of the shares. When a trade went badly, the sisters took the losses.

By the time the widows realized what he had done, they were so poverty stricken they had to fire their caregiver of 30 years.

Hendry generously offered to provide his aunt with three-months' severance pay out of his own pocket. She wouldn't be tossed out on the street while she looked for another situation. She didn't make it the three months. Heart-broken over the evil she had visited upon the sisters, she committed suicide.

In total, $5 million of the widows' worth of nearly $12 million went right into Hendry's pocket. Another $2 million went to intermediaries to disguise some of the trades and $1 million went to bribe those who helped backdate the transactions. The rest was lost to trades that went sour.

With the $5 million to prime the pump and a template that had worked so well, Hendry played the same game over and over again, this time as a successful 30-year-old financial whiz with a new Cadillac, a mansion and expensive tastes, adding embellishments here and there until his net worth was close to $20 million by age 35.

That's when he stepped up his game again. He found that bribes to field workers and geologists and occasionally 'salting' samples, to make prospect land look better and sometimes worse, dramatically affected the price of potential resources properties. If his timing was right and with a bit of leverage, he made good money on the way up, and more money on the way down.

He parlayed that trick to bring his net worth to $200 million before blowing out the candles on his 40th birthday cake at a lavish party he threw for himself.

With that kind of money behind him, Hendry elevated his game to the next level. He was in the habit of paying traders for inside tips on major plays to squeeze in his trade. That's when one of them approached him to do 'the big one'.

Whenever a customer had a huge order – so large that it had to be filled by breaking it down into many smaller trades at different stock exchanges around the world – the trader secretly pre-purchased the same securities on one exchange for Big Ed and sold those shares milli-seconds later for a higher price at a different stock exchange when pieces of the original customer's order came through.

By repeating the process dozens of times a week, he made a tidy profit with zero risk. Hendry, who by this time was known exclusively as Big Ed, loved this game.

When the trader initially walked him through the scheme, Big Ed cackled with excitement. "It's like playing poker when you know what the other players have in their hand."

Thirty-thousand transactions later, before the SEC closed the loophole, and just shy of his 45th birthday, Big Ed bought a huge bloc of shares in Empire Exploration & Energy [NYSE Listing: EExE] of Irving, Texas. A few deft business maneuvers that swapped the interest in his Canadian oil sands venture, propelled Big Ed to the chairmanship of EExE and made him the corporation's largest individual shareholder.

At 61 years of age, he now ranked among the world's richest people. Depending on the price of oil, he placed as high as #47 and no worse than #91.

Now all of Big Ed's work, the mighty enterprise he had built, and the fortune he had amassed were threatened. From out of nowhere, came not just salvation but the potential for something truly extraordinary. Something worthy of Big Ed. Something that will be his crowning achievement.

And from all places and all people, the key to everything was Cleopatra.

Of the hundreds of women he had known, only Cleopatra stood out in his mind. And she was the one who got away.

Despite his vast reach, she had disappeared. Girls like her never disappear but, then again, there was no girl quite like her. He had paid the hundreds of women brought to him, not for sex, not to fulfill his particular tastes, but to go away and stay away afterward.

She'd be older. Too old to get his juices flowing the way they did that day.

But she had a new use. He would pay Cleopatra what she asked to come back. She had returned, not to be his plaything this time, but to be an asset, possibly his greatest asset.

How did she transform herself from that shivering, naked 14-year-old to a major power broker with the balls to demand $10 million and a plan to transform that bankroll and Big Ed's vast fortune ten-fold?

The thought of Cleopatra and the money started a stirring within his large frame. As he had done countless times over the past 15 years when the fragrance, memory and taste of Cleopatra squirmed like a worm in his mind, he opened his safe and withdrew that special DVD. Soon he wouldn't need a DVD to stir those memories because Cleopatra was back.

Big Ed inserted the disk into his computer. The screen lit with the image of him hovering over the girl with the letter opener flashing in his hand. Within seconds, he was hard and, within minutes as the video played, without any stimulus other than actions on the screen, he reached orgasm.

"She's the only one who ever got to me. I think it was the scar. Yeah, it was the scar."

—

10

THE SCAR

HENDRY LOVED THE NICKNAME, Big Ed. Although he barely reached 5-10, it was a symbol of his wealth and, possibly, weighing in at 225, his girth. He was wide but not too flabby, built like a brick shithouse, as the saying goes.

Big Ed also had appetites befitting his name. Huge steaks, bold Italian wines, big love – meaning lots of it. He had never married. Never had a girlfriend. The idea repulsed him. After all, what's the good of all this money if you can't do whatever you want, to whomever you want, whenever you want?

His taste usually ran to beautiful, tall, thin blondes. And he preferred hookers. You didn't pay them for the sex. In his mind, all women get paid for sex. You paid a hooker to leave.

He always wore condoms – just in case. Not in case the girl had AIDS or other STD, but in case the sex involved normal coitus, which, usually, it didn't.

Big Ed had a unique specialty. He liked to beat up the girl. Not beat, as in S&M, but beat up. Slap, punch, kick, and in one exquisite case, cut, in that order. His 225 pounds versus some bitch's 120 pounds. Sometimes, when he put his weight behind a punch, he was Babe Ruth knocking one into the bleachers.

In those cases, it was usually a model-thin junkie flying across the room and crashing into his antique furniture or English walnut walls. It made him laugh when a piece of furniture broke or a wall panel cracked. It meant he really put his heart into it. The younger and prettier the girl, the better – 16 year olds, 15 year olds, 14 year olds, but not 13. After all, he wasn't a pedophile. There had to be some womanliness in the girl or the beating wouldn't be satisfying.

If the girl went two rounds as his punching bag, he'd give her $5,000 for the usual, black eye, bloody lip and bruising. If he got a little more excited, and there were broken bones, or some permanent scarring, he tossed in another $5,000 plus hospital bills.

That's the kind of guy he was, generous to a fault. These tramps often get pounded by their Johns for normal rates. Sometimes the John take off without paying. If the girl told her pimp, and she had to eventually, she'd get a second thrashing. The girls and pimps that do business with Big Ed get a much better deal, he reasoned. With the cash he flashed, pimps were lined up to feed their girls to him.

Big Ed never wanted to see the same girl again. What he wanted was to work his way through hundreds and maybe thousands of them leaving his mark like Genghis Khan whose conquest of half the known world was surpassed only by his appetite for the thousands of beautiful women, who, willingly or not, would bear his children. Big Ed remembered seeing an article where scientists verified the Mongol emperor's prowess.

The researchers found Khan's DNA in 16 million men in the area stretching from China to the Middle East, roughly the Mongolian Empire. It was living proof that they were the progeny of the emperor's dalliances.

Children weren't Big Ed's goal. He relished only the thought of thousands of women with marks on their bodies or their psyches from injuries he inflicted on them. To him it was a numbers game. The total number mattered, not the individuals. He didn't remember or want to remember any of them – except that one girl.

It was almost 15 years ago. Of all the hundreds of women, only she stood out in his mind – beautiful, slender, 14, tall for her age. She was different, not because of her straight, jet-black hair but because she had an incredible innocence and resilience, possibly the result of her Muslim upbringing.

She had no track marks, no tattoos or any of the markings of a girl who walked or lived on the streets. No marks, that is, before she serviced Big Ed.

At first, he was unhappy when her pimp brought her. She wasn't a blonde. She lacked the paleness that showcased bruising so well. He should have figured it out by her name.

What did Honeymoon call her? Ah yes, Cleopatra. However, he had an appetite and she was there. What was it that his mother used to say to him? Oh yeah, 'Eat what's in front of you.' So eat he did.

He started by slapping her hard across the face, a full roundhouse swing of an open, meaty paw that terminated with a thunderous smack on her cheek. He expected her to collapse to the ground in a teary pile. The force spun her around, but she didn't fall. She adjusted her balance and stood there.

If at first you don't succeed, Big Ed mused . . . So he did – slap, Slap, SLAP, SLAP!

Each succeeding wallop was harder than the last. Each time the girl's body spun around or lurched sideways. But she didn't fall. She didn't plead. She didn't duck. She didn't cry or beg for mercy like the others.

His hand throbbed from the impact but there was another, more important sensation.

This sensation – a dramatic warmth and rising in his loins – came on Big Ed so fast it startled him. It caused him to take fast shallow breaths matching those of the girl as she dealt with the pain. It was as if they were at the height of passionate, breathless, synchronized lovemaking.

All of this shocked him and, the shock at being shocked, aroused him even more. This never happened and certainly never so quickly. *Interesting, really interesting*, he thought as those devious neurons in Big Ed's limbic system fired creatively.

A deep crimson washed the left side of the girl's face. That colouring would be replaced by black and blue tomorrow.

Big Ed often played a little game that amused him at this stage. He would take a little break to lull the girl into believing the worst was over.

He'd usually smile gently. He'd ask the girl to undress or move in a sexy way. When the next strike came, sometimes when her shirt was over her eyes, the girl would be unprepared and the horror and fear would make her fall to pieces. Big Ed loved that part.

It was just so . . . so wonderful. It would then end with a few hair tugs that lifted the girl off the ground interspersed with kicks to the stomach and the back. He wouldn't kick her in the face. That would be too cruel. Besides, the pimps wouldn't be happy if the girl had to be off the market for long.

But this girl was different. She deserved so much more. But what to do? What to do? He couldn't decide. To buy himself a few minutes to think, he punched her in the stomach, hard, his full 225 pounds behind the blow. The punch lifted her off the ground before she came crashing down, folding her over on the floor like a piece of origami.

She grunted as the hard landing knocked the wind out of her. She gave short gasps as she struggled to catch her breath. But that was it, no tears, no begging for mercy. Big Ed was impressed.

He would allow her time to recover before resuming. This Cleopatra was different. This girl was exciting. He needed to remember this, to savour it.

There was something he was at a loss to explain about her. Even now as she struggled through the pain, there were no tears, no cowering. She lay there trying to get her breath but staring up at him with an amazing intensity.

Then he saw it, an inch above her hip, a ragged scar, four-inches long, all knotted with tiny tucks and eddies of white and pink like a tapestry the width of a finger. The scar was her golden skin's solitary imperfection. To Big Ed, the scar was a thing of beauty.

In an instant, he had an erection. Of all the girls he 'encountered', never before had he experienced anything like this. As much as he wanted to videotape the other girls, he didn't. He wanted no hard evidence that might be used against him. In this case, it was worth the risk. He needed a video of this strange, but incredibly alluring creature.

He almost skipped to his desk, pulled open the top drawer. Next to his pearl handled Colt 45, sat a mini video camera. He set the camera on his desk with a small tripod, focused at a wide angle on the girl, and clicked record. Then his eye caught a reflected glint. Next to the camera lay a long, sleek, sterling silver blade.

I wonder, he thought to himself, weighing the letter opener in his hand. It had a very sharp tip but, relatively speaking, the blade itself was dull, exactly what was needed to leave a ragged scar.

Fifteen minutes later, Big Ed was satiated. Blood covered the girl's stomach and chest.

She winced from the pain and grunted but did not cry out even when he had pressed the silver point through her golden flesh and then slowly, excruciatingly so, dragged the dull ripping edge from above her breasts to below her navel, once, twice, three times, leaving a trio of gory, ragged furrows.

The wounds were too shallow to be life threatening. The salacious part, the part that caused multiple eruptions in Big Ed's now soggy drawers, was the thought that these rough tears would heal into meaty braids but never, ever disappear.

He didn't worry that she'd talk. All the pimps handled their girls well. They all made it clear that if the girl called police or anyone else, they would disappear, as others had before them. As for the pimps, Big Ed was by far their best customer.

If the girl had to 'disappear,' no big deal. He made it well worth their while. Perhaps, he was too generous.

A month ago, that skinny blonde, Dolores, didn't seem the type to talk but, for her pimp Frenchie, a quick 20Gs may have been too tempting a prize.

He didn't say she threatened to talk, only that he thought she might talk and that was enough for Dolores to disappear and for Frenchie to claim the bounty.

—

11

THE ESP TEAM

THE MENTAL IMAGE of someone being shot into space without a rocket or spacesuit left Bonnie and Nathan speechless.

"We'd never find the body and without a body, there's not much chance of a conviction," said Jordan.

"Many industries, especially in the energy field, would be very concerned," added Beauchemin.

"Much of Canada's wealth comes from the export of energy – oil, gas and electricity. When goods and vehicles transporting people no longer have weight, the energy required to move them drops to near zero. That will turn our energy-driven economies in North America and Europe on their head."

"Why haven't we heard of this?" Bonnie asked.

Jordan sighed heavily.

"When Plank first released the information to the university, the administration realized the potential negative impacts and contacted CSIS. CSIS contacted the FBI and between the two organizations, we made sure it didn't get out. We feared it might cause panic, cause the stock markets to crash, cause governments to fall, cause who can tell what else. At the same time, if we can harness this technology, it would be the greatest boon to mankind since . . . well, ever."

"Yeah the rich just get richer," said Bonnie.

"Not really," said DeRoach. "The super rich dominate because they own the means of production, meaning energy that drives machines and makes the products and food that we need to survive. They also own prime locations close to where people want to live and do business"

"And this would change that, how?" Nathan asked.

"Just think about it. If you can turn a gigantic steel tank into something with zero weight or negative weight, the cost of transportation becomes almost zero. Put food, clothing, whatever into that container, get a toy airplane to tow it, and instantly anybody can be in the transportation business," said DeRoach.

"It also means no more shortages, no more famine if there's food somewhere in the world. It will do for goods what the Internet did for services, directly connect consumers with providers. No middlemen, no bankers eating up all the profits," Jordan said.

"It's a total game changer," Flynn added. "Location, other than a great view of the ocean, doesn't matter. In fact, forget my comment about the ocean. If you want to move a cubic mile of ocean water into Death Valley, you can. You now have an ocean view.

"There's a water shortage in California. Put a few negative gravity plates under an iceberg and you can use a toy airplane to tow it from the Arctic to the Sonoma Valley. No more water shortage."

"You'll still have to heat and cool your home and our cars still need gas. We'll still need energy for that," said Bonnie.

Jordan shook her head. "Maybe, maybe not. If negative gravity can be turned off and on, you can have a teeter-totter piston system that literally becomes a perpetual motion machine, generating electricity that will supply heat in the winter and cold in the summer. Zero weight cars would be easily propelled through solar power alone."

"What I don't get is how all of this relates to me," said Nathan. "I can't smell gravity."

"No, but we think you can help us track down the terrorists who kidnapped Dr. Plank and stole his research. We want you to go through the materials that we gathered at the lab."

"Are they asking for a ransom?" It was Bonnie's news reporter side coming out.

"That's just it. They haven't asked for a ransom. In fact, they haven't even claimed credit for the kidnapping or theft. That's why we need Nathan to find out who they are."

"Then why are you classifying it as a kidnapping?"

Flynn raised his hand. "Number one, Plank is missing. Number two, there were signs that someone rummaged through his files and removed them. They hacked his computer and downloaded the electronic files. Once they finished, they erased all Plank's files from the university's computer.

"Number three, they took a number of pieces of equipment. Number four, we located his car at the Toronto airport but there was no record of him catching a flight."

"Unfortunately, that's it," said Jordan. "We don't have any leads where Plank may be. That's why we need Nathan to pick up the scent from here. But first, we need to introduce you to our ESP team."

"Uhhh. ESP? Like extra sensory perception? Mind reading?" said Bonnie.

Flynn gave a big toothy grin that someone new to the scene might mistake as friendly.

"A lot of politicians think that's what it is and that's why they keep funding the program. To them, ESP sounds sexy. But that's not it any more. Special Agent Jordan is the expert on this and, in fact, she's the team leader."

He nodded to Jordan and she took hold of the reins of the conversation. "ESP stands for extraordinary sensory perception – people like you Nathan who have enhanced abilities.

"You didn't think you were the only one, did you? However, even among our ESP team, you are exceptional because your gift is incredibly powerful and you don't have any of the downsides."

Bonnie's chair squealed as she thrust her body forward. "Downsides? There are plenty of downsides, such as being suspected of murder at age 14 and being threatened and hauled in by federal officers from not one but two countries."

"Nathan, you've imagined what I'm talking about. Haven't you?" Jordan ignored Bonnie's comments entirely, which added to the Girl Wonder's growing dislike of the FBI Barbie.

"The ESP program started with the U.S. government looking for telepaths, people who could read minds or people with telekinesis, the ability to move objects with their minds. We soon discovered that nobody had the ability to use their mind to move things. Mind reading was another matter."

The special agent described how subjects were given an ESP aptitude test using Zener cards. The cards had a series of five symbols presented in random order. A tester looked at a card, concentrated on the symbol he had seen and the subject was asked to determine the correct symbol. A number of subjects showed markedly better results than random guessing could provide. The ESP program leaders believed they were onto something.

"That's when an 18-year-old American of Japanese heritage named Seiji Mushima arrived for a test. He scored 100% in test after test. The ESP staff, especially the director, was ecstatic. That's when Seiji dropped the bomb."

"I'm no mind reader. I cheated."

The researchers told him there was no way for him to cheat. They held the cards below a screen and they were scientifically shuffled.

"I can see your faces and that's all I need."

When researchers took Seiji through the cards to familiarize him with the five symbols, he perceived each tester had emotional responses specific to each card expressed in micro facial movements. He spotted the expressions easily and correctly named the corresponding card.

Seiji's comments shocked the program director and all of the researchers. They interviewed all subjects with high Zener card scores to learn if their success was the result of mind reading or something else. In every case, whether the subject was aware of it or not, each had heightened abilities in one of their five senses, rather than possessing a sixth sense.

—

12

SOUND & SIGHT

JORDAN CONTINUED HER EXPLANATION while she led the group to an elevator and placed her palm on a hand shaped pad.

"That's how it all started. Two of our team are ready to meet with you two now. We'll be seeing Reyanna first."

A sign on the door spelled out in large red letters:

Authorized ESP

Personnel Only

The elevator doors opened, startling Nathan and Bonnie because it made no sound. When they entered the small cubicle, Nathan and Bonnie both sensed something odd but traded looks of puzzlement meant neither had the answer.

Jordan pressed a square button on the panel's bottom that was marked with the letter 'R'. It lit at her touch. The door closed silently.

Individuals in the party breathed; Flynn shifted from one foot to the other; Bonnie and Nathan's eyes flitted metronome-like from the elevator door to each other. Nothing happened. Absent was the click of the lift engaging. They had no sense of the elevator moving. Bonnie finally broke the silence.

"What's happening? Is the elevator broken?"

"We are descending 12 storeys underground. The elevator has a unique hydraulic system that runs without the normal noise and vibrations. Without them, you have no sensation of movement," said Jordan.

"We are on our way to meet Reyanna Cortez. Reyanna has an extraordinary sense of hearing and can pick out the most minute sounds and dissect them. For her benefit, we've designed everything around her to be as silent as possible. She started life normally although quiet and introverted. Her parents and the doctors believed that she was autistic.

"A few weeks before her ninth birthday, things changed rapidly for the worst. She complained incessantly about noises. Sounds her parents could scarcely detect bothered her. In those early weeks, their hushed whispers slapped her like a succession of sonic booms. They sent ripples of pain through her body and, at times, made her physically ill. Miranda and Felipe Cortez gave their daughter ear plugs and then noise protection ear muffs to put over them."

"I can relate to that," Nathan said. "I was eight when my sense of smell kicked into high gear."

The doors of the elevator swept open soundlessly and, therefore, without warning.

Jordan motioned to the group to follow and directly addressed Nathan as they walked.

"You are about to learn how fortunate you are. All other individuals we have worked with in the ESP lab have a profound downside to their enhanced abilities. Reyanna is one of our two most gifted ESP team members. Both live here because of the specialized facilities that allow them to function in a somewhat limited but functional lifestyle. Before we see Reyanna, I need to tell you a bit more about her.

"The whispering, the ear muffs and all of the other obvious things the Cortezes put into play failed to help. Reyanna continued to become more sensitive. Any amount of noise made her violently ill and often caused her to go into convulsions. The Cortezes insulated her room against sound. They tossed out their radios. The doorbell blinked rather than buzzed. The phone would flash instead of ringing. The couple watched television in closed-captioned mode only.

"It wasn't enough. The electronic hum of the TV set, the refrigerator and all other appliances became torture. The Cortezes went the summer without air conditioning and without opening a window. They worried how they could survive a Detroit winter without turning on the furnace.

"When Miranda and Felipe Cortez's sole means to communicate with their daughter, the written word, became a painful exercise – taps on a computer keyboard or the scratch of a pen on paper were heard as AC/DC decibel-level bangs and screeches, the Cortezes sought our help. That was eight years ago.

She was 10. Reyanna has lived here ever since."

Surfing over the balm from an institutional cocktail of cleaning products and plastic furnishings, two new streams of flavouring hit Nathan's nose. The first came from Bonnie. One look confirmed her alarm. The second, Nathan realized, came from himself. His clenched teeth and balled fists affirmed what his nose told him. He was afraid, afraid of a vulnerability he had never contemplated.

Bonnie took Nathan's hand and gave what she hoped was a smile of reassurance. Her friend felt freakish and alone when he discovered his powers. His pain was nothing compared to what this teenager had experienced.

Jordan interrupted Bonnie's thoughts.

"Before we go in, I need to ask you to keep all sounds at a minimum. If you speak, whisper as softly as possible and use as few words as possible."

Jordan placed her palm on another panel marked with the outline of a hand. A large section of the wall opened, again silently, revealing a cavernous white space with large waffle patterns on the walls and ceiling and dozens of similar panels hanging like banners throughout the chamber. The lair of a James Bond villain, Nathan thought.

A huge egg-shaped, crystalline structure rose at the rear of the room. Within, a frail-looking teenager with straight, jet-black bangs, dressed entirely in white, greeted them with a big smile.

"Hello, I'm Reyanna," she mouthed silently, as the words appeared as large, green, illuminated, 3-D letters, floating magically before the group.

"Reyanna, this is Nathan," Agent Jordan whispered while motioning to the newcomer.

The chamber squeezed the sound strangely, like a big mouthful of cotton candy that melts into nothingness. Nathan wasn't sure he had heard the words or just read the glowing version floating in front of him.

Those thoughts vanished when Jordan placed her arm over Nathan's shoulders, sending shivers of excitement through his body and ice through Bonnie's.

"He's like you." Again, Jordan spoke to Reyanna in hushed tones.

"I'm Bonnie, by the way. I'm Nathan's friend." Her cheerful up front response carried an nasty tandem rider as she directed an 'if only-looks-could-maim' glare at Jordan.

"What is all of this Wizard of Oz, floating letters stuff?" she asked, making circling motions with her hands at the huge chamber, Reyanna's crystalline pulpit, and her own shimmering electronic dictation.

"It's what I need to keep from going crazy. It's a bummer but I need it," Reyanna mouthed/wrote.

"Just because you hear too well?" Bonnie said, noticing the emphasis in her voice was translated into bigger and brighter letters, tinged yellow-white at the edges. She took the changed colours as a signal she was speaking too loudly.

"Don't take this the wrong way," she said in a much softer voice. "If I were in your shoes, I'd prefer to have my ear drums surgically removed so I had no hearing at all."

"I had that done six years ago." Reyanna mouthed the words glumly but in a weird contrast to the flashy electronic word display.

"Turns out my whole body, my skin, my bones, my nervous system, all act as a type of whole body noise magnet and ear drum. After that my eardrums grew back good as new. "No wonder the ear muffs didn't help. The only way I can leave the chamber is by wearing a special spacesuit that cancels almost all noise and vibration."

"Reyanna, we have to go now," Jordan said. "We're off to see Seiji. Time to sign off."

For a second, Nathan and Bonnie thought Jordan was unaware of the words she used. A faint smile by the agent, highlighted by the glowing 'Time to sign off,' that hung in the air, gave it away.

Bonnie involuntarily groaned at the joke and was surprised to see it rendered in large, iridescent green script as, "Uuuuhhhg."

"I'll tell Seiji you're coming." As Reyanna mouthed the remarks, the same message appeared in glowing green.

"What kind of a life is that for a teenager?" Bonnie didn't expect or get an answer. As they walked away, she felt a lot less sorry for herself and Nathan.

"Not much of a life, but a better one than she had. We keep coming up with advances that give her more opportunities to interact with people. Two years ago, we came up with the current version of the silent suit she mentioned that allows her to leave her cocoon. The suit can be set to dampen sound and vibration by more than 99.99%. The cocoon eliminates 99.9999% of all sound and vibration."

The group exited through the wall panel, which opened automatically, and stood before the elevator door which, unnervingly, opened so soundlessly and suddenly that again it startled Bonnie and Nathan.

Agent Jordan moved her long, immaculately manicured index finger midway up the row of numbered and lettered squares and pressed on one marked with an 'S'. Again, sound and a sensation of movement were absent.

"This Seiji . . . does he live like that, too?" Nathan's question broke the silence, his face varnished with uneasiness.

"No, the limitations on Seiji are nothing like those Reyanna has to live with. Still, we are concerned because his vulnerabilities seem to be getting worse. When he first came to our attention at age 18, he had almost no side effects other than the need to wear very dark sunglasses, a propensity to get easily sunburned, and an obsession with complete darkness."

Jordan explained that after Seiji's gift was uncovered, he worked on an as-needed-basis for the FBI's ESP Team.

"Otherwise, he lived a normal life. He trained as an engineer and worked for a company that identified weaknesses in boilers and other machinery. Seiji's natural abilities allowed him to see infrared hot spots and electrical failures in their earliest stages far more quickly and accurately than the best equipment."

The agent with the super visual abilities made a good living until his late 20s when his powers outstripped his ability to control them.

"At age 28, he came to stay with us. He's 39 now and must wear large, specially designed goggles indoors and outdoors. He can't tolerate any daylight on his skin. When he ventures outdoors, he must to be covered head-to-toe in a special fabric."

As direct as always, Bonnie let loose at Jordan. "And you keep him caged like Reyanna?"

"No, Seiji is free to come and go as he likes. He lives here but also has a private apartment near here to keep himself sane. He can only be there for so long before he needs the absolute darkness that only our facilities can provide."

"His exceptional sensory perception is . . . super vision, like Superman?" asked Bonnie.

"We describe Seiji's ability as being extreme vision. His vision captures the full range of vision in all animal types. He can see further and clearer than a golden eagle. He can bring things up to five kilometres away into clear focus as long as humidity isn't high.

After we taught him how to read lips, he became a star in our intelligence arena.

"He sees light beyond normal vision wavelengths, in the ultraviolet and infrared ranges and beyond. He can focus on extremely small objects, microscopic objects and identify them. It isn't just his eyes. His whole body acts as a form of light funnel, much like the giant mirror an observatory may use to gather light and concentrate it for viewing. He can see things happening behind his back."

The elevator doors opened into complete darkness beyond the lift's threshold.

The blackout was so complete, Nathan hesitated making a move for fear his foot would paw at nothingness, before his body tipped to its screaming doom into a bottomless void.

Agent Jordan ventured a shapely leg outside the elevator. A nanosecond before her heel touched ground or nothing, introducing her to her ancestors, a faint glow illuminated the path ahead. Bonnie and Nathan followed her single-file, neither daring to test a toe beyond the edge of the glowing path that vanished into the gloom behind them. Twenty paces later, the path broadened to encompass an area with three egg-shaped chairs.

"Please be seated Ms Nakagowa, Mr. Sherlock and, of course, you Rebecca," came a disembodied voice.

"Forgive me if I keep the lighting low. I've had a trying two days in Toronto. I prefer not to overdo it. I'm trying to see if I can possibly shorten the usual five days of migraines and nausea when I hit that state. But, enough of me. I am very glad to see you. Albeit, it's a bit one-sided. Despite what you perceive as darkness, I see all of you as clearly as festively-lit Christmas trees. I do have a question, however, for Ms Nakagowa."

"And what is that," Bonnie asked.

"Your family name is Japanese as is mine, Seiji Mushima."

"Yes, I'm aware of that."

"What area of Japan does your family come from?"

"I can't answer that. My parents were both born in an internment camp for Japanese- Canadians in the interior of British Columbia during the Second World War. They never talk about it and that includes anything about our family's past in Japan. But why do you ask?"

"I suppose it's silly but my gift allows me to see things that are imperceptible to others and be able to piece them together in ways no one else can."

"And you see something in me, perhaps something about where in Japan my family originated?" said Bonnie.

"Precisely."

"Do tell. I'd be interested in anything you can pick up."

"I hate to toss you a curveball, especially on our first meeting, but your family lineage originates in Korea, not in Japan."

"Korea? But that's impossible."

"Not really. Koreans and Japanese have crossed the Sea of Japan, or as Koreans call it, the East Sea, for thousands of years. It's not surprising that many Japanese and Koreans have blood originating in the other country. What I find interesting is your bloodline is pure Korean. Koreans bear the closest resemblance to Japanese and Japanese to Koreans of all the other Asian nations. Natives of each country may have difficulty identifying whether certain individuals are Korean or Japanese. That would certainly be true in your case. However, the height and width of your cheek bones, your forehead, the colour of your skin, your ears and how you move, while close to Japanese, are all undiluted Korean."

"I'm sure you're mistaken."

"I can tell from your infrared heat signature that I have insulted you and that in your mind your bloodline is pure Japanese. I am sorry. I apologize profusely."

Bonnie said nothing but Nathan's nose told him Seiji's interpretation of her reaction was spot on. There was also no acceptance of the apology. Nathan determined he'd better direct the conversation along a different path because, with Bonnie's attitude toward Agent Jordan and now Seiji, things were about to get really ugly.

"So what were you doing in Canada?" Nathan chimed in as cheerily as he could.

Nathan heard a tiny hum and then a faint glow lit the head and shoulders and outlined the surroundings of a man wearing big, dark goggles, who he presumed was Seiji. The man, sitting in a floating oblong bubble like Reyanna's, began to speak.

"It's the same reason why you're here."

"I'll take it from here," said Agent Jordan. "In this case, it is Seiji's ability to see the tiniest objects, things much smaller than the average human being can detect with the most powerful magnifying glass. After Dr. Plank was reported missing, police dispatched a crack CSI team to search for clues. They found none. There were no fingerprints, no bits of spittle or other fluids, and no hairs with follicles intact. There was nothing found that could provide a DNA sample.

"We thought Seiji could do better. Over the last two days, Seiji went through Dr. Plank's office, the lab he worked in, his car, and the equipment lockers – anywhere a potential kidnapper might have been."

Seiji started in again. "When I leave the Egg, I use a special set of goggles that allows me to walk freely in society, if you consider it walking freely when everyone looks at you like you're Cyclops from the X-Men. The goggles can be adjusted so my eyes are not absorbing more light than necessary and only the type of light I want.

"I set the goggles at as high a light level as I could take for 15 minute intervals. During that time I collected microscopic samples that no CSI could see let alone collect. I sorted the samples into groups that looked the same.

"For instance, I collected hundreds of skin samples too small for the human eye to detect. The trouble is, even with my great eyesight, most dead skin samples pretty well look the same. We figured if you could sniff out the difference, it could save us months of trial and error."

"I'll certainly give it a try."

"That's all we're asking," said Jordan.

That's all we're asking, Bonnie mockingly repeated in her head, adding, *I think that was the same pitch she made to Doctor Faustus.*

—

13

NOSING AROUND

THE GROUP BADE the goggled agent adieu and retreated to the elevator. Seiji's story alarmed Bonnie. She noticed how quiet Nathan had been with both ESP agents. She felt a foreboding for Nathan that she never experienced before.

Nathan's hyper acuity to odours, as Bonnie often explained it, or a super sense of smell, according to media reports, had given the two of them the good life.

The Toronto Clarion food review, the Nate the Nose Food & Wine TV series, and the 2.2 million Twitter followers whisked Nathan from dull, old Etobicoke to become the world's most celebrated chef and wine connoisseur by the age of 21.

The public's appetite for his food and wine insights was insatiable. Within the past 12 months, the Nate the Nose series ranked as North America's No. 1 TV food show. He had three foodie specials and appeared as a judge on television programs in the UK, Australia, France, Japan, Italy, and Brazil. Three weeks ago, hooked by an eight-figure salary, Nathan became adviser and celebrity pitchman for international food conglomerate, Let's Eat Inc. Let's Eat threw in the Mercedes supercar as a signing bonus.

They knew that those afflicted with hyperosmia are often debilitated – rendered unable to function because they are overwhelmed by an extreme sensitivity to a vast array of odours. But not Nathan. He never experienced any side effects.

In interviews, he alternately described scents in terms of colours, musical tones, harmonies and textures.

"I'm not repulsed by any odour to any degree, even the ones that normally nauseate people," he told Ascot Magazine. "I sense it differently. I may not love the odour but, at worst, I wince like someone not liking a specific colour scheme, the feel of worms, or a sour note in a piece of music. Conversely, if an aroma is magnificent, I'm in a rapture as if entranced by great music or a powerful emotion. Some amazing scents bring me to tears."

It was all good and kept getting better. The question never arose whether his rare form of hyperosmia might one day impact his health or quality of life.

Seiji's experience rattled Bonnie. Like Nathan, Seiji functioned well in society but then something caused his powers to overwhelm him.

Slowly, the agent with the immaculate vision had to withdraw from normal society and now lives like a high-tech hermit.

The worst side effects hit Seiji when he turned 28 . . . . 28. Nathan is 27. Bonnie had noticed the faint signs that Nathan's breathing had been slow and steady, his typical way of taking inventory of all the scents while in Seiji's chamber. Possibly he was testing himself, testing to see if he was experiencing any of the side effects. Was his nose functioning normally with no nausea or hint of a headache? Reyanna was nine when her powers overwhelmed her. Could this be something Nathan will face months or years from now?

Bonnie snapped back to the present. Agent Jordan was saying something and moving.

"Our next stop is the forensic evidence lab."

The foursome entered the elevator and after a silent ride up a few floors to level F, the doors opened to reveal a traditional looking hallway with glassed in offices and labs on either side. Agent Jordan walked to the third door on the left, opened it and motioned the others to enter the laboratory.

Flynn walked up to a tall woman in a white lab coat. The woman stood beside a table stacked with a variety of electronic and other scientific equipment, including an isolation glove box, and a half dozen lab coats. At the back of the lab, they saw an older model Mazda 3 parked snuggly inside something resembling a giant, glass cake cover.

As Nathan went about sniffing through the scientific equipment, Bonnie asked, "What's up with the car?"

"That six-year-old car is owned by Plank," Jordan explained. "We believe the kidnappers used it to take Plank to their hideout and abandoned it at Toronto's Pearson Airport."

"You brought the car all the way here from Toronto?" Bonnie asked incredulously.

"Weren't you afraid of corrupting the evidence on the drive here?"

"The car's been sealed since we found it at the airport. We airlifted it here."

"You airlifted a car here?" Bonnie's taxpayer voice emerged once more.

"We airlift everything. We have a Marine Corps Air Facility next to us and when it comes to terrorism, everybody cooperates. We needed the car and all the equipment from Plank's lab here because we have the best people and the best forensic tools in the world.

We thought we could crack it without Nathan's services. We were wrong."

"Well, you should have left everything back in Toronto. Nathan's compiled a list of everything he smells in a database. We can pinpoint scents not just by name but by their locations," said Bonnie.

"We're looking for specific things. I'm sure those resources won't be needed. Besides, the car is here," said Jordan.

"Question!" The Girl Wonder waved her hand, in a mock impersonation of a high schooler trying to impress the teacher.

"Yes?" Jordan's single word response played on Bonnie's tone and countered it with her interpretation of an impatient teacher forced to tolerate a troublesome student.

"How the hell did you even find the car? There's got to be tens of thousands parked at Pearson."

"We lucked out. They parked it in one of those long-term outdoor lots so it was easy for Seiji to pick it out when we flew over."

"He picked it out from the air?" Bonnie's face showed genuine astonishment.

"It wasn't as easy as that. We had to find a car of the same vintage and colour for him to use as a comparison. Then we flew across Toronto six times. We passed over every shopping centre and commuter parking lot before we received clearance to take a peek at Pearson. Believe me, that was the hardest part, getting leave to fly over an international airport in a nontraditional pattern."

"But he . . . he could pick out one car from a thousand feet up?" Bonnie's respect for Seiji's abilities rose like a rocket.

"Actually, 2,000 feet. I told you. He's like Nathan," said Jordan. "Speaking of which, Nathan, can you use your spectacular nose to help us continue Seiji's work? I think we'll get the best results from what you find in the car. All your comments will be recorded."

Nathan nodded his consent. As he walked toward the car he realized why Seiji was burnt out. If the roles were reversed, his nose wouldn't have detected a thing from a high flying plane.

Seiji spent hour after hour in total concentration to spot that car, thought Nathan. My job is easy. I sniff. I categorize. I calculate what it means. Everything's done in ten seconds.

As he neared the vehicle, the giant cake cover lifted and disappeared into the ceiling. Nathan stuck his head through the open driver's side window. He sniffed deeply. Billions of molecules battered against cooperative olfactory receptors. Each triggered a signal that scurried to an individual neuron, awakening Nathan to the new knowledge.

"I detect the tailing essence of a variety of people and things. To be exact there are 473 distinct odours, which fall into 3,942 main sub-scents. The sub-scents are ingredients. I'll eliminate them. Next are gasoline, motor oil, cleaning products, an air freshener, four types of plastic on the seats and the trim, greases used on cars, rustproof undercoating, and adhesives used during the auto assembly process. This removes all of the scents that are native to the car.

"I'll also strike out scents that are pretty well common to everyone. There's the scent of car exhaust and other smog ingredients, tree and plant pollen, flowers, concrete, and tar. Then there's what I characterize as the secondary scents of every day living that sticks to clothing or skin such as fish, vegetables, spices, deodorizers, etc. from a walk down a grocer's aisle and sewage, garbage, compost, etc. that cling to shoes when you walk on any street.

"Now I'll target the direct odours of organic materials that were physically in the car. The kidnappers grabbed Dr. Plank three weeks ago. I'll drop anything that hints of decay older than four weeks. I sense three people were in the car in the last month. Until I get something from these individuals for comparison, I can't say any more on that.

"I'll move to the aromatic trail of food consumed in the car around the time of Dr. Plank's disappearance. There's bacon, lettuce, tomato, mayonnaise, bread, I'm presuming a BLT sandwich. There's the unmistakable musk of French roast coffee, definitely Starbucks, bold with soymilk and honey. Perhaps only one had the soymilk and another had the honey or one had both and the others were black. I can't distinguish it any closer than that, other than the force of the scent tells me there were two large or three medium coffees. I think they call them 'grandes' and 'talls' at Starbucks.

"Chewing gum. I can't tell you which brand exactly but here are the ingredients: xyledol, sorbitol, a gum base, maltitol, artificial and natural mint flavor, acacia, acesulfame, potassium, aspartame, BHT preservative, a milk derivative called calcium casein peptone-calcium phosphate, beeswax, glycerin, sodium stearate, soy lecithin and titanium dioxide."

"I'll compare that list to chewing gums on the market." Jordan efficiently typed the ingredient list on a keyboard that displayed the words on the lab's smartboard. "Wait for it; wait for it . . . There it is. Breathless Freshmint Gum, manufactured by B. Chewsy Inc., a gum and confection contract manufacturer in Marietta, Georgia.

"Hair tonic," said Nathan, who had moved to the next scent.

"Who uses hair tonic any more? Mineral oil, gibberellins, cider vinegar, alcohol, and two high-quality essential oils – Tea tree oil and chamomile. The mineral oil is used in the hair tonic to increase manageability and to make the hair shinier. Gibberellins are used to stimulate the scalp and hair growth. The essential oils give the hair tonic a pleasant smell and strengthen hair roots.

"Hair tonic suggests a man who takes care of his hair a lot better than Dr. Plank and I remember that scent on a chef from Georgia. Whenever I come across a scent I don't know, I ask what it is, and Gilbert, that was the chef's name, told me it was Darby's Hair Tonic, a product sold in the Southern U.S. states, mostly in Georgia."

Bonnie's inner detective, honed since she was 14, joined the pursuit. "So we're likely looking for a male Georgian, who chews mint gum likely to sweeten his breath and hair tonic to look sharp and stimulate hair growth. That means he's in that still-hopeful mating age, under 35. The fact he drinks Starbucks, with soymilk or perhaps with honey, indicates that he's 30 or younger and enjoys an urban lifestyle. Starbucks, soymilk, and honey in Georgia probably mean we should stick to bigger cities and the hip ones at that."

Agent Jordan returned to the smart board. "Here are the main choices: Atlanta, population 443,775; Augusta, population 198,413; Columbus, population 197,872; and Savannah, population 142,022. All four cities have at least one Starbucks. That's about as far as we can go with that information. Let's cross reference it with the other evidence that Seiji found."

Agent Jordan passed copies of a single page report to Nathan and a file box containing 92 clear, plastic envelopes.

"Seiji spotted residue too small to be normally detected, mostly skin samples that can't be seen to be collected by anyone else. What we want you to do Nathan is tell us which skin samples are from the same person. The bags marked with red lettering come from Dr. Plank's lab and the ones marked in blue are from his car."

Bonnie picked up the bags, examining one after another. "They're all empty."

"They only look empty. As I said, Seiji collected skin samples too small for anyone else to see but it is my belief that they are big enough for Nathan to identify and match."

"Okay, let's do it." Nathan grabbed the first bag, opened it and took a whiff.

"I mostly smell the plastic but there's a definite human odour present. Let's call that one Person A."

Jordan grabbed the envelope and placed a big green A on the package.

Jordan passed the next bag. Nathan sniffed. "This would be Person B."

The sample in envelope three, Nathan pronounced as Person C.

Bag four produced a match. "Bag five is B again."

The sixth envelope produced another Person C.

The seventh registered a Person D.

After going through all 92 envelopes, Nathan had identified that the skin samples came from seven different individuals – Persons A through G. Three of the people had been in both the lab and Plank's car. Four had been only in the lab.

"That leaves us with three people who were in both the car and the lab and, presumably, Plank was one of them. Can you run DNA on samples too small to see?" Bonnie asked.

Jordan produced a knowing smile. "If you use a magnifying glass, you can see the samples and even if you couldn't, it's not a problem. It takes only one nanogram of skin cells to determine DNA and we have DNA from seven people each providing multiple samples. We have enough to identify all seven people if the database can come up with a match."

The beautiful Agent picked up the box containing the samples and motioned for the others to follow. Halfway down the hall, Jordan entered a forensic laboratory and placed the box on a table before a tall woman in a white lab coat.

"Hi Alice. Here are the DNA samples. Create a profile for each of the seven individuals and see if there are any matches in our databases. I need this done right now."

Turning to her guests who were still caught in the doorway, Jordan fanned at them to clear the entrance.

"It'll take a couple of hours to get results. In the meantime, let's go upstairs for dinner and discuss next steps."

A late dinner at the FBI offices consisted of a stringy hamburger steak, a pallid, lumpy puddle of creamed corn and reconstituted mashed potatoes, all prepared in the best hospital-meal tradition and served with exaggerated ceremony by Flynn who completed his task by sliding foam plates and plastic cutlery toward Bonnie and Nathan like he was dealing blackjack.

"This ain't exactly what you're used to, eh?" Flynn's feeble attempt at a chuckle and an ingenuous smile was as heart-warming as the food.

Both Bonnie and Nathan played fork hockey with the lumps of potato and meat on their plates but decided to pass on eating.

"Here I am sitting next to a three star Michelin chef, and this is what we have to eat?"

"An honourary three star Michelin chef, not a real one," Nathan replied.

"Well, Mr. Honorary Michelin Chef, I'm about to make a withdrawal from my memory banks. It's one of those dinners that made you a culinary star."

—

14

NASCENCE OF THE NOSE

AFTER BONNIE LEARNED of Nathan's super sense of smell, the teenagers fulfilled their role of dynamic duo but covertly. All through high school they used Nathan's power cautiously . . . to secretly help friends get together "Whenever Bill's around, Cindy's pheromones go off scale but Bill's too petrified to talk to her" and academically . . . "Mr. Tripp was sending a five-alarm signal during the bit on South Africa. That's on the exam for sure."

Occasionally, they'd pitch in to help police in secret. Bonnie wrote anonymous notes providing police with valuable crime clues after the break-in at Marty's Variety Store, after Mrs. Holly's schnauzer Pepper was dog-napped, and once to alert police to the body of a homeless person who crawled into a sewer to spend his last night on Earth under it but, at least, in a warm environment.

Upon graduation, crime fighting went on hold while they set about building individual careers. Bonnie's parents insisted on a university education but didn't mask their disappointment when she enrolled in journalism and not medicine. Nathan, who had gained an interest in cooking from Aunt Lucy, took a chef school program. His keen sense of smell pushed him to create unusual food combinations that shocked observers yet pleased their palates.

He became the star student, winning national student competitions and receiving rave reviews from guest chefs and food critics drawn to the school to witness the birth of a culinary genius. Nathan had three distinct, and perhaps unfair, advantages over the other students:

1. Before food preparation began, Nathan's superlative sense of smell gave him a decided edge in the selection and rejection of ingredients. The peach

that stood out from the rest in sweetness, flavour and ripeness flew into his basket. The singular red snapper that best transitioned from ocean to market found its way into his kitchen. He passed on the bay leaf that failed to pronounce its attributes profoundly.

2. Aspiring chefs are advised to taste the food continuously. With his unerring nose, he understood how to pattern the dish as it cooked to achieve the desired taste. He detected ingredients that were not coming together as expected and made adjustments – a bit of fat to boost richness, a drop of lemon for tartness, cumin or coriander for a savory note, a few flakes of chili pepper for an added jolt.

3. Top chefs are trained to balance time and heat for the best results. Nathan didn't rely on learned steps, a timer, or the look of a dish. His nose declared, as clear as a trumpet blast, the amount of heat needed and the precise instant of cooking perfection.

Once in the real working world, Nathan's culinary flair vanished under the shadow of a reputation for insolence. His special insight into ingredients – how to select them, substitute for them and blend them – placed him in Toronto's finest kitchens but never for long. Every executive chef's blood pressure spiked when he argued vociferously with the kitchen crew to swap ingredients or vary the proportions in their boss' signature dishes.

After three years, Nathan had been all but banished from Toronto's upscale dining industry.

He had few options. Other talented maverick chefs ran their own restaurants, but the usual money men shied away, partly because of his reputation for causing problems and partly because he had angered the top chefs who had their ear.

One exception was Henri Meunier, the renowned Executive Chef of the prestigious Obsidian Club. Meunier confirmed Nathan possessed something special when he acted as a judge in one the chef school's competitions.

In the competition, Nathan presented two dishes that unanimously wowed the judges.

The first offering he called a Trio of Figs. It featured a fresh King fig drizzled with fig vincotto, a port poached Blue Celeste fig, and Natalina fig ice cream. The freshness of the figs astounded the judges. They marveled at how each element's flavour in every course spoke boldly without conflicting with or overpowering the others.

"The fig dish is astonishing," said Mandrake Lee, executive chef of the Toronto Triomphe. "So beautifully presented and the taste is fresh, clean. I could taste the difference in each fig variety. The Canadian grown figs in this dish surpass the best I've eaten in Italy and the Middle East."

The second course possessed deceptive simplicity, a BLT salad featuring organic crispy bacon on Bibb lettuce, sliced heirloom tomatoes in a French vinegar, dressed with a roasted garlic mayo.

"This Nathan Sherlock is someone to watch," said Kurts Jennings, a three-star Michelin chef who owns 20 restaurants. "The superb match of heirloom tomatoes and the use of Banyuls, the famed vinegar from Southern France, is wizardry."

Chef Meunier took Nathan aside after awarding him the top prize.

"All of the judges were impressed by the exquisite tastes. The heirloom tomatoes and the figs amazed. Who supplies you with such fabulous produce?"

"I grow them myself and take only the best and at their precise moment of ripeness. When you start with the best ingredients, you end with the best product."

"But how could you do this? How could you know so exactly?" the renowned chef asked.

Nathan gave a toned-down explanation of his gift to Meunier.

"I smell the ripeness, the sweetness. In a dish that's cooking, one sniff and what's missing is obvious. I'm like a composer whose ear tells him to add a line for woodwinds or perhaps a designer who sees balance in colour and shape by adding a specific belt or piece of jewelry. My nose says what's needed."

Since that day, Meunier kept his eye on Nathan. He decided the brash prodigy needed one more chance, but as a lowly kitchen assistant to instill some discipline and humility. After two weeks with the kitchen staff in revolt, he fired Nathan. Before Nathan could utter a word, Meunier offered to hire him back to replace his retiring sommelier once Nathan completed the appropriate training.

"You will work with me rather than against me," Chef Meunier decreed. "Your nose gets you in trouble in my kitchen but if you worked with me in the dining room, we might create magic."

Chef Meunier told a rattled Nathan that he had enrolled him in the North American Sommelier Association (NASA) course in San Francisco and paid for his tuition, room & board. "Pack your bags. Your plane leaves tomorrow at 2."

"But my apartment . . ."

"Our new kitchen assistant will move in."

"But the money . . ."

"You will definitely pay me back one way or another."

As much as Nathan could visualize food through the scent of ingredients and their changes while cooking, wine was his natural world. From the first day of classes he astounded his teachers through an ability to dissect the elements of wine in ways that baffled most seasoned sommeliers and wine tasters. Once he sampled a vintage, his nose never forgot.

"In technical terms, Nathan's abilities make sense," the school's master sommelier Gregor McIvor explained in an interview with WTW (Wines That Wow) Magazine.

"Most of what we perceive as taste is detected by our nose. Nathan simply has a God-given ability far beyond anyone we've ever had in our schools."

With the added knowledge of great vintages, soil conditions, microclimates, wine growing regions and what were traditionally considered the perfect matching of food and beverage, Nathan's virtuosity soared.

Before Nathan completed half the silver pin program, McIvor took him under his wing to complete his gold pin at the same time. McIvor was a great teacher but also an amazing observer. In the school's test restaurant, he saw Nathan match sea bass with the wine cellar's Xuri Dansa 2005 Irouléguy for one male guest and at another table, Nathan selected the Xuri Dansa 2006 Irouléguy for a woman who ordered the same sea bass.

"Why the difference," McIvor asked.

"Her body chemistry lent itself to a fresher, fruitier wine."

No other person on Earth could make such a call and with such absolute confidence, McIvor thought.

When Nathan graduated, McIvor gave him advice that would stay with the young sommelier for the rest of his days.

"Nathan, you are the most gifted sommelier in the world, bar none. No sommelier, no wine maker, no wine judge, no wine buyer in the world can do what you can do. The one quality that may prevent you from being one of the world's great sommeliers is humility. You must work on that. Your gift pushes you toward arrogance, but your arrogance is born of insecurity. You must be confident enough in your own abilities to accept that the customer is always right.

"Lack of humility destroyed your career as a chef and it could destroy you even quicker as a sommelier. When a guest asks for a specific wine or vintage, you may offer an alternative suggestion, but at no time are you to do anything other than make a suggestion. The guest chooses the wine, not you."

Nathan fulfilled Chef Meunier's wish by returning to Toronto's Obsidian Club as sommelier. The matchless combination of Chef Meunier's cuisine and the wine pairings by Nathan created a sensation.

Rarely was a star born in so spectacular a way.

—

15

A STAR IS BORN

FOUR YEARS LATER AT QUANTICO, Bonnie placed her fingertips on her temples like a cruise-ship mentalist. She started moaning in her campiest Hollywood-horror flick voice.

"Hmmmm, I'm getting a vision. It's getting clearer. It's the spirit of great meals past. I see a single skillet. Now it's turning. I see your Spanish Chicken with Green Beans. Ah yes, you laughed it off as a one-skillet wonder that even I could make. But, oh, the aroma, and those flavours. Juicy chicken with a touch of smoky paprika. The crunch of slivered almonds. Better than chocolate.

"And the wine, a 1991 Las Rocas Garnacha. I'll forget the name of the first boy I kissed before I forget Las Rocas Garnacha. Give it a little swirl in the glass. Breathe. Then it all comes out to play. A touch earthy with soft tannins, and lots of fruit to link up with the paprika in the meal. Um um, good. I take it back, it was definitely better than chocolate. And maybe better than sex."

Nathan was about to protest when the words *better than sex* sunk in. *Bonnie's had sex? And with who?*

"Earth to Nathan. I'm looking for a little back-up here."

"Oh yeah. The food's horrible but we're out of here in a day or so. Why go on remembering the great meals when you know this is what they're feeding us? You're amping up the torture."

Bonnie shrugged and turned to Flynn. "It's like prison food but even prisoners get to protest the food. Are you going to lock us up for the night, too?"

"There's no lock on the door, but since we're six floors underground and your hand has to be coded to use the elevator, you might say you're our guests until you aren't," Flynn said with that sickening, ever-present sardonic smile.

"So tell me, how did your boy here get so famous?" he asked.

Bonnie produced a smile that reflected reawakened memories.
"You really want to know?"

...

Randolph Westeen, President of the Obsidian Club, was so pleased with his diningroom duo of Meunier and Sherlock, he invited the food editor of the Toronto Clarion, Dianne Kingsmere, and the Clarion's publisher, Jonathan Graves, to be his guests for dinner.

"I assure you. It will be memorable. Oh, and be sure you bring your spouses as will I," he added with a wink.

Chef Meunier prepared five courses and Sommelier Sherlock created the suggested flights of beverages with each course.

The premier plata - Chef Meunier's Red Snapper and Calamari Ceviche with a fine drizzle of Venta del Juliette White Truffle oil and Perfumed Ruccola was a singular triumph. Now it was Nathan's turn. He gave each guest a small, shallow bowl with a teaspoon of an amber liquid in each and a champagne flute with two ounces of a slightly golden elixir.

"The bowl contains a splash of Don Julio Tequila Real and the champagne flute, a tasting of Peller Estates' Signature Series Riesling Icewine 2011."

"Tequila?" interjected Kingsmere. "And ice wine to start?"

"Yes, I am straying from the normal boundaries of a sommelier. It may seem a bit odd. Of course, you may choose whatever you like but, if you follow my instructions exactly, I promise an experience like none other."

Bemused smiles and nods rounded the table.

"Inhale the aroma of the bowl, then take the smallest sip possible bringing in plenty of air at the same time."

The guests complied.

"Now try the Ceviche."

"I was going to say you were taking things to the silly level but this is amazing," announced George Kingsmere, a world-renowned cardiologist.

"Now breathe in the Ice Wine as you sip it."

The group complied. Silence ensued.

Mrs. Graves started to weep.

Mr. Graves silently shivered with delight when he noticed his wife and gave her a squeeze. "And that ladies and gentlemen is merely a taste of the first course."

At the end of the meal, a chocolate mousse infused with Armagnac ringed by what appeared to be miniature grapes – achieved through the spherification of Castello Banfi Brunello grappa – there wasn't a dry eye at the table.

Dianne Kingsmere stood, rounded the table and clasped hands with Nathan and Meunier.

"I don't know how to describe this experience."

She began to clap and every patron in the dining room stood and joined her in the applause.

When Kingsmere returned to her seat, her husband stood and tenderly embraced her. The Graves were as tightly entwined as side-by-side seating allowed.

"I suggest all of us go home. I have limousines waiting," Westeen declared, his arm securely wrapped around his wife whose dewy eyes were all for him.

The three couples bowed to Meunier and Sherlock. It seemed the natural thing to do. They left quietly, still holding their partners closely.

Kingsmere's column two days later put the pairing of Meunier and Sherlock on the world stage.

" . . . a feast to the emotions as much as to the palate . . . couldn't wait to get home to make wild, crazy love all night. We were like teenagers with our first love and hormones on a rampage . . . Afterward, we both cried like babies, emotionally and physically satiated in every way."

It started in coffee shops just after midnight. A shift worker with the Clarion's early edition in hand read the article aloud to strangers who salivated over every word. "I swooned, I actually swooned."

For the first time in his career, a taxi dispatcher used his radio for communications other than business. "My legs turned to jelly . . ." he read to his enraptured drivers.

The early morning appointments at the hair salons shunned the dryers while stylists and customers huddled, taking turns reading the best parts. "Honestly, four hours. He kept coming back for more and the word no wasn't in my vocabulary."

The morning drive DJs put on their own spin. "I'm not making this stuff up. It's here in black and white but my face is red. It's supposed to be a food review but it makes Fifty Shades of Grey read like a grade school primer."

By noon, the story was trending around the world.

"What did your publisher say when he read your column," asked TV host Ellen.

"He just gave me a wink and a nod and added: 'Go to print'."

"So —?" said Ellen.

"I have no idea. I don't ask my boss about his sex life."

Never wanting for members from Canada's elite, the Obsidian Club came under global siege for membership. In the ensuing month, the club turned down a dozen Hollywood frontliners, two members of the Saudi Royal family and an assortment of new tech billionaires. Despite a nine-month queue for a dinner date, the club found none of the new members wanted their six-figure initiation fee returned in order to maintain their position on the waiting list.

—

16

I DREAM OF GINI

FLYNN STARED AT NATHAN with a new level of respect.

"And that's absolutely true?"

"Scout's honour," said Bonnie. "Any chance that buys us some better food?"

"Sorry. No chance."

Bonnie shoved her untouched plate into the waste bin and looked to Nathan and Flynn.

"Might as well crash for the night."

Flynn ushered his charges through a series of corridors to a sitting room that fanned out into four cell-sized rooms, each equipped with a computer, a desk, a bunk and a tiny bathroom and shower.

"We have some clothing you can wear while you're with us. I think it'll fit. Take your pick of rooms. Lights out at 10 p.m. Reveille's at six."

Flynn retreated to the exit.

Bonnie and Nathan glumly looked at the rooms and the unisex blue tracksuits and what they guessed were prison issue underwear.

"It's like we're trapped in a bad spy movie. Jack Bauer has nothing on us. The last 10 hours have been, well, interesting and the next 14 hours could easily fill the plot of his next 24 series," said Bonnie.

"I thought I was going to a birthday party and then there's a murder, special agents from Canada and the U.S., international terrorists, a mad scientist with a weapon that could destroy the world, and then a couple of people who have abilities like me but . . ."

"Don't say it Nathan. No need to get worked up about something that hasn't happened and may never happen. Let's focus on getting the job done and returning to our normal, uneventful lives."

They both laughed heartily at that one.

...

The next morning, breakfast was as grim an affair as their dinner.

"Yummy! For you sir, we have Star Trek replicator food. Fakon and reconstituted eggs."

Bonnie used her Jeeves-the-butler accent and completed the announcement with a regal bow before switching back to her normal voice.

"Nathan, if we're going to be here any longer, you've got to take over the cooking."

"Not much I could do about it. Everything comes frozen and then it's microwaved. They don't have a kitchen or any ingredients."

"What I wouldn't give to be back at that wonderful villa in Tuscany. Remember that simple breakfast of Italian Fritatta – free-range eggs, roasted red peppers, garlic crumbled spicy sausage and fresh basil. Incredible, simple and hearty but better than any French omelet. And the coffee – strong with warm milk. It was so easy, you even let me do some of the cooking."

"If you can persuade Flynn to get some fresh eggs, go for it. I'll gladly stand back."

"Don't blame me. Before I met you, my big treat was fries with gravy and a Coke. You've ruined me for normal, or in this case, sub-normal food."

Other than a bite of brittle toast and a sip of weak, tepid coffee, the two ignored their plates. When Jordan arrived, they declared themselves done. The threesome walked to the lab where they were met by Flynn and a middle-aged but very tall woman in a lab coat and a man in his mid-20s, about a head shorter than the woman. He wore jeans and a Green Lantern sweatshirt.

"This is Alice. She's been looking into the DNA samples. Davis is our computer guy. Once we get a lead on the DNA, he'll track the perp.

"Good morning Alice, what have you got for us?"

"Good morning Special Agent Jordan. We've run all of the samples and found that of the five, the DNA from one group, as expected, belongs to Dr. Plank. Two samples found only in the lab belong to university personnel. The other two DNA samples were found in both the lab and the car and belong to persons unknown."

Jordan gave an audible sigh of disappointment. The tall lab tech adjusted her over-sized gold-rimmed glasses and with a knowing smile added: "We didn't get a direct hit but we did get a close match to a relative, a sibling for one of the two. Davis, show then what we found."

Three sets of eyes peered over Davis' shoulder as he pulled up a profile on his screen of a black man, possibly in his late 30s.

"James DeSoto, 38, of Savannah Georgia was arrested for dealing marijuana five years ago. He received a 10-year sentence. This guy had the misfortune of not smoking a joint the day of his arrest. He was caught with 28.2 ounces of marijuana and Georgia law states anything over 28 ounces is automatic trafficking and 10 years in jail. If he smoked a single joint, he would have been out in 60 days. He was released five months ago after six years in the can but remains on probation. Mr. DeSoto is on early release. You've got some leverage there if you need it."

"Can you find out who his siblings are?"

"Already done," said Davis. "James DeSoto has three brothers. Carl DeSoto, 34, is a cable guy for Communicast Systems in Savannah. Solly DeSoto, 33, is a dental equipment sales person, and Delroy DeSoto, 30, is a cinematographer and small-time filmmaker."

"Delroy DeSoto, Delroy DeSoto . . . where have I heard that name before?" Jordan puzzled aloud. "Get me everything you can on Delroy DeSoto, arrest records, parking tickets, library fines, anything."

After a few minutes, Davis sat back and said, "This is interesting."

"What?" everyone said or thought.

"There's no criminal record but the Internet is full of references. Delroy DeSoto produced a documentary film six years ago titled, Underground. It was seen as a stinging indictment of the oil and gas industry running rough-shod over average property owners' rights and health concerns over the release of sour gas. The film, by all reports, was an Oscar contender in the documentary category. That's when the oil and gas industry let loose their PR and lobbyist dogs to discredit both DeSoto and his film.

"From all quarters, the Academy was pressured to drop Underground from the list of nominees on the premise that the film failed to meet the standard of research required to be taken seriously. As an example, they cited that no counter-balancing comments by representatives of the gas industry were featured in the film. A rebuttal by DeSoto stated that more than two dozen requests were made for interviews with no fewer than five corporations but all requests were turned down. DeSoto mentioned it in the film."

"I'll bet Underground was never nominated for an Oscar." Bonnie's face projected a frown equally divided between disgust and resignation.

"You got it. And the distributor, Reel Events Media, dropped the film. No other distributor wanted to touch it after that. So basically, the film died and DeSoto's career was gassed, if you pardon the pun."

"It's obvious," Nathan piped in. "DeSoto saw the oil and gas industry ready to suppress negative gravity technology. He stepped in and now has the opportunity to give the world negative gravity and destroy the oil and gas industry at the same time."

"Exactly, but he couldn't have done it alone. Any indication of DeSoto's associates?" said Flynn.

"This is where it gets really interesting. He's referenced as an associate of a guy named Jason Sage."

"That's it!" said Jordan. "I remember now. DeSoto was a member of the Gini Group or the Gini Conspiracy. The name Gini originates from an Italian statistician and sociologist named Corrado Gini who came up with the Gini Coefficient, a measure of a society's income inequality. It was a name the FBI gave the group. I'm not sure they called themselves that but we took it from references on one of their flyers."

"If the FBI knew about the group and DeSoto's membership, why wasn't he in your database?" asked Bonnie.

"They broke no law. They used the system so cleverly that most of us in law enforcement gave them grudging respect," said Jordan.

"We didn't want to go overboard by putting marks against their names that would prevent them from success in the future. Even hard-ass lawmen really want to see justice done. Usually it's the rich that use the law to their advantage to screw the little guy. So when a bunch of little guys use the law and the rules to screw the rich, why would we do anything to stop them?"

...

When the group broke, Flynn rode the elevator to the parking garage. He drove to a Papa John's restaurant and ordered a small pizza to go. After placing his order, he walked into the washroom and checked all of the stalls. He was alone.

The CSIS officer pulled a prepaid phone from his breast pocket. There was one message from a number with the area code 312.

He hit reply.

"Summers here," came the response.

"It's Flynn. They definitely have Plank. There are six of them. The leader's a guy named Jason Sage. He's the one who turned the corn commodity market inside-out back in 2012. Look him up. He did that to equalize the wealth between rich and poor and did a pretty fair job of it. Now they want to do the same thing with negative gravity."

"Are they sophisticated enough to pull this off?"

"Yes, they have worldwide a network to help them and access to money if they need it."

There was a long pause marked only by exasperated breathing.

"Do you have a location for them?"

"No, other than one cell is in the general Chicago area and the other somewhere around Toronto. There may be other cells in Europe and the Middle East."

"That's not going to make Mr. Hendry happy," Summers said. "Mr. Hendry has made it clear he personally wants to own this technology."

"I only give you reports. The rest is not my problem."

"How naive you are. If this goes badly, it goes badly for everyone, you and me included.

I'm not just talking about losing your job or going to jail, if you get my meaning."

This time Flynn paused to reassess the situation. "Okay, I'm on it. I'll locate them."

...

Frank Flynn graduated in 1994 with a Master's degree from Carleton University's prestigious School of Public Policy in Ottawa. He was undecided on law school or becoming a PhD candidate when one of his professors called him aside to introduce him to an old friend. The friend was a recruiting officer for CSIS. After more conversations, a battery of tests, and six-months of training, Frank Flynn became an operative for the Canadian Security Intelligence Service.

Unlike most spy agencies, CSIS advertises for recruits although anyone who's hired has to keep quiet about his place of employment. CSIS jobs also carry unglamorous titles. No 'Double O' denotations. An operative in the field is simply known as an intelligence officer (IO) and one who analyzes what's collected, an intelligence analyst (IA).

Ten years into the job, Flynn worked as a threat management analyst. He looked for the potential of a terrorist act at special events, against public figures, and actions such as hijackings or bombings. His career held great promise until local cops scored Canada's biggest terrorist bust, right under the nose of the federal agency assigned to do the job.

Toronto city police and Ontario Provincial Police infiltrated a terrorist cell, and seized bombs destined for government buildings, major businesses and trains. They arrested 15 suspects, all with Al-Qaeda links.

Two of the 15 had been on CSIS's radar but, from Flynn's assessment, neither appeared to present a danger to the public. The inter-policing embarrassment to CSIS landed like a fallen tree on Flynn's career.

It didn't matter that the two suspects Flynn investigated were recruited after he filed his report. For the next eight years, any job more important than shredding files bypassed him. With it, Flynn's self-esteem imploded, as did his body conditioning after he retreated to a diet of junk food and developed a fascination for hillbilly reality TV shows.

He gave serious consideration to pitching himself down a flight of stairs at work and finagling a disability pension when Wilbur Harding, vice-chair of the Canadian Senate Security Committee approached him.

The senator urged Flynn to apply to be part of the U.S.-Canada joint anti-terrorism task force.

"I can ensure you get the job. It's a good one. It puts your career back on track. Your pay goes up two grades, and you get to see real action again."

"Why me?"

"Let's just say that I recognize you've been made a scapegoat. You need a friend with the power to help you put your mind and talents to good use."

"So, you're my friend."

"Yes, I am. As friends, we do favours for each other."

"And I suppose by *each other* you mean you'll be asking me for favours in my new job."

"Favours but nothing that compromises the greater good or Canada," said Sen. Harding. "You are there to protect the interests of Canadians. I just want to make sure you protect Canada's economic interests at the same time. Any threat that will impact our economy must be reported to me immediately and confidentially. I'll ensure the right people get the information after that."

Flynn nodded his agreement.

"And so you understand me perfectly and you keep our arrangements just between the two of us, there's a little something that will be deposited into a bank account in your name in the Cayman Islands each month. Absolutely no one else must know of our arrangement."

Sen. Harding extended his hand and, with a resigned shrug, Flynn took it and shook it.

Two years later, on April 9, 2014, Sen. Harding's cell phone rang.

"Sen. Harding. It's Flynn. I have something you need to know. I don't have all the details but this could be big, really big and it would really affect energy prices."

"Well that would certainly be a concern considering oil and gas represent the third biggest chunk of the Canadian economy after real estate and manufacturing. Will it make prices go up or down and how long do you think the effect might occur? I just might want to put a little money in play on the market."

"I don't think you're understanding what I'm saying senator."

"It couldn't possibly be anything to rock prices too much. All the troubles in the Middle East haven't hurt the Canadian oil and gas business at all. It would take all out war to do that."

"Senator, please stop and listen to me. I'm talking about oil prices going from whatever they are today, more than $100 a barrel to zero, maybe less because everyone would be paying to get rid of it."

Flynn heard a gurgling noise on the other end of the line followed by a fit of coughing.

Finally, a hoarse-voiced Harding said, "This better not be a joke."

"I assure you, it isn't."

He explained.

"I need time to think, to talk to some people ... I'll get back to you ... No, a man named Summers, Rick Summers will call you. He's with a company that has big holdings in the Alberta oil patch and has significant investments in the tar sands. He will have the ability to deal with this."

—

[17]

THE CONSPIRACY

FIVE WEEKS EARLIER, in a modest rented house on the south side of Chicago, a computer screen flashed, "Welcome Dr. Plank. Access permitted: April 6, 2014, 12:03 a.m."

With that, a jubilant Morris "Mo" Hatcher leaped from his chair, both arms raised in triumph. "I'm in. I'm in."

Jason Sage rushed forward with a double high-five and chest bump. The rest of the crew, Alessa Reese, Delroy "DD" DeSoto, Jasmine "Jazzy" Irianto, and Olga Kalata surrounded Mo, slapping him on the back and leaning in to see the stream of data cascading into his laptop.

"And we're sure we can delete the original data and then erase the trail," Sage half stated/answered.

"Positutely!"

"Considering we might all go to jail, 'positutely' doesn't give me a keen sense of assurance."

"Look Sager. I designed it. You checked it. Alessa checked it. Bulletproof."

"I want to be sure. We've got heavyweight dudes super pissed over our manipulation of the corn commodities market," said Sage, holding his hands in a defensive posture.

"If they sniff out our cyber trail too soon, we're done. We've got to buy time for Jazzy to go through the data and see if she can figure enough of it out on her own."

He directed a hard stare at the exotic beauty.

"Jazzy, the game's on. Now it's all on you to save humanity."

"Gee Jason, you're batting a thousand. You needle Mo about being perfect

89

and now a lowly physics PhD dropout like me is supposed to crack the secret mathematical code that holds the universe together."

"That about sums it up. Think you can have everything all wrapped by, say, afternoon coffee break?"

"I'll set the alarm on my atomic clock for 2 p.m. Would that be okay your Highness?"

"Perfect," Sage pronounced while puffing up his chest imperiously. In an instant, he was laid flat as the rest of the crew piled on him, delivering not-entirely-tender punches and pinches.

When the laughter subsided, Olga, a former top-10 U.S. college gymnast, eyed the others grimly.

"The rest of us have jobs, too. Alessa stays with Mo and Jason to coordinate the data and operations but Jazzy, DD and I will head for Toronto this afternoon."

"I wouldn't mind having Jazzy with me to help with the computer tracking." Mo tried to sound casual but no one mistook his intent.

"Mo, you know we need Jazzy in Toronto because of her knowledge of the city and her physics background. She has to be part of my team."

He didn't meet her eyes or anyone else's. "Okay Olga. You're right as usual."

Olga did her best to move past Mo's awkward moment. "Afterward, we all disappear. We make our collection. We go to ground. No contact at all with any relatives, friends, no one but us. Our lives will depend on it. Agreed?"

All six exchanged solemn glances. "Agreed," they said as one.

...

The group reconvened an hour later. Bonnie posed her question. "So just what did these Gini Conspirators do to get everyone so riled?"

"For that, we're going to have to start at the beginning."

Flynn punctuated his statement by plopping his briefcase on the table.

"Davis has been busy puttin' this stuff together for us." He withdrew a thick portfolio and placed its contents on the table in piles, one of them a stack of 8x10 photographs. He spread the photos into two rows of three.

"This is Jason Sage. He's the leader. He was in the financial world when the banking crisis hit. His career, like a lot of the others in his field, took a big dump but that's not what turned him. He came from a small town in the Mid-West and the banking crisis destroyed the town's economy. A lot of farmers went under when they couldn't get credit. A favourite uncle committed suicide when he lost his farm.

"So Sage packed up his bags and his career and joined the Occupy Movement, camping out on Wall Street, a few blocks down the street from his former office. There he met with the others. This is a photo of Morris Hatcher. He's a computer science dropout from Indiana U. but seems to be a hell of a hacker because he turned the whole financial industry inside out with the automated trading system he and Sage put in place to max their returns on corn futures.

"This beautiful lady is Alessa Reese. She seems to be romantically linked with Sage. Before she joined this radical cell, she was an actress-in-waiting, doing the waitress thing to pay the bills. She was instrumental in persuading a lot of the farm families to put their faith in Sage's plan.

"Delroy DeSoto, you already know about him.

"Jasmine Irianto, she's another looker. Her parents left Sumatra and moved to the States with their three children. Jasmine was the middle child. When she was 13, something happened and she was left an orphan.

"After that she moved to Toronto and lived with her foster mother. She followed in her foster mother's footsteps and became an activist in a whole range of social justice causes. Jasmine was pretty smart, too, and became a graduate student in sciences working on her PhD in physics in Canada before she dropped out to join up with Sage and crew. She's also a whiz with computers and linked up with Mo Hatcher via the Internet. We think that's how she got involved with the Ginis in the beginning.

"Olga Kalata is another member of the team. She's small but mighty. She's second in command to Sage. She stands about five feet nothing but is incredibly athletic. She just missed the cut for the U.S. Olympic gymnastics team, mostly because her dedication to athletics came second to her activism. She's the most radical member of the team and has been active in a number of causes for years. We suspect she was responsible for the release of lab animals from two universities in 2009. Only someone with her physical skills could have bypassed the university alarm systems by scaling five storeys up the side of one building and then wiggling through the ductwork to get to the labs.

"We believe she may have used the same skills to enter some of the key traders' offices to set up email and computer taps to get passwords and access notes so that Hatcher and Sage could anticipate counter moves being made to thwart their corn trading strategy.

"There's some suspicion that couldn't be proved that they were the first to send buy orders that spiked corn prices. The account reps, whose accounts were used, didn't complain because they ended up making a lot of money and getting credit as the first ones in."

Bonnie interjected. "Isn't that breaking and entering? Those are crimes."

"Yes, but proving it is another matter. She left no trace she was there and neither did Sage and Hatcher's computer hacking. We only suspect they did it because of the results. There was no evidence to be found. And after all was said and done and the markets got over their initial tantrums, everybody wanted to forget about what they considered a truly embarrassing episode," Jordan said.

"So you're telling us a bunch of kids is behind this crisis and they are not to be under-estimated," said Nathan.

"That's it exactly," said Flynn.

...

Those who remember Jason Sage as a child recalled an energetic, freckle-faced kid with flaming red hair who never walked if he could run. The only child of Marianne and Jesse Sage, a fourth-generation farming family in the Iowa Corn Belt, young Jason's life as a fifth-generation corn grower seemed to be preordained.

In the closing years of the 20th Century, nothing was that simple any more. His mother died of cancer when he was eight and a farming accident claimed Jesse's life four years later. When the dust settled, the farm sold for what was owed. Jason's Uncle Jed and Aunt Ruth, who owned the adjoining farm, took him in and raised him until he was 18.

After that, he headed to college. He graduated cum laude from the University of Illinois with a business degree in 2006 and went to work for the Wall Street financial services firm, Torcher Associates.

It wasn't long before Jason saw a number of things that alarmed him. His job title was Financial Security Advisor.

"I was anything but," he told his friends later. The emphasis, as constantly drilled into him and his associates, was maximization of corporate profits and his personal income with financial security for the client's investments far down the priority list.

"It was like a religion but their god was greed."

Jason placed a high percentage of his clients assets into safe, solid-performing companies, going against the higher fee-earning portfolios recommended by his bosses at Torcher. At the end of the first week in January, 2008, Torcher's management fired Sage for under-performance and failing to follow orders. Nine months later, that same environment of greed at Lehman Brothers imploded under the weight of risky investments and falsified records. The financial services company filed for bankruptcy protection under Chapter 11. The ensuing $600-billion financial collapse, the largest in U.S. history, sent shockwaves through the financial sector collapsing many smaller financial houses that adopted the same risky strategies, among them, Torcher Associates.

Even before the financial troubles of Lehman and Torcher became evident, Sage had enough of the world of finance and what he believed was a system so perverted, the original objectives – to provide the money needed to create businesses, jobs and wealth for all Americans – was lost to anyone in the industry.

He joined a small, informal think-tank composed of others his age who found the financial system and American economics had become an abomination. In time, Alessa Reese, DD DeSoto, Mo Hatcher, Olga Kalata, and Sage became fast friends.

When the Occupy Movement began its protests to bring attention to social and economic inequality, the group joined the frontline. They were among the first to rally at Occupy Wall Street in New York City's Zuccotti Park, which began on Sept, 17, 2011. Within three weeks, Occupy protests were in more than 951 cities across 82 countries, and over 600 communities in the United States.

In the first week, Mo brought in Jazzy Irianto to join the group. Jazzy was a friend he had corresponded with for years on the Internet. She had been a PhD student at Western University in London, Ontario and was thinking of quitting her studies to join the Occupy Movement in Toronto. Mo persuaded her to join him at the New York protest.

Sage soon demonstrated his leadership qualities by staging a masterful publicity coup.

During his time with Torcher Associates, Sage seethed with embarrassment whenever CEO Harrison Torcher *put on the show*. The epitome of the show was the CEO's personal, gold and royal purple-trimmed cocktail tent that had its own built-in bar and hot serving table. The cocktail tent seated Torcher and whatever arm-candy he had at the time on purple, throne-like chairs with plush divans spread out for 12 special guests.

What Torcher's employees called the pre-TENT-ious was ferried in all its gaudiness to the golf tournaments, Indy Car Races, and other premier events that Torcher sponsored.

When the cocktail tent with: "Torcher Associates – Your Trusted Advisors" imprinted in big, bold golden lettering on its roof came available on eBay for $299, thanks to bankruptcy trustees, Sage couldn't resist.

TV news crews and newspaper photographers at Zuccotti Park bored of the same old, same old sign-holding bearded ex-hippies and braless moms holding wailing babies were itching for new images.

Enter Sage and friends.

The all-important ironic story hit the news and circled around the globe.

The Pulitzer Prize winning shot captured a dozen rag-tag protesters gen-teelly seated on upside down buckets in the Torcher pre-TENT-ious. All 12 had their pinkies raised in the air, as they sipped black coffee from mugs bearing Lehman Brothers, Bear Stearns, and AIG logos .

The tent lasted only two days before the powers that be ordered New York's Finest to take the structure down.

Sage didn't oppose them. The point had been made.

"Sorry bud, we have our orders." The sergeant in charge looked sympathetic.

"I understand." Sage signalled his group to dismantle the tent without a fuss.

He extended his hand and the sergeant shook it. After that, police turned a blind eye to everything the group did.

Despite all the publicity and its worldwide reach, after a month Sage ad-dressed his clique and admitted defeat.

"We're making a lot of noise but the real money guys don't care. At best, a bunch of people camping out on Wall Street is an inconvenience. They're not going to change unless they have to."

"What do you suggest we do?" said Olga.

"We've got to hit them where it hurts – in their wallet."

—

18

THE CORN CAPER

THE 2012 DROUGHT in the Corn Belt proved the turning point. Sage's Uncle Jed had mortgaged the farm to the maximum after a series of disastrous years culminating in a flood in 2011 that wiped out his crop and his last hope of saving the farm. He hadn't been able to afford crop insurance. With the bailiff's notice of foreclosure nailed on the farm gatepost, he hung himself in his barn.

Sage was devastated and bitter. Having worked in the financial sector, he watched those who worked the commodities market take no risk while farmers broke their backs and spirits.

The traders complained of bad markets but still drove Jags and decorated their bodies with Rolex watches and $200 neckties. The farmers mortgaged everything for a tractor. Dirt farmers like his uncle risked everything and, like his uncle, many lost everything.

The commodities market is designed to play one farmer off on another, Sage explained to his friends.

"People who trade commodities say it is the perfect system that ensures rewards to the most efficient producers. Inefficient growers step up or go out of the business. Mega industrial farms bloom. The farm family becomes extinct.

"But who really wins? Certainly not the consumer. Big corporations and the financial markets suck up the profits and hundreds of thousands lose their livelihoods and their way of life."

Sage's crew started by travelling across the Corn Belt talking to every farmer they could.

"You stand together and prosper together or you fall as individuals," said Sage.

Alessa became a warrior with farm women who were often more determined and tougher than the men.

Sage talked about his father and how he gave his life to the land and about his uncle who took his own life when he lost the farm. The farmers were sympathetic and shared his and Alessa's concerns but they still couldn't see how it could be done.

It wasn't until they came across a group of farmers in Iowa who had known Sage's family that he found an audience that would act. There was a looming corn shortage brought on by the drought of 2012. A shortage meant higher prices and usually that evened things out. This time the markets, driven by smaller fees on smaller volumes, were demanding pricing that, because of lower yields, would be below the cost of production. The Iowa farmers were among the best producers but, by their calculations, they would still lose money in 2012.

Sage tried to negotiate on their behalf but there was no one to negotiate with. The answer always came back: "It's the market that dictates pricing. It's a matter of supply and demand."

His experience in the markets taught him there was something else the market responds to and responds to in a big way – fear.

During his brief dance with the Occupy Movement, Sage forged alliances with hundreds of organizations around the world. He passed along an idea for a crowd-funding project.

The idea was to raise enough money to buy crops at the same price farmers would get from the traders less the cost of harvesting.

It was Alessa who persuaded two women farmers to press their families to commit a small portion of their farmland to a three-step plan:

• Step one, the activists would buy the corn crops on 500 acres from each of two farm families, worth about $500,000 each.

• Step two, they would not get the money directly. Instead, it would go into buying the equivalent in corn futures held jointly by the farm families and the activists. The farmer's risk was if corn prices fell, the loss would be theirs. This was no different than the normal risk of pre-selling a corn contract. If the price of corn rose, the two farmers would get the base price plus some of the surplus. The rest would be ploughed back into a fund to make the same deal with other farmers.

• Step three, each of the two farmers was to set fire to the 500 acres of corn that the activists had purchased.

"Set fire to our fields when those crop prices are high?" The farmers were dumbfounded when Sage first proposed it.

"It's the only way to get their attention."

And attention it got. When the local news media and commodity brokers witnessed the 1,000 acres ablaze with dozens of other farmers privately telling the brokers this was just the start, the market panicked.

The news allowed Sage's crew to raise an additional $1 million through crowd funding and had purchased another $10 million in crops on margin with a $500,000 stop loss. The corn prices immediately rose by 32 per cent providing the original farmers with the profits they needed for their crops and a nice payback on crops from the rest of their land. Sage now had more than $3 million, $2 million of it in profits. He used the money to engage six more farmers in the same scheme and purchased a $30 million contract on margin.

By this time, more than 400 farmers in the Corn Belt had signed on with Sage's program vowing to burn their crops.

...

Bonnie gave out a gasp in wide-eyed astonishment. "So how many farms were set on fire and how come I never heard about it?"

"Key social activists and those who work the markets knew the full story but Sage never let the news media in on the fact the fires were set purposely. I'm guessing it was easier to negotiate without a lot of publicity. It was publicized locally as accidental fires and it ended there. It never came to being more than the original two farms, just 1,000 acres in total," said Jordan.

"How could anyone keep that a secret," Bonnie asked.

"Of course there were leaks but the only reports to be carried widely were in the tabloid press. Sage managed it all so tightly. The farmers didn't want to talk. No one in the markets would admit they had so easily been held hostage."

"And what happened to this Sage guy?"

"Nothing. He and his friends disappeared after that. Now that I know a little more about him, I'm sure he had no intention to burn more. His bluff worked. Corn commodity prices rose to profitable levels for the farmers and the Gini Conspirators hit a homerun for the little guy," Jordan said.

"That's a pretty crazy strategy," said Nathan.

"Crazy as a fox. At first Sage tried negotiation on behalf of the farmers. That didn't work. He tried to threaten that farmers would store the corn for a year. That didn't work. The financial guys called their bluff because the cost of storage would kill any profits and, if the next year was a bumper crop, they'd lose both in price and quality."

Jordan paused a second for dramatic effect before firing off the line. "So he used fire to fight fire."

Even Bonnie groaned good naturedly.

"And what happened to the Gini Group? Surely, they'd be charged with arson or something," Nathan said.

"What could they be charged with? The farmers freely admitted they set fire to their own fields. There was no fraud, no arson. They didn't apply for crop insurance or insurance of any kind. And Sage's group owned the corn outright so what they did with it was their business. The people who run the markets wanted us to charge them but what could we nail them on? I don't think there's a judge in the country that would convict them of public mischief. It would be a local charge and the local police were on the farmers' side."

Flynn pointed out that every recourse the powerbrokers looked at met a dead end. "The lawyers for the commodity traders talked about charges for inciting people to violence but burning corn, in and of itself, isn't violence and it isn't a crime. There may have been a pollution law that was contravened but that would be opening up another can of worms for no purpose."

"Did the Gini members get rich, too?" Bonnie had seen too many false prophets swaddled in the robes of a social cause who were really only in it for the money and power.

"They did and they didn't. They made a few million in the transaction and by all accounts they were investing it in grass-roots environmental enterprises and NGOs working toward equalizing wealth around the world."

"So why would they get involved with this negative gravity?" asked Nathan.

"My profile of the Gini Conspiracy is that they are looking at all ways to find balance in the economy. They want to knock a few digits off the wealth of the super rich and distribute it to those at the bottom of the socio-economic ladder."

"And this would do it?" Nathan directed his question to Jordan.

"In their view and ours, yes."

At that point, Bonnie jumped up and started pacing while giving voice to her thoughts.

"Okay, all of this is fantastic, a miracle, incredible. They give negative gravity to the world and the poor get richer and rich get poorer. Why the hell would we ever want to put a stop to this. Agent Jordan, it's like you said before. Even cops are people. We should be helping the Gini Brigades or whatever they call themselves. I think we should be giving Dr. Plank and the Gini guys Nobel Prizes for their contributions to humanity."

"Yeah, that's the good side," said Flynn. "Here's the bad news. Canada weathered the financial collapse better than most countries because a big chunk of our economy is based on resources – mostly oil and gas. If you make energy worth nothing tomorrow, the economy of Canada and the world collapse. This thing has to be introduced gradually. And that's just for starters."

Jordan signaled her agreement and added, "We've put out an APB. All law enforcement agencies in the U.S. and Canada are putting on a full-court press to hunt down the Ginis. Thanks to you Nathan, we now know who they are."

"I'm not so sure that we're really happy about that. Their goal is to help average people, after all. You're still just talking about super rich people protecting their interests," Bonnie said pointedly.

"In a perfect world, that would be wonderful, but this isn't a perfect world," said Jordan. "What made us seek out Nathan and makes his role so important is the potential – no the reality – of negative gravity being used around the a world as a weapon – the ultimate weapon."

—

19

THE HUNT

MO SHOWED SAGE AND ALESSA the alert on his computer screen that identified each member of the team by name accompanied by a photo.

"The cops are on to us."

Alessa remained calm, pulled out a large manila envelope and slid it toward Mo.

"Knowing who we are and finding where we are is a different story."

Sage smiled in agreement.

Alessa's job had been to secure false identities, cars, anonymous credit cards, bank accounts and places for group members to stay in Toronto, Chicago and elsewhere where they wouldn't be detected.

"We have a great advantage over other people who have tried to change society." This was Sage's opening line to the group right after they learned of Dr. Plank's technology.

"We have money enough to pull this off. But money is also our great weakness. Once authorities figure out that it's us, they will follow the money trail, find us, and shut us down."

Alessa stepped forward. "I guess that's where I come in."

Alessa Reese grew up in a working class neighborhood – as the song goes – on the south side of Chicago. Like all of those who are born to a work-a-day life, she had her dreams.

The moment she walked on stage in Grade 3 as Dorothy in an abbreviated version of the Wizard of Oz, she set her sights on acting.

That early incentive plus God-given beauty, indefatigable drive, and a good helping of talent started to pay off in her mid-20s. She landed a few commercials, and progressively larger guest spots on TV series and secondary character roles in films. Her career needed one more thing, full-time residency in Los Angeles – more exposure and more opportunities than the Windy City.

As a career decision, it was the right move. From a personal perspective, it couldn't have been more wrong. Alessa was horrified by the extravagance and mindless pursuit of money. One Rodeo Drive address had a six-pack of super-cars sitting in the driveway and who knows how many other luxury vehicles parked in the garage. The Hollywood parties thrown by young entertainment execs, not yet 30, cost more in a single night than most people back home made in two years.

"Has the world gone mad? Do these people understand there are people in America who are starving? How can they not know people in Chicago are dying because they can't afford medicine or an operation?" She poured out her heart to boyfriend Jason Sage.

"It's the same on Wall Street, worse. They take people's money pretending they are working for them. It's all a scam."

Alessa told him she was done with Hollywood and was coming back home to Chicago for Christmas and for good.

"I'll see you over Christmas. I haven't finished moving all of my clients' accounts to safe investments. It should take me until the end of January. After that, I'll quit unless they fire me first."

Back in Chicago, Alessa's incredible head for numbers landed her a job in a bank. It didn't hurt that as teenager she she'd been a babysitter for the manager Mrs. Owens.

Alessa had another extraordinary talent. Her natural openness coupled with the empathy and presentation skills honed as an actor put customers at ease. They'd tell her their full story, a key to judging the character of visible minority customers who distrusted authority figures. The result was more successful loans extended to people who, on paper, the bank perceived as too much of a risk. For others, who the bank was more than willing to toss money at, she found inconsistencies in their stories and documentation.

On one occasion, she looked at auto ownership documents offered as collateral on a loan. The papers looked superb but were forged. Alessa lived in the same neighbourhood as the applicant, Mrs. Fernandez. She knew the real owner of the expensive SUV.

Alessa did not call her manager or the police. She took the woman aside and told her she had destroyed the loan application and all related documents.

"Why do you need money so desperately that you are willing to commit fraud. Once they checked the truck's ownership with State records, everything would blow up in your face. You would not get the money. You would go to jail."

The woman broke down and cried for a long time before Alessa got her to talk.

"I need the money for my sister's operation. If I don't put down the rest of the deposit, another $4,000 this week, they won't give her the operation and she'll die."

"I can't promise you anything but you can apply for the loan again based solely on your character. I will vouch for you. It just might work."

"You would do that for me?"

"I know this was an act of desperation, driven by your love and loyalty to your sister. I need that same level of commitment to me and to the bank. If we give you this loan, do you swear you will do your utmost – legally – to repay it?"

"I swear. I swear I will pay it all back."

"One last thing, who forged those documents for you?"

Mrs. Fernandez admitted her 20-year-old son Pedro, a graphic artist, created the documents.

Alessa submitted the loan but had one last condition. She wanted to meet with her son first. Pedro had talent as an artist but in these depressed times his career was heading nowhere. She asked about the forgeries. He showed her computer files for the hundreds of fake driver's licences, birth certificates and a few passports he had created. Pedro promised her that side of his life was over.

Through her contacts in the entertainment industry, Alessa put Pedro in touch with agencies that agreed to direct work his way. The rest was up to him.

"We owe you so much. If ever you need anything of me, you ask and we will do any thing to help you," Mrs. Fernandez said.

Two years later, Alessa found herself back at their door.

Pedro earned a respectable income, thanks to Alessa and the diligent performance of his craft. He and his mother had no reservations doing anything that Alessa required.

"I know I am sounding very two-faced after my speech on morality to you but this will help a lot of people, perhaps millions who need help," Alessa said.

"I see it in your eyes," Mrs. Fernandez replied. "You are like me when I was desperate to save my sister. I believe you. I believe what you are doing is a very good thing. We will tell no one about this."

With the money that Alessa brought to the table, Pedro had access to high resolution scanners, printers, specialty papers, materials and a 3D printer to create a range of flawless pieces of identification based on the identities Mo plucked via cyber space from records of people who disappeared or died in their infancy.

As instructed, Pedro created three new identities for each of the six team members.

Moving money was another challenge. It wasn't prudent to carry more than a few thousand dollars in cash. More than that would arouse suspicion when team members crossed the border into Canada. Again, Alessa came up with the answer.

...

"Surely, you can trace where the money goes," Flynn said.

"They've been very clever."

To emphasize his point, Davis called up a screen where the bank account showed more than $600,000 had been withdrawn from the Gini's bank account and investment portfolio over a month.

"How is it possible that you can't track the money?"

"They took it out in cash," Davis said.

"Six hundred grand in cash? How's that possible without leaving a trail?"

"There's a bit of a trail. After that, it goes cold. Where do you think each of them can withdraw $5,000 to $10,000 in small bills every day for three or four weeks without raising suspicion?"

Before anyone could respond, Davis blurted out the answer. "Las Vegas, Atlantic City and other places with casinos."

He described how $500,000 went directly into chips that were later redeemed for cash. Other sums were used to buy prepaid credit cards that each of the Ginis created under a false name. They'd also use the card's balance to buy chips. Later in the day, they'd return the chips for cash.

"In the days before we were on to them, the Ginis who went to Canada travelled around from casino to casino gathering the money they needed."

"There are other ways to track them if they went to casinos," Flynn said. "Those places all have cameras. We can use facial recognition software, track their movements in the casinos and once we know when they left, pick them up on other cameras."

Davis shook his head.

"These guys are smart. Facial recognition isn't an exact science. The position of the eyes is central to most systems. Big sunglasses will thwart most systems."

Flynn leaned in with a more serious look than he'd shown before.

"We've got to step it up. The Ginis' connection to the Occupy Movement gives them allies everywhere. There were Occupy protests in nearly 1,000 cities in 82 countries. We're dealing with the potential for hundreds of thousands of terrorists, any of them can trigger an unimaginable weapon."

"It's not hundreds of thousands. It's seven billion, the 99% who have been left out," said Bonnie.

"Once the majority holds the power, as it should, we'll have détente like the U.S. and U.S.S.R. over nuclear weapons."

"Yeah. Remember détente meant that at any moment we could blow the other guy off the face of the planet," said Flynn.

Bonnie shook her head at the CSIS officer.

"The Occupy Movement's goal is to moderate how large corporations and the global financial system manipulate the world. The system hurts 99% of the people to benefit the richest 1%. This undermines democracies, economies, our food supply, fresh water supplies, and even the air we breathe. This negative gravity stuff will level the playing field."

"Really good, idealistic thinking but very naïve," Jordan said.

"The Occupy Movement has direct links with the folks behind the Arab Spring, the Portuguese and Spanish Indignants Movement in the Iberian Peninsula and, if you can believe this – God-loving, gun-toting members of the Tea Party.

"We're talking about technology in the hands of people who strap bombs on their bodies and blow themselves and everyone around them to kingdom come. We can hope everyone who gets a negative gravity chip will use it for good.

"Human nature tells us not everyone will. Each of them will have the power to pass negative gravity to the next guy. Who knows how many psychopaths will possess a negative gravity sample and goodness knows what they will use it for."

Flynn offered an example.

"Suppose a couple Al-Qaeda members are hiding out in a cave in Afghanistan. They use the technology to pick up a medium size mountain, float it into the edge of space until it's somewhere over New York City and then let it drop. It wouldn't have to be close. They could cause a tsunami.

"It doesn't have to be a mountain. It could be an iceberg, discarded ships, tanks, cars, even garbage. You don't have to make a bomb. When something falls from the edge of space, it's going to make a big hole in something or someone."

"Is it easy to reverse the effect back to normal gravity to let it drop?" asked Bonnie.

"We don't know that but we're not going to be taking chances," Flynn said, reverting to matter-of-fact cop speak.

"Yeah, we got the Ginis in our sights and we're trying to nail them but you have to understand that they are really the least of our worries and it's not just terrorists that keeps us up at night."

Nathan screwed up his face. "Then who are the other enemies?"

"Well, basically everybody," said Jordan. "The oil and gas industry sure doesn't want this out. I'm sure more than a few would kill to suppress it. Some of the most valuable companies in the world will become worthless overnight."

Flynn jumped in again. "Even our allies may see this as a way to get an economic leg up. Any number of foreign countries with a bone to pick with the U.S. and Canada would love to get their hands on the technology. How safe would we be if North Korea possessed it?"

"So what's the Ginis' game? Why haven't they released it?" said Bonnie.

"Our best guess right now is that the Ginis, being really smart people, have thought of all the downsides that we've come up with and it terrifies them, too," said the blond agent. "They aren't bad folks and I don't think that they see themselves as terrorists. From their past work, they certainly don't appear to want to hurt people."

"So what will they do?"

"I think they'll ask for a ransom, a big one, in keeping with the Occupy Movement's objectives. It might not just be money. It may be legislation. It may be a gun to the head of corporations and government to operate in certain ways that benefit the majority and limit the power of the 1%."

"But so far no ransom demand, right?" Bonnie said.

"Not only haven't they asked for a ransom, they haven't claimed credit for the kidnapping or technology theft. That's why we needed Nathan to find out where they are," Flynn said.

"Just how do you know all of this if no one has reported the scientist missing and there's no ransom? Besides, I don't see these kids being the type to forcibly kidnap Plank," said Bonnie.

"We do have some additional information and, as you suspected, it shows Plank willingly going along with them," said Flynn.

"Willingly? Why would he do that," asked Bonnie.

"Through the oldest trick in the book. Here's a video that Davis found from one of the cameras on the U of T campus. The time stamp says it happened on Tuesday, April 8."

The camera captures an image of Plank leaving the physics building. Immediately, a beautiful young woman approaches him. After a few minutes, the two walk together out of camera view. The video jumps to a scene captured by another camera a few minutes later, which shows Plank and the woman entering the St. George Subway station.

"After that, Plank disappeared and has not been seen since," Jordan said.

"What happened to the student?" Bonnie asked.

"Take away the big sunglasses and the phony wig and that was Jasmine Irianto," said Flynn.

"And he just walked away with her, not knowing who she was? I know she's great looking but why would a guy as smart as him get sucked in so easily?"

"We see that a lot. It's called the MBS syndrome," Flynn replied with a smirk.

"MBS syndrome?"

"Yeah, Male Blood Supply syndrome. Basically, a male has two heads but only enough blood to supply one of them at a time."

—

[20]

THE RANSOM

AFTER A LUNCH consisting of what appeared to be day-old, vending-machine sandwiches and juice boxes, which the two chose to eschew rather than chew, Bonnie threw up her hands and demanded that Jordan and Flynn make some menu changes.

"Agent Flynn, news flash! They've invented something new. They call them fresh vegetables. If you eat them before they rot, they taste good and they're good for you. Surely, everybody in this building can't be eating the slop we're getting. I mean, don't a lot of them carry guns?"

"I'm afraid security allows only inspected and approved things on security levels. This is a security level. Food is covered by the same protocols and must go through the same security measures. It takes between one and two weeks so we can't have anything that will go bad," Flynn said.

"Gee, the stuff you give us can't go bad because it is bad. Look, I'm not beyond giving a food bribe. Surely, there must be some meal, some restaurant somewhere you want to try. Nathan can get you a table anywhere. Just give us some god damn fresh ingredients and Nathan will whip up a meal that you'll remember for the rest of your life."

Getting no response from Flynn, Bonnie turned to Nathan. "How about a little support here. Remember that incredible Salad Nicoise that your friend Jill Wilcox whipped up for us – heirloom baby potatoes, haricot vert, quail eggs, and Spanish tuna. Yum."

Nathan shrugged and angled his head toward Jordan for her take.

Jordan's apparent lack of interest in anything Bonnie said or did turned the sidekick's mind to thoughts of what it would be like to yank a few clumps of blond hair out by the roots. A knowing gaze from Nathan, whose nose is a world-class angst detector, swung her back from violence to a verbal path.

"That's enough! Nathan's helped you identify the group responsible. I think our work is done."

Jordan straightened her navy jacket and matching skirt, in contrast to the sloppy tracksuit Bonnie was wearing, as if to frame her words as an adult would to a small child.

"Nathan has proven himself to be extremely valuable to us and we may still have need of his skills. We need both of you to remain with us until this investigation is completed."

Whether consciously intended or not, the Special Agent's use of her business power suit as another control mechanism had Bonnie seeing red – blood red. Visions of tuffs of blond hair between her fingers resurfaced so vividly, her wrist began to twist and, with it, she could almost see and hear the golden strands popping out of Jordan's head like hundreds of guitar strings snapping in unison. Nathan stirred next to her but she held up her hand to indicate she would, again, wage words, not war.

"Now wait a minute. What if your investigation takes a year or more?"

"We don't think it will take long one way or another," said Flynn. "They didn't steal the technology and kidnap Plank to sit around playing tiddlywinks for a year. They're planning something right now. They know the longer they take doing it, the more likely it is we're gonna get 'em."

Jordan nodded vigorously in agreement. "We're hot on some leads right now. Davis's scans of the Internet are collecting any messages, coded or otherwise, that speak of negative gravity or Dr. Plank. We think we're on to something."

"And that would be?" asked Nathan.

"We found some terrorist groups were using a ploy to get email back and forth to each other without transmitting them over the Internet. The tactic specifically prevents authorities from intercepting their messages using key words and other snoop programs," she said.

"They send email without sending email?" Bonnie asked.

Flynn produced the broad, cocky grin of someone who had just performed a three-move checkmate.

"Exactly. It was a brilliant idea to start but now it's such an old trick that it's even been used in the plots of a couple of spy novels. Lucky for us, they don't read spy novels."

The CSIS officer said the communication system works by creating a web-based email account but instead of typing in messages and sending them, the notes are saved. Others members of the group use the same user name and password so that they can access the account to read the saved correspondence.

"We now have sweeper programs that signal if email accounts are being used by multiple IP addresses. We scan those email accounts for anything suspicious. I guess in this case IP stands for Idiot Perps." The grin devolved into a series of half-muffled guffaws and snorts.

Nathan prodded for more information, ignoring Flynn's self-congratulatory laughter.

"And you've obviously found something suspicious."

"More than suspicious," said Jordan. "It's definitely the Gini Conspirators. The un-sent emails date back over the past two weeks and they make reference to a Dr. P, un-gravity and even the nicknames of a few of the team members – Mo, Jaz and DD. We just found a very fuzzy phone video clip that was put up two days ago of one of them trying the negative gravity experiment and they were doing it without an isolation box to create bigger objects with negative gravity."

"Then overnight, they literally gave us the smoking gun." It was a beaming Davis who seemed to pop out of nowhere, inserting himself into the conversation.

"It's a video of Plank. Again, the video was loaded as an attachment on the email site but was never sent. I believe the intention was to allow all members of the group and perhaps their international friends to view the video before it was made public. Obviously, there's some kind of delay or they didn't like the video because it hasn't been released yet."

The video showed a sad and disheveled-looking Plank trussed up to a chair with two people in hoods, each carrying an automatic weapon.

The smaller of the two, a woman, walked straight up to the camera and delivered a scary, almost maniacal rant that at times planted her hooded face, with only crazed, fanatical eyes visible, taking up the entire screen.

"We have Dr. Plank and we have the technology," she screamed, flailing her left arm like a crazed conductor and, in her right, an M-16 waving a bit too carelessly for Davis' liking. "We will send samples of materials that possess negative gravity to our friends all around the world unless you follow our instructions exactly."

In a non-stop staccato as rapid and nearly as lethal as her weapon, the woman's rant continued, escalating each minute in volume, pitch and ferocity.

"The U.S. government provided the filthy rich with a $700 billion bailout to save their butts during the financial crisis. That money came from everyday taxpayers. We want that money returned to the people, every penny of it through an immediate tax on the rich and corporations in the financial sector. We demand $100 billion a week placed into the following seven areas over the next seven weeks."

"Whew, Seven Hundred Billion Dollars?" Flynn nearly choked on the words. "We were expecting a ransom, but $700 billion?"

"Sshh!" Bonnie gave a stern stop-the-chattering glare, simultaneously pointing to the screen as the woman began her explanation how the ransom is to be paid.

"The first $100 billion is to fund an upgrade to the pension and benefits and health support available for our veterans. In week two, an additional $100 billion will be allocated to the Affordable Care Act (Obama Care) to provide extra support and services to our most vulnerable citizens.

"In the third week, $100 billion will be distributed to all states on a per capita basis to support public education at inner city schools. Week four's allocation will go toward measures to clean the nation's air including $1 billion toward the hiring of more EPA inspectors to shut down and/or fine polluters.

"The $100 billion in week five will be used to provide clean drinking water for all U.S. citizens including $1 billion to hire more EPA inspectors to shutdown and/or fine polluters. In week six, $100 billion will be injected into programs that deal with addiction issues.

"The seventh and final week will see the direction of $100 billion toward solving the nation's homeless crisis with a minimum of half of the amount going toward mental health services for the homeless."

The hooded woman stepped back from the camera, paused, and spoke directly into the lens.

"Don't think for a second that you can move around money and pretend to have it go where I've told you. This must be new, unallocated money. You must do exactly as I have directed or pay the consequences. We are the 99%. We are everywhere. We see all. We know all.

"Our associates in Europe and the Middle East are ready and will be making similar demands. Make no mistake. If you try to deceive us, we unleash negative gravity on the world."

Bonnie rocked back in her chair, heaved a huge breath and placed her hands on the top of her head as if to keep it from exploding with all the information that had gone into it.

"That is one scary lady but, wow, can she ever deliver a ransom demand."

"Not exactly a ransom. We're not supposed to know about it because they haven't released it, yet. I guess they're trying to coordinate things with their buddies around the world," Flynn speculated.

"I guess it's all over for them now that you're on to them," Nathan said.

"Not yet. None of the messages gives us any idea where they're located other than one group is definitely in the Greater Chicago area and another in the Greater Toronto Area.

They've accessed the account from libraries, Internet hot spots, you name it. But we do know they have Plank and we do know who they are. It's just a matter of time before we get them," said Flynn.

After yet another sad dinner where the two ate white bread but left the rest untouched, Bonnie and Nathan assessed their position.

"Nathan, I'm afraid it's not just the mission. You've done your work and there's not a clear next step for your powers. I believe they will resist letting you go. I think they want another elite member of the ESP team."

"That's my conclusion, too. First, they'll use every means possible to get me to stay voluntarily. My celebrity status helps, but I'm not ready to press them just yet. If you make a fuss, they have to let you go. I need you on the outside so you're free to act. Let me explain."

—

21

THAT SPECIAL AGENT

BONNIE WALKED INTO the dining room the next morning with her hand blocking her view of the table.

"Okay, let me guess what's for breakfast. I just know they've decided to surprise us. How about a reprise of that fantastic primo colazione in Tuscany. Grilled ciabatta topped with a slice of beefsteak tomato, wilted spinach, poached egg, finished with a Mornay sauce and garnished with crumbled, crispy prosciutto.

"Don't tell me about the beverage. Is it freshly squeezed grapefruit juice with pomegranate juice and a splash of sparkling water to go with it?"

Bonnie removed her hand with an even greater theatrical flourish for the grand unveiling.

"Uhhhh, no. What is THAT? Are you purposely trying to torture us?"

Bonnie walked by Flynn, making gagging noises and grabbing at her throat. She snatched a fork and poked it into a chubby sausage that resembled moldy steel wool. The poke inspired a gush of greyish liquid that merged with a semi-liquid, yellow goop that she presumed were eggs.

"This stuff elevates hospital food to epicurean standards."

"Yeah, the grub's not the best. But it's supposed to be super nutritious."

"You sound like one of those mothers from the Stepford Wives."

Spinning sideways to face Nathan, she positioned the plate below his nose. "And what in hell's name is in this sausage and these uggs."

Nathan reflexively moved his nose away from the plate. "I could tell you but, believe me, you really don't want to know."

With that, Bonnie jettisoned the plate onto the table as if it held a cobra.

"We've been here three days and the last decent thing we've had to eat was Aunt Lucy's latkes and cabbage rolls on the plane."

"Maybe, you could order a pizza?" Flynn had a smug look on his face as he held out his cell phone. "But I doubt whether the delivery guy could make it through security."

"I want out. You say you need Nathan, okay. You got Nathan. You don't need me. Unless you charge me with something, you need to release me today, in fact, right now."

Flynn contemplated the thought for a minute, shrugged and decided it was above his pay grade. He walked toward the intercom on the wall next to the exit and hit a button.

"Rebecca. We need you in the breakfast room."

A few minutes later, Jordan breezed into the room, alternately glancing at Flynn, Nathan and Bonnie. "What's up?"

Flynn pointed a thumb toward the scowling young woman. "Bonnie wants out."

"I told you that we need to keep Nathan here."

"Nathan yes, me, no."

"Are you sure? I thought you two came as a set."

"You're so funny. You're in the wrong career. You should be on Vegas Strip delivering one-liners between has-been crooners."

"Uuhh, let's get back to what we were discussing," said Nathan. "Bonnie wants to leave and I don't see any purpose in you holding her here. I promise to keep cooperating fully without her."

"I guess it's decided. Bonnie, you can leave. We'll arrange for a flight home this afternoon. Any more requests?"

"Just one. Get Nathan some decent food."

...

Jordan pulled up in the big black Suburban and Bonnie hopped in. They drove to the airstrip in silence and shared no words as the Special Agent ushered Bonnie into the Learjet. Jordan waited 20 minutes while the jet taxied into position and lifted off into the late afternoon skies.

From a hidden compartment beneath the seat of the car, Jordan withdrew a cheap burner phone and dialed a number.

"She's gone."

"Good. Good. No more interference from Ms N. You have Mr. S's full attention?"

"Yes, absolutely. He will follow my instructions virtually without question."

"I need you to come in. We need to talk about our next steps and you need to regenerate."

"With the usual precautions, it will take me just over an hour."

There was a click at the other end and the line went dead. Jordan was used to such abruptness. It had been like that since the very beginning.

...

Thirteen-year-old Rebecca Jordan had been prescribed a medicine cabinet full of supplements and, for the past two months, blood transfusions twice a week.

"There's nothing abnormal internally. That means all we're doing is treating the symptoms. We haven't touched the surface of what's behind this. We're doing all we can but so far, we're stumped," said Dr. Rodgers, a gynecologist.

"There's got to be someone, somewhere who knows something about this," said Emily Jordan, Rebecca's mother.

"There is a physician who's doing some experimental work. Normally, I wouldn't point anyone in that direction, but I'm afraid there's nothing more I can do for Rebecca, and unless someone can get to the bottom of this soon ..."

"What's his name and how to we get in touch with him?"

...

"Rebecca Jordan-an?"

"Yes, that's me," said the slender, pasty-faced teen, seated next to her mother.

The doctor, a stocky man with brown hair and a goatee,. stood about six feet. He looked to be 40. He wore a white lab coat and held a laptop under one arm. His lapel badge displayed the name Dr. J. B. Menck.

"My name is Dr. Julian Menck-enck," the doctor said, pronouncing his last name like the word 'mink' but stretching the last portion like an echo dragged unwillingly over a gravel road. "Mrs. Jordan-an, I'd like Rebecca to come with me-e, but I need you to remain here-ere."

114

Mrs. Jordan flinched slightly at the odd and irritating vocal creaking on the final word of each phrase but she dipped her head twice in consent. Dr. Menck led down a long corridor with armed Marines on guard at each entrance. Rebecca wasn't shocked.

It was, after all, a medical facility on the Marine Corp base at Quantico, VA. She and her mother had seen many armed Marines when they went through the checkpoint at the main gate and cleared security again at the medical office.

Dr. Menck stopped at the last doorway and beckoned Rebecca in. The examination room was typical and so were the medical tests. First up were the questions about family history, medical past, health habits, and other symptoms.

Father still living-ing? Father and mother's health okay-ay? Any siblings-ings? How is their health-ealth?

At the end of the long list of questions, Dr. Menck gave no hint about Rebecca's issues.

The physical part came next. He listened to her heart, lungs, and abdomen. Examined her skin, ears, mouth, and eyesight. Next came the reactive process. Reflexes, a press on the abdomen to check for masses or get a reaction of pain. The lab and testing portion followed with a blood pressure test, measurement of her heart rate and tests for cholesterol and blood sugar.

When everything was done, Dr. Menck confirmed a severe case of anemia but otherwise none of the usual indicators showed anything out of the ordinary.

"So Rebecca-ca, I've read your medical file-ile but could we go through it again-ain?

Tell me-e, what is happening to you-ou?"

"It just doesn't stop," she said, with tones of despair and panic colouring her voice. "My family doctor said I could become too anemic and die."

"So how long has this been going on-on?"

"Well, I had my first period about eight months ago."

"And when did it start-art?"

"I told you I had my first period eight months ago."

"And it hasn't ever stopped-opped?"

"It's been constant. Every day and some days so bad I can hardly get out of bed. And the blood flow. It's a lot worse than anybody I know. My mother had to buy me some new outfits because the old ones were ruined. Can you help me? I was told that you were the one who could help me."

"Yes, I believe I can-an. But for my therapy to work-ork, you will need to make certain sacrifices-ces."

...

Agent Jordan drove north on I-95 for about a half hour before taking the turn-off for I-495 and I-395 to D.C.

Once on Washington Boulevard, she took a meandering route before quickly veering into the Arlington Residence's underground garage. She parked in area 2B.

Reaching into her purse, Jordan found a second car fob. A press on a button and a familiar honking came from a Jaguar two rows over.

She approached the Jag, popped its trunk, and gave a quick glance to see the coast was clear. She swopped her navy blazer for a long, hooded Armani coat and slid a pair of Roberto Cavelli jeans under her skirt before shedding it. Designer sunglasses that covered a third of her face and a dark brown wig completed the transformation.

She grabbed the clothing she shed, stuffed them in a bag and put everything in the Suburban. She gave one quick glance in a compact mirror and departed in the Jag.

A few minutes later, Jordan motored along trendy Dupont Circle in George-town, arriving at the swank boutique hotel and private meeting place, La Casa on O Street. She tossed her keys to the valet and disappeared inside.

She knocked on the door of a third-floor suite and without waiting for a response, walked in and locked the door behind her. Dr. Menck stretched out on a divan.

"Come here-ere. Come here-ere," he said impatiently. "You should have been here two days ago-go."

"It was impossible to get away," she said, doffing her coat and rolling up the left sleeve of her blouse.

Dr. Menck opened a black physician's case and scooped out a plastic tube. He removed the top and tipped out a syringe with a pale, pink liquid in it. He pulled off the guard, sent a tiny spurt from the needle, and jabbed it into Jordan's arm.

"How was your control in the past two days-ays?"

"Still functional but certainly not at peak."

"And this Nathan Sherlock does not suspect-ect?"

"No, he is fully engaged in the project. However, his palate for fine dining has meant he hasn't been eating much of the food we've provided to him. You're sure he can't detect what's in it? His powers are amazing."

"He can detect that the food is full of hormones-ones, but that's just like all processed foods these days-ays. He won't be able to figure out what they do-o. No matter, he has to eat sometime-ime. That's when he'll be ours-ours, just like Seiji and Reyanna-na."

"I'm not certain he needs enhancement like the others. His power seems to have no limit. He gave us an amazing demonstration two days ago when he identified hundreds of compounds in seconds."

"It's not about his power-er. We need him to eat the food-ood or he won't be compliant-ant, the way I want him to be compliant-ant. The way you are compliant-ant. Do you understand me-e?"

"Yes sir."

"Good-ood. Have Seiji or Reyanna given you any problems-ems?"

"No. They know what will happen if they do."

"And what about your boss-oss, Assistant Director DeRoach-oach, and that Canadian Flynn-ynn and his boss Beauchemin-min."

"Beauchemin's a pompous ass. He's more concerned about his appearance than getting the job done. Besides, he's already returned to Canada. Flynn's another story. He comes off as a bumbler but that's just a façade to put everyone off guard. He's hard to read, but I'm certain he doesn't suspect anything about our arrangement. DeRoach is the one we've got to worry about. At the moment he has bigger fish to fry and isn't thinking about anything else, certainly not about you. Still, he does know about our past connection and he forgets nothing."

"Yes, Agent DeRoach-oach. My nemesis-sis. We could have wiped out all the terrorists-ists, solved many mysteries-ies but for that meddling fool-ool. I don't have to remind you-ou, it would be the end of you-ou as well as me if he finds out-out."

With that, Jordan left, a seething rage hidden beneath a well practiced veneer of aloofness.

...

For the first time in more than a year, Rebecca Jordan smiled without reservation. In a few days, it would be her 14th birthday. She actually had thoughts of celebrating it – go out or, maybe, have a birthday party with friends. She felt healthy, strong and even pretty.

Since returning to school she noticed that all the boys she liked, seemed to like her.

Not that any of them told her that. It was the way they looked at her and got tongue-tied and clumsy whenever she came near.

Even that gorgeous Bobby Wade couldn't take his eyes off her during algebra class. His girlfriend Sissy, the most popular girl in school, sat next to him and kept stomping her foot to get his attention.

It's a good thing I acted like I didn't notice or Sissy and the Sissters would have been all over me, Rebecca thought.

"How have you been Rebecca-ca?" Dr. Menck asked during her regular monthly checkup.

"Fantastic. I feel really good. I've caught up with my school work. I've got all my friends back."

"What about the boys-oys?"

"The boys?"

"Yes, the boys-oys. Do they seem interested in you-ou?"

Rebecca's face flushed. She shifted her gaze away from Dr. Menck. "Well, yes. Some boys seem to be paying more attention to me these days."

"And do you return their attention-tion?"

"Well, uh, umm, well, no. I sort of pretend that I don't notice them staring at me."

"Good-ood. You must be careful-ful. At your age you don't want to be acting rashly-ly."

"Dr. Menck! I'm not that kind of girl. I never . . ."

"I apologize-ize. I think you misunderstand-and where I was going-ing. It's time to tell you more about the true nature of your condition-tion – about your hormonal therapy-py and its possible side-effects-ects."

. . .

118

When Rebecca completed high school, on Dr. Menck's recommendation, the FBI recruited her for a special program where she could work for the bureau while completing advanced university studies in criminology and psychology. Dr. Menck placed her in the ESP unit, where he was the chief scientific officer and director.

Rebecca's intellect and hormonal abilities gave her star status in the unit along with a bright, Japanese-American named Seiji who possessed extraordinary visual abilities and a young man named Kirk, who had a super sensitive sense of touch.

Rebecca learned – under Dr. Menck's tutelage, continued hormonal therapy, and with much practice – she had the ability to detect the chemistry of any male near her and adjust her own body chemistry to exude the ideal pheromone cocktail to leave him panting like a love sick puppy.

This gave her a significant edge when she interviewed male suspects. While their love yearnings rarely resulted in outright confessions, her enchanting aura threw them off their game. Bewildered subjects often blurted out clues that contributed to their undoing and the case being solved.

—

22

BONNIE'S MISSION

ANOTHER BLACK SUBURBAN dropped Bonnie off at her two-storey, brick home on Indian Road, a tree-lined neighbourhood at the edge of Toronto's largest green space, High Park.

Bonnie loved the area.

She, like Nathan, had been raised in Etobicoke, a Toronto suburb, known as Canada's first planned community. The west end burb boasts great traffic movement and few squabbles with neighbours over property lines. But all that planning scrubbed the suburb clean of everything that makes Toronto unique, its spontaneous, and sometimes crazy multi-cultural character.

When she moved to Toronto to work with Nathan, there was no question where she'd live. It had to be High Park. The park and the community around it wasn't part of any master plan like Etobicoke. It just evolved into one of the best parts of the city. That's where her grandparents lived when they were still alive.

The thought of the area revived emotions and memories that never failed to lift her day.

With everything that had happened and was still happening, she needed a jog through High Park, at least in her mind's eye.

To Bonnie, the park was magical. It gave life to diverse vegetation, provided an uncluttered view of Lake Ontario, housed greenhouses, made homes for a zillion squirrels, raccoons, skunks, and other critters. It was nature's temple for Torontonians to seek and find momentary sanctuary from big city life.

One of her fondest memories was of crazy grandpa and grandma Naka-gowa, wearing his and hers straw hats with big canvas bags slung over their shoulders, lurking through the bushes with their granddaughter, in pursuit of the greatest of all treasures – wild mushrooms.

"Here grandpa," a six-year-old Bonnie said, a giant puffed fungus overflowing her twin cupped hands.

"Thank you so much Bonnie. We will use this as decoration. You see the spots along the edge and pink underneath? That means you can't eat it. It will give you a bad tummy ache."

And so it was that Bonnie learned about finding wild mushrooms, the right ones, just outside her grandparents' door. And there were other treats as well – fiddleheads and garlic mustard, mallow, stinging nettle, wild alfalfa, burdock, and sunflowers that, back in the 80s and before Bonnie's birth, found their place in the diet of the elder Nakagowas.

When Bonnie returned to High Park, she learned big city rules and conservation ordinances now prohibited the gathering of mushrooms or any plants from the park. Still she loved to spot them on her many walks. She pointed them out to Nathan.

He crawled on hands and knees for a better sniff and rose with an incredible smile on his face. "I've got an idea."

That night, Nathan assembled a High Park centric meal for Bonnie: Wild Salmon pan seared and served with a Wild Mushroom Ragout and fiddleheads. The ragout included golden chanterelles, morels, and giant puffball mushrooms acquired from a specialty dealer and shiitake, king oyster, and porcini mushrooms from the local market, all sautéed in butter and finished with a few drops of truffle oil.

The meal, at Bonnie's urging, led to Nathan's best-selling Inspirations of High Park Cookbook.

That was the cookbook that directly resulted in the Let's Eat Inc. contract.

Unfortunately for Bonnie, her dose of High Park this day would be only visual – a sward of green backing into a forest, framed by her livingroom window. She had a lot to do and not much time to do it. She linked her laptop with the server in the office, entered the parameters Nathan provided and set the computer to follow the instructions.

This was but another secret mission for Nathan and a major part of her job since she took his call four years ago.

...

Bonnie stifled a monster yawn to maintain professional appearances while performing as a 'two-way man,' journalism parlance for a reporter/photographer, covered a $5,000 cheque presentation by the Lindsay Memorial Hospital's Women's Auxiliary.

Snap.

Forever frozen in time, six blue-rinse bobs frame wide smiles over a poster-sized cheque handed to the Armani-suited hospital CEO.

This was Bonnie's scoop of the day, which she dutifully covered for her employer, the Peterborough Daily Express, circulation 12,000. In this Ontario backwater, her dreams of becoming an investigative reporter for the Washington Post or 60 Minutes seemed far-fetched.

Fellow Ryerson journalism grads had been called up to the media major leagues in the past. A year in the field, Bonnie found herself stuck on a hamster wheel. The job kept her crazy-busy but for all the energy expended, her career remained in the same spot.

While waiting for the end of the CEO's long-winded speech, her cell phone rang.

"Bonnie . . ."

"Nathan! I was waiting for you to do something like this. I read the Toronto Clarion food review . . . Amazing. Amazing."

"They were talking about it on the radio this afternoon. The Clarion's Food Editor Dianne Kingsmere was the guest. She pretty well told everyone that your food and wine pairings give people multiple orgasms. You're a star."

Bonnie hit the last sentence like the final notes of an aria.

"What are you doing tonight?" Nathan posed the question, barely containing the Vesuvius of news that threatened to erupt.

"Well, of course, I'm working. Small town reporter, town council meeting. If things get really exciting, they might hold an emergency library board session or announce cancellation of the talent show at the fall fair. No rest for cub reporters."

"Yes, you'll be working tonight but not in Lindsay. Come to Toronto right now. As of this moment you're working for . . . er . . . with me, Girl Wonder."

"I can't, really. I've got my job, my career."

"That's not a career and they may never recognize your talent. I've just been offered my own food and wine reality TV show and I need you to help write it, be my publicist, my best buddy, my Girl Wonder, whatever. You have the talent I need. I can't do it without you."

"But I just can't quit like that. I'll never get another job."

"That's what every chef I worked for predicted about me. You don't need another job. I know how much, rather how little you make. I'll move the decimal point on your paycheque one digit to the right, and I'll cook something really special if you come tonight."

Bonnie tried to think of other reasons to back out. There were none. Like all newspapers these days, the Daily Express' declining circulation laid off loyalty along with most of its long-time staff. It wouldn't take a day to replace her, if it replaced her.

As for Nathan's offer – a huge raise and a chance to work with her best friend – was there a decision to make?

"Sure. If I leave now, I can be there by 7."

As much as he'd prepared himself, Nathan was stunned when Bonnie arrived. They'd been in touch by phone and email at least weekly but the only thing worse than a reporter's schedule was a chef's.

It occurred to him, he hadn't seen her in person in nearly two years and even then only briefly. Gone was the baby-faced girl with the Harry Potter spectacles. An attractive woman in designer glasses stood in her place. Exit the sloppy jeans and sweatshirt that she wore in high school. In their place, a casual but smart and professional pantsuit provided the perfect outfit for a reporter on the go. And were those actually curves? She certainly had filled out.

Their discussions covered the show's theme and every conceivable role Bonnie might play in its development, Nathan's brand, and all spin-off businesses.

Nathan's generosity astounded Bonnie. She was not to be an employee but a partner. She had to take his offer. It was better than a dream.

There was no turning back. Quitting her newspaper job without proper notice put paid to any notions of progressing in journalism where everybody in the industry knew everybody.

Still, when Nathan offered his hand to shake on the deal, she didn't take it. She told him she would sleep on it and give him an answer in the morning.

Nathan stepped back and redirected his energy to preparing a dinner of crab cakes with a Lemongrass Aioli – Bonnie's favourite – accompanied by a sharp tomato salad and polenta with a fine Napa Valley Sauvignon Blanc to wash it down. The meal was simple but lovely, with incredible flavour combinations that only Nathan could create.

The wonderful dinner, the far-reaching business discussions, and the spectacular career opportunity, served up an infinite menu of delicious ideas that whirled through Bonnie's brain through the night. She and Nathan shared a special relationship. Now new and unknown business pressures might test its limits.

She kept hearing her father's words that business and friendship are like oil and water. They don't mix.

The prospect of working with Nathan, the person she trusted and liked most in the world, was exciting, inviting, and scary. If his TV career foundered, their relationship might be at risk. Logic directed her in the past. There were too many emotions in play today for critical thinking.

...

The old memory made Bonnie laugh aloud. They were a great team – maybe a super team. The super part was about to come into play but as foodie fanatics, first things come first, she thought.

I need to save Nathan but even he would agree that after our near fast for three days, I have to refuel first.

She hit the speed dial for Queen's Pasta Café on Bloor Street West.

Scanning the online menu, her eyes and stomach found accord with the Penne Tapenade – black and green olives, capers, artichokes, garlic, sautéed in olive oil and a fresh tomato sauce, and a Caprese Salad – bocconcini cheese, tomato, fresh basil, and balsamic drizzle.

"It's Bonnie. One Penne Tapenade and one Caprese Salad to go. I'll be by in 30 minutes."

"You got it girl."

Sophisticated Bonnie plated the penne and salad on white bone china as recent training dictated. She set the plate on a table that Carson, Downton Abbey's butler, would nod at approvingly – linen on linen, sterling silver, and a delicate claret glass filled with a superb 2011 Palazzo Maffei Ripasso. Then ravenous Bonnie tucked in.

Savour it. Savour it, she kept reminding herself as her days of deprivation won out.

The computer had completed its work by the time she demolished her dinner. She printed the results and dashed out the door.

—

23

CLEOPATRA

BIG ED'S THUNDERING voice called out yet again.

"Summers!"

The frail CFO, half out of breath, rushed into his boss's office.

"Where are we on those trades?"

"Here's today's report – April 18th. We completed sales of over two million shares today. That brings the total to just over $3.7 billion over the past week. That leaves $8.2 billion to go. The way we've assaulted the market, I think it'll take at least three more weeks to get it done without sparking a run."

"Why were there so few trades today?"

"Uh, it is Good Friday. We did the sales mostly on the Nikkei and, in dollar terms, just a few mill on exchanges in South Korea and China."

"This has to happen faster," said Big Ed, chomping on a fat Cohiba and blowing a dense plume of Siglo VI toward Summers.

"Mr. Hendry, selling off $11.9 billion worth of EExE shares is one thing but selling off that much without the market sitting up and noticing is a very different thing. It will take at least another three weeks at minimum. Everything has to be broken into several dozen pieces so it all looks just like an active market rather than a big sell-off. Still our average price was way down to $127 a share."

Big Ed's fingers drummed impatiently, swelling in a crescendo and finally ending with an open hand slamming on his desk.

"$127? EExE hasn't been that low in three years."

"Shall I halt the sell-off?"

"Did anyone say anything about stopping? No, this is Big Ed you're talking to and Big Ed never quits early."

Not great at $127 a share, Big Ed thought. *In the big picture, peanuts. Some sucker thinks he just nailed a huge bargain of a million shares of EExE at $127.*

Cleopatra says the shoe will drop on May 16. By then, I'll have sold all of my EExE shares and use my nearly $12 billion or so to buy short positions in every big oil company in the world. Who cares if I cause a panic after that?

Big Ed realized all this thinking aroused him.

Is it the money? Is it Cleopatra? Ah yes, it's the money and Cleopatra. What a wonderful combination. Could it be just 10 days ago that I got that handwritten note at my Chicago office? Cleopatra needs to speak with you.

Beneath those words was a telephone number to what he presumed was a burner phone.

I respect that. People can't be too careful these days. She doesn't know what I'm thinking and I sure don't know what she's up to.

"Hello, Cleopatra?"

"This is Cleopatra. I presume that you remember me."

"I do, indeed, if it is you. I don't recognize your voice. We didn't do much talking."

"But you did have a ripping time," she said.

Her bluntness caught Big Ed off guard and put him in the unusual position of being at a loss for words. He regrouped his thoughts before responding. "Whew! You continue to be one surprising lady. I'm sorry you disappeared. We had unfinished business, you and I."

"That kind of business will never happen between us ever again. I have a different kind of proposition for you, one that I believe you will find equally intriguing."

"Go on."

"There is a new technology that very few people in the world know about. This technology is about to be released and when it does, it will render all current energy resources unnecessary and expensive. I have the inside track and can keep you apprised in advance. If you follow my instructions exactly, you will become the richest man in the world, by far."

She provided a few of the details and then said, "Ball's in your court."

"Sounds like a bunch of bull to me. What's your angle?"

"Don't take my word for it. Use your own intelligence networks. Get confirmation. Just understand that I have the inside track."

"Say I follow your advice. What's in it for you?"

"I believe you owe me, but I don't expect a man like you just hands out money. I won't make my demands known just yet. As I indicated, check it out and then get back to me. You have my number."

Big Ed softly cradled his phone and considered Cleopatra's words for a full minute.

The girl certainly has balls. And she's right, I do owe it to her. I'll think about it and maybe check it out in a few days.

Two days later, Summers walked into Big Ed's office.

"Mr. Hendry, I'm not sure we should do anything about this but it is troubling. The senator is insistent that we make contact with an individual who has information he says will greatly affect your company."

"What state does Senator Harding represent?"

"Uh, no state, sir. He's Canadian, a Canadian senator."

"Canada has senators?"

"Apparently so."

"And what's he to us?"

"He helped us in the past with our oil and gas acquisitions in Canada. It worked out very well."

"Okay, make the call. Find out what his informant knows."

An hour later, Summers reappeared, looking more nervous and pale than usual.

"I had a conversation with the senator's informant who related very unsettling news. It could severely impact your company and all of the resource sector."

"How?"

"It's a new technology that will replace oil as an energy source. If word gets out, the value of your stock will tumble."

"Replace oil?" Big Ed made a series of half-human noises that disgusted Summers. "Ridiculous. Nobody's going to scare me off with some cockamammy story about a replacement for oil. Still, rumours alone could hurt us. Do some more checking and then run the numbers."

When Summers returned the next morning with supporting documentation from other sources and a projection of a free fall in EExE's share value, Big Ed started to panic. Then his eyes lit on his silver letter opener. The blade's twinkle ignited and linked two memories, one 15 years old and another just two days earlier.

The angry, red face transformed into a barracuda smile that Summers recognized only too well. His boss had a devilish scheme in the making.

"I want regular updates on this. Leave out nothing. Include financial projections for me every day to see the ongoing effect on our share value."

When his CFO retreated from the office, Big Ed eyed the handwritten note. He dialed the number.

"Cleopatra?"

"Ah, nice of you to call me again Big Ed. May I call you Big Ed."

"All my friends do and I believe we are destined to become very good friends. I've confirmed what you've told me. I'm ready to play by your rules. What do you need?"

"Here's my proposition. You pay $10 million into a numbered bank account in the Bahamas. I'll send you authorization to use the money to execute trades. The bank will hold the shares.

"You are to make investments that leverage your money and mine at least 10 to 1. That will maximize your wealth and make sure my $10 million is always in on the action. That will turn your $12 billion into $120 billion. You'll easily be the richest man on Earth and I will be worth a paltry $100 million."

"I like that. It's really win-win. If you double-cross me, you lose, too."

"Exactly."

After a further exchange of information, Big Ed hung up the phone and looked to the open doorway.

"Summers!"

"Yes, Mr. Hendry."

"Here's a numbered account in the Bahamas. Set up a transfer of $10 million into the account but I don't want it triggered until after I get documentation that allows me to use the money for trades on behalf of that account. You gettin' this?"

"Absolutely."

"Make sure it all happens today."

Smart girl that Cleopatra, Big Ed mused. *She must have learned it from me.*

When Cleopatra saw the request for documentation, she sent it immediately. Within a minute, a $10 million deposit landed into her numbered bank account. Cleopatra gave a broad satisfied, smile.

She thought back all those years to her youth when her parents, devout Muslims, moved to the United States for a better life when she was 11. Life in

America was different but her memories of her homeland came in only brief flashes of colour, screams, and days when there was little food on the table. Her father had been a physician back home. In America, he drove a taxi.

Then came the day of the accident. A drunk driver crossed the centre-line and crashed head-on into her family's car. Her parents and two siblings died. She had a nasty gash on her hip that took 30 stitches to close but she had no lasting injuries.

At 14, she was alone in the world and nearly catatonic. In Chicago, there were few members of the Muslim sect her family belonged to and her mental state made a match impossible.

Child welfare bureaucrats placed her into foster care with the Ramsays. The couple that had experience with girls deep in their shell.

The Ramsays liked girls that way because they needed no care at all. They'd leave them alone in a room day and night and collect the money. One night the man put hands on her. Something deep inside awoke. She fled the next day.

It didn't take long for a lone, pretty, 14-year-old to attract attention. A black man in a gold suit and a broad-brimmed, not-quite-matching-gold, Panama hat offered to buy the starving girl a burger. He introduced himself as Honeymoon and he was, indeed, a sweet talker. He asked her if she had a place to sleep. She didn't. "Come with me. Me and my girls, we'll take care of ya."

Honeymoon had a traditional breaking in process. He'd go first and be gentle. Gradually he'd introduce a couple of clients he could count on to go easy before subjecting the girl to the full ride.

Honeymoon looked at the frail, innocent girl and wondered to himself: *This just might work out really good for me.*

He had a special client who wanted girls who weren't broken in. And she was the right age, 14, pretty, exotic, and completely innocent. He hadn't asked the girl's name and didn't care to know it.

"I'm gonna call you Cleopatra because ya got straight black hair and bangs and those beautiful, big brown eyes."

—

[24]

BONNIE IN THE SKIES

WHEN JORDAN RETURNED TO QUANTICO the next morning – May 14 – a frantic-eyed Davis greeted her.

"There's more activity on the email site. You need to see this before Nathan does."

Jordan held her questions while they walked to her office. Davis opened his laptop and clicked on a file. A fuzzy, jumpy video, obviously shot with a cheap cell phone, showed two people gagged and bound to chairs. Two people, off camera, argued.

"It's tough enough to have Plank. We can't handle anyone else." A woman, unseen but obviously in charge, angrily shouted the words. This was not a debate. It was a command.

"Well what . . . what do you propose we do? We just can't let her go." This time it was a male responding but in a halting voice that seemed tinged with fear.

Jordan looked closer at the fuzzy video images on the monitor. She let out a gasp.

"It's . . . it's Bonnie . . . as well as Plank. She just left yesterday afternoon. How could they have her?"

"We've got to get rid of her." The woman barked out the command just as her shoulder, but not her face, came into the camera's view. "And stop shooting that video."

"You know the rules. Jason wants a video of everything," came the voice of a second woman.

The unseen man spoke again, his voice carrying a rising sense of panic.

130

"What do you mean get rid of her? We can't kill her."

"We have the perfect way to get rid of her. We'll never be caught. You know what I'm saying."

"No way. Using anti-gravity that way is . . . it's just plain evil. It's murder. I never signed up for this."

With that, a slight but athletic woman appeared on the screen. She kneeled next to Bonnie's chair. She attached what appeared to be a diving belt to the chair's legs.

There was something strange about the belt. The woman stood on the belt while she attached it. Ends of the belt not under her foot reached upward like arms in surrender. She left the picture for a moment to retrieve a second and then a third belt and repeated the process. When she brought a fourth diving belt into the picture, she lost her grip on it. It hit the ceiling with a *thunk*. She retrieved it by pulling on it hand over hand like the raising of a flag.

Bonnie, visibly terrified, struggled against the ropes to no avail. When the woman wrapped the fourth belt around its legs, the chair lifted off the ground. The woman held onto one of the legs and pulled Bonnie out of the room like a helium-filled balloon.

The woman suddenly whirled toward the camera and, with her free hand, made a grab for it.

"Turn that phone off."

The video shook as the shooter jumped backward but maintained its wobbly focus on the action. The man shouted.

"Olga stop! You can't do this. We've got to talk to Jason first. He'll know what to do."

"I know what to do and I have the balls to do it, even if you don't."

The woman dragged the floating Bonnie toward the back door and swung it open to reveal a dark, moonless sky.

A black man entered the shot and grabbed the woman by the arm. The woman released the chair, which floated upward. Bonnie's head banged hard against the ceiling. The woman ducked under the man's arm while grabbing it in a rising, twisting motion and, in a incredibly quick move, spun her much larger adversary down to the ground. She followed up with two kicks to the head.

The man remained motionless while the woman regrasped one of the legs of Bonnie's chair, dragging her to the open doorway. The woman stuck her head out and peered in both directions to ensure the coast was clear.

With a sudden spinning movement like an Olympic hammer thrower, the woman flung a horrified, struggling, wide-eyed Bonnie out the doorway. At first, the seated figure floated smoothly, horizontally across the backyard before carving a lazy, upward arc. Then with an appalling abruptness, like a kite caught in an updraft, Bonnie shot straight up into the night sky. In a second, she was gone.

"Give me that," said the woman, making a grab for the cell phone recording the events.

"No way," the other woman screamed. "You're crazy. Jason needs to see this."

The video ends.

Jordan leaned on Davis' desk for support.

"I think I'm going to be sick. That had to be Olga Kalata. She murdered Bonnie and we've got it on video."

Flynn walked into the room and looked from anguished face to anguished face.

"What's up?"

"Bonnie's been murdered."

Davis' voice and face seemed drained of life.

"Murdered?"

Flynn's mouth made more movements but uttered none as his mind flashed to what Summers told him about Big Ed. Finally, he composed himself.

"But who, how?"

"It was the Ginis," Jordan said. "We saw it. We saw a video of Bonnie's murder."

"How did they know about Bonnie? And murder? I thought they were just a bunch of kids. They didn't even break the law before."

"Frank, I can't think about the Ginis right now. I've got to figure out how to break the news to Nathan. He'll be devastated."

"We can't tell him until after we get a line on these kids. We can't have him distracted."

Flynn's accompanying glare carried an unmistakable message.

Don't break ranks. We're in a war.

Jordan disagreed. "He'd smell it on us the first time Bonnie's name comes up. I'd rather meet this one head on. Besides, once he knows they killed Bonnie, he won't stop until he's tracked down the killers."

A sharp series of raps came from the door, followed by Jordan's voice.

"Nathan, can we talk?"

"Sure Agent Jordan, come in."

He stood at attention to greet her, smoothing out his shirt and sleeves like a boy trying to impress a girl he had a crush on. A stupid smile held his face as her presence intoxicated his senses.

"Nathan, I need you to focus."

Jordan's stomach twisted. Her mind cursed her regenerated powers. They made the task doubly difficult.

"The Ginis captured Bonnie . . ."

"Bonnie left," Nathan said.

"Nathan!" she said, grabbing his arms and shaking him. "The Ginis captured Bonnie in Toronto."

"Bonnie? Captured? The Ginis captured Bonnie in Toronto? Uhh? What do they want?" he asked, as the message seemed to sink in. "I've got lots of money. I'll pay any ransom."

"No ransom. We can't get her back. I'm so sorry. They murdered her."

Jordan watched as her words seemed to catch hold and snap Nathan's brain into gear.

"What do you mean Bonnie's been murdered? That's impossible."

"We have it on video."

Jordan led him back to her office. He watched the video, twice. Nathan looked like he was ready to faint or throw up. After a long pause, his head jerked up.

"I want Seiji to look at it, to make sure it's for real."

His request was reasonable. Jordan nodded agreement and led Davis, Nathan and Flynn to the elevator where they descended to level S. Nathan stepped forward.

Jordan noticed Nathan was so nervous he kept rubbing his arms erratically and fidgeting with his sleeves as he gave a brief and grim introductory explanation to the agent with the exceptional vision.

"I need you to tell me, is it real, or is it some kind of CGI fakery? Please take your time to be sure."

Davis hit a few keys on his laptop computer. The video image seemed to leap from his computer, expanding to the size of a movie theatre screen that floated before the group. Then it played under the scrutiny of the agent's unmatched vision.

Seiji didn't speak for several seconds and then responded slowly, soberly, considering every word.

"I'm afraid it's true. Sorry Nathan, I appreciate how much she meant to you."

Nathan reeled as if kicked in the gut. He fell to his knees. His head nearly pitched to the ground with his arms hugging and writhing about his body. No one moved. No one had words of comfort. Jordan started toward Nathan but he angrily waved her off.

An awful hollowness tugged at her. She bore much of the responsibility for Nathan and Bonnie's involvement in the Gini chase. She might accept it if Homeland Security was her sole motivation. It wasn't. Her actions were designed to keep Menck happy.

The ESP team long identified Nathan as a potential candidate. Menck forced Jordan through threats and chemical torture to lure him to Quantico. He needed his olfactory abilities and cellular makeup tested.

Jordan understood the disastrous path she set for Nathan but never considered it might end in Bonnie's death. She enjoyed using her power to manipulate Nathan partly because it drove Bonnie crazy.

How could I have been so petty?

The emotional spasms wracking Nathan's body proved he and Bonnie had something special. Now it was gone.

As Nathan wished, she kept her distance. Through a combination of will power and distance, she'd prevent her pheromonal emanations messing with his natural grief.

Everyone allowed Nathan a few minutes to compose himself before Seiji broke the silence with the words rolling out carefully, hesitantly.

"There is one thing, however, that you ought to know about Bonnie."

Nathan took another minute to compose himself enough to respond. "And what is it that I should know about Bonnie?"

"I hate to say this with her gone but I might as well come out with it. I believe she was a sleeper agent, probably for North Korea."

"Wha . . . How . . . how dare you say that."

Jordan saw the meter on Nathan's emotions swing from grief to confusion.

"She's been my best friend since we were kids. If that were true, I'd have detected it years ago."

"You're too close to her. As a youngster, she might not have been aware herself. But if the idea were introduced to her slowly like a game, she wouldn't send off signals because she was comfortable with you. With me, that's a different story."

Seiji braced himself. He knew that his next statement would trigger an explosion. It was a statement that Nathan and the others needed to hear.

"She collected and sent information about negative gravity to North Korea. I believe I can prove it."

Jordan held her breath as she watched Nathan's meter do another 180-degree swing from confusion straight into the red zone.

"That's the biggest pile of BS I've ever heard. I'm not going to be here for another minute and listen to this crap. And I want out of this place. I know I can track down Bonnie's killers and clear her name at the same time. North Korean agent my ass."

Nathan stormed out of Seiji's lair without another word and headed straight to the elevator. On the ride up, Nathan seethed with rage.

"I want to see DeRoach! I want to see to him now!"

Nathan screamed the words just six inches from Jordan's ear and then refused to look at her or speak to her again. The words stung Jordan in tone and in volume.

"Okay, I'll take you to him."

As much as she was capable of dishing it out, Jordan had little armour when it came to taking abuse. Her beauty, grace and special abilities prevented all men and most women from speaking harshly to her. When she couldn't control a woman, it was usually jealousy marshaling her adversary's emotions. Nathan's grief-stricken state appeared to have the same effect, making him impervious to her charms.

In a minute, they stood in the open doorway of DeRoach's office.

"I'm sorry Nathan. I just heard about Bonnie."

"In the three days since I've been here, my entire life has been turned upside down. I'm not without some public presence and unless you want me to hold a news conference and tell the world about the mess your task force has left us in, I want to leave right now."

"Okay, we can do that, but you have to calm down," DeRoach said, using his gnarled fighter's hands open and relaxed like a conductor cuing the strings for softer tones.

"Forget about calm. I want out and then I'll be calm." Nathan's eyes were wild, crazed.

Perspiration poured from his neck and brows. "I need you to take me to the airstrip right now."

"All right, Rebecca . . ."

Nathan cut off DeRoach. "I've had enough of her. Assistant Director DeRoach, I want *you* to drive me. Is that too much to ask?"

"If you like, certainly," said DeRoach.

Three hours later, Nathan found himself back in his Toronto office. He checked his server.

The reports Bonnie had created were still open and, in the server's mailbox, he found the message he expected.

—

25

THE ESCAPE

IT WAS 15 YEARS AGO that Honeymoon got an unexpected call. Six hours earlier, he had ushered Cleopatra into Big Ed's limousine.

"Cleopatra was delightful, absolutely delightful. My man will be dropping her off in a few minutes. He will have a package for you. I expect you will be pleased. Cleopatra will be in need of some TLC. Be sure to follow my instructions precisely."

Big Ed never called, never ever, until today. Honeymoon was, well, over the moon with excitement when the long limo pulled up. His ecstasy turned to horror when he saw the girl. Blood covered her blouse. She appeared to be catatonic.

A fat manila envelope made everything good. He counted the $100 bills – $15,000. He unfolded the accompanying note. It directed him to get the girl medical care and provided the name of a doctor who had been paid to do the work.

Cleopatra spent three weeks recovering in a relatively luxurious setting, a private bed at the back of a private medical clinic. She had no visitors other than two people identified only as Dr. Bob and Nurse Jane. Nurse Jane looked in on Cleo to give her breakfast, lunch and dinner and for the twice-daily bandage changes. Dr. Bob's daily appearances in week one soon slipped to every second and then third day.

Dr. Bob and Nurse Jane were paid well to ensure Cleopatra received nothing but the best: antibiotics to fight infection; a good healthy diet; regular bandage changes; and a sponge bath every second day.

There was one more set of instructions. No stitches, no nips or tucks, nothing to interfere with the natural healing of three brambly knots of flesh that formed serpentine scars the length of her chest.

Cleopatra had so few moments of lucidity during her 20 days at the clinic that Nurse Jane thought she was once more talking to the proverbial wall. The nurse casually mentioned she was leaving her a change of clothes. Honeymoon would be coming to get her the next day.

The girl's mind, while scarcely functioning, managed to capture snippets of the nurse's words. Three syllables, HON – EY – MOON, spun into the outer ear, funneled their way to the tympanic membrane that relayed the vibrations through a series of auditory partners ending at the cochlea. The cochlea magically transformed the physical vibrations into electrical information.

The electrical signals wandered on a seemingly aimless circuit through layer after layer of grey matter until they found a willing partner – a specific neuron that in its dedication to its job, processed the information, then conspired with its brothers to initiate a chemical cascade. The flush of chemicals stopped the demon dance in Cleopatra's head long enough to trigger that most human of emotions – fear – and its instinctive response, fight or flight.

Cleopatra chose flight.

She threw on the street clothes Nurse Jane left, slipped out the back door, and walked. She walked until she came to a bridge and collapsed from exhaustion. At sunrise, she started walking again without a destination in mind. She recognized one of Honeymoon's girls, returning from a late date. The girl, perhaps a year older, waved at her. Cleopatra had to get out of town.

She saw workmen loading a rig and waited until they took a break. She crept into the trailer, behind a stack of boxes. After a time, she heard someone shout, "That's everything," followed by the slam of the trailer doors and a sharp click of the lock.

A transport trailer's cargo bed was not designed for comfort. Every bump, turn and urgent braking translated into a stomach-rattling jolt and, occasionally, a full body-slam into a crate or the side of the trailer. Absent, too, were climate controls to take the edge off the heat and flush out exhaust fumes.

Late evening, the truck stopped. Workers opened the trailer to unload. A girl stepped out without a glance or a word.

The truck took her to Toronto, a city in Canada she had vaguely heard about. It stopped at a market area that combined the scents of fish, fresh baked bread with exotic spices and sweat.

Like the odours, the people presented a kaleidoscope of humanity, every skin and hair colour imaginable. The noise of market life, including loud jabberings in different languages, buzzed about her. They spoke what she supposed was Greek at one store, Chinese at another.

Other establishments provided a mix of accented English and a variety tongues she couldn't begin to guess.

A skyscraper-dominated business centre lay ahead. She walked toward it. Like Chicago but unlike Chicago. The glass towers looked newer. No big river cut through the downtown. She wanted a river because she needed shelter from a slow drizzle that gave no sign of letting up. With a river came bridges. Bridges gave shelter without the need to provide explanations.

A kid in a hoodie told her to walk 40 minutes 'that-a-way.' When she came to the river, it seemed barely more than a creek, dwarfed by a major highway running beside it.

As the low-point in a huge valley, the creek had once been a mighty river.

"What happened to you?" she said aloud. Then as strange as the circumstances were, she began to laugh.

"I guess you might ask, what happened to me? We both started out so grand. Now you're just a polluted trickle and me, I don't know what I am. At least you know where you're headed."

The unbroken grey grew darker and paid out heavier rain. She ran under the bridge. The river may have been tiny but the bridge was immense, soaring more than 100 feet above her and almost a mile across. It was so high, she didn't know whether it would provide much shelter.

The sky turned to charcoal.

This is as good a place as any to spend the night.

The girl found a platform half way up the rise where the bridge offered better shelter but there was a trade-off. For the first part of the night, she didn't get much sleep. Subway cars ran on a track beneath the bridge and every few minutes a screech/swoosh accompanied by a gust of wind signaled yet another train's approach. In the wee hours the trains stopped.

She'd scarcely fallen asleep when something awoke her. A very tall, very pale man stood before her. His appearance was frightening but his manner and words soothed. He caressed her cheek. A calmness she'd never known engulfed her. Soon her mind floated into a dreamless serenity.

The next morning, he was gone and so, too, were her demons. She felt confident and as happy as she had been when her parents were alive. The mysterious man left a green and yellow plastic bill with a large '20' on it.

Canadian money, she guessed. The mysterious visitor said she'd need it to buy food and fluids. She was ravenous and thirsty.

She found a pathway that wound gently up the hill. Twice she stopped while the dizziness passed. At street level, she saw a pizza restaurant. She walked to the counter where the clerk stared at her open-mouthed. So did the other customers.

What are they looking at?

A glance in the mirror revealed two large wounds on her neck and dried blood down her neck.

"Do you want me to call an ambulance?"

She was too confused to respond.

Seven minutes later, police and ambulance attendants were firing questions at her. She didn't know what happened, she repeated over and over. When a cop asked her name, she feigned total amnesia. She didn't want him to send her back to Chicago, back to Honeymoon.

They took her to a hospital and, unlike Chicago, they were treating her injuries without asking for money but they did want something that puzzled her at first.

"Dearie, we need your health card."

She remembered that in Canada health care is free, if you're a Canadian. She thought it advisable to keep quiet and get the help she needed first. If they figured out she entered Canada illegally, she'd deal with it later.

The neck wounds and health card took a back seat after a doctor examined the long, ragged scars on her chest. Torture and abuse, he determined. She spent the day and night under observation to buy time for doctors and police to confer. When she awoke, a middle-aged woman smiled at her. The woman had a kind face beneath an explosion of fuzzy hair that showed the last wisps of red yielding to grey.

"Hi Honey. My name's Sally. I'm here to help you."

—

26

MARKET MOVES

Thursday, May 15, 2014, 10:46 a.m.

"MR. HENDRY, I have Orville Tennesen on the phone."

"Orville, What can I do for you."

"What in hell are you up to?" Tennesen's *don't-give-me-any-of-your-BS* tone, wrapped in a thick, yesteryear-Texan twang, was a not-so-subtle reminder of the rough cowboy-code of justice that he lived by.

"What are you referring to Orville?"

"Look asshole. We've tracked shares of EExE going on the market and it all comes back to you. We own substantial holdings in EExE and if there's some underlying rot in the company that's going to hurt its value, you better tell me right now or you'll find yourself in court for withholding information from shareholders."

"Hey Orville, I'm just getting a little tired of the oil game. If you look closely, I held interests in a number of oil and gas plays and I'm out or getting out of all of them. Surely, you can't believe the sky is falling on the whole industry. Ha ha ha. I'm 62 and I think it's time to enjoy the better things in life. You know what they say. You got to stop and smell the flowers."

"There's something that smells all right and it ain't the flowers. I don't know what you have up your sleeve, but you're not going to get away with it," he said, slamming down the phone.

At 75 years of age, Tennesen remained a formidable presence. Through the strength and sweat of his arm when he worked on oil rigs and sheer force of will against Eastern blackhearts, Tennesen had battled them all to become one

141

of the most influential and trusted men in the oil and gas industry.

Tennesen loved the oil business but he hated how it provided "that lyin', cheatin' jackal Big Ed" the opportunity to get rich by harming so many others. Whatever he was planning, it was sure to be at great cost to somebody.

One of these days, he'll outsmart himself. I'd give half my wealth to see that bastard burn.

Big Ed heard the abrupt click, smiled to himself, and turned to Summers.

"Where are we now?"

"Down to our last $1.4 billion."

"Dump it out today. All of it. And then take whatever money hasn't been put into short contracts on EExE or any other energy resource company and use it to buy more. Just get it done today."

"But Mr. Hendry. If you push out all $1.4 billion over the next six hours, we'll be lucky to get half the value and it could very well start a run on not just our stock but all oil and gas holdings."

"Summers, you are my CFO are you not?"

"Yes, I am."

"And you hold your Chartered Accountant's degree and license."

"Yessir."

"And you've been following everything that's been going on over the past month."

"Yes, certainly."

"Then what the hell? Has your brain gone for a walk? Do you know what I'm about to do here?"

"But Mr. Hendry, if prices rebound, everything's gone."

"Again with that prudence thing. Big Ed didn't get to where he is by being prudent. I'm all in on this one."

"I'm only saying we should be careful, not put all our eggs in one basket."

"When Big Ed knows the cards everybody else is holding, he always goes all in. Get going. I don't want to see your ass in here until it's 100% done."

...

"Franz?"

"Yes, Mr. Tennesen."

"Time to pull the trigger on everything. Big Ed knows something and

I'm not going to be standing there with my dick in my hand when it all goes down."

"Mr. Tennesen we have more than nine dozen contracts totaling in excess of $300 billion that just need to be signed by you and the other board members to execute. It seems the pension funds and a few Third World Nations are most eager to get bargain prices on our oil shares."

Tennesen winced at news of who the buyers were but shrugged at the inevitable.

"Have the papers ready for me and the others to sign before the close of business today."

"Yes, Mr. Tennesen. Would 4 p.m. work? I'll round up the others."

"Just make it happen."

...

Big Ed saw the spread between his short position and the average price of EExE and other oil holdings. He laughed heartily.

A $4.2 billion gain in my net worth in just three hours today.

He couldn't wait till the markets opened on Monday. Just then his private phone line rang.

"It's Cleopatra."

The voice carried a sharp edge.

"Cleo. Good to talk to you. I'm kinda busy right now. Lots of financial moves in play."

"I know there are but haven't you forgotten a certain part of our deal?"

"I put the money into the account – $10 million."

"And you were supposed to invest it the same way you were investing your money, just as I told you, and on the timetable that I explained to you. Everything in short positions before Friday morning and cash out like crazy on Monday."

"Well, I had a little change of plans. I couldn't get all of my money in, still don't; so, your money is gonna have to wait."

"You haven't waited. You spent my full $10 million on EExE shares this morning. I told you they won't be worth a dime on Monday."

"Well my dear, that's $10 million of my EExE shares taken care of."

"That wasn't the deal."

143

"The deal was I have the exclusive right to make the investments in your account until the markets close on Friday and unless I'm done before then, you're going to have to be happy with that. Besides, if EExE falls to 10-cents a share and you cash in, that's $10,000, huge money for a carved-up honey like you."

"You're a pig."

"And you're a two bit hooker well past your prime. I don't know what I ever saw in you."

Big Ed slammed down the phone. He had a wicked smile on his face. Cleopatra had served her purpose once more and that was that. Just thinking about her no longer did anything for him. Just as well, there are still thousands of other girls out there who need tender lovin' bruisin' from Big Ed. They'd literally be lining up to go a few rounds with the world's richest man.

Big Ed looked at his watch. It was now 11:59 a.m. Time to turn on the radio and tune in the noon news.

"At the top of the news," the announcer's resonant voice rang, "market watchers are stunned by the fall in value of the world's most valuable integrated energy company EExE. Its shares have gone from its high this year of $143 to a morning low of around $97, that's a decline of 32 per cent. A full 27 per cent of the 32 came just in the past week. EExE's value has influenced the entire industry, which, including EExE, has fallen by 18 points in the past three days.

"For insight into what's happening, we turn to Roger Cochran, Chief Market Analyst for six major mutual funds, two of the country's biggest pension funds and a host of portfolios held in trust for a number of Third World Nations.

"Roger, what is going on with the oil industry and especially EExE?"

"I've triple checked all the fundamentals. None of the majors have significant issues or liabilities that we haven't taken into account. Demand seems strong, no hiccups with production, and there are no big surpluses to drive down prices. The Middle East is as stable as we've seen it in more than two years. Unless someone has come up with something that will replace oil and gas as our chief energy source, this makes no sense at all."

The announcer snickered.

"The market seems to be spooked by the sell-off by Ed Hendry of all his holdings," Cochran said. "Some people think he knows something the rest of us don't. In my opinion, there's a better chance that Big Ed has just lost his mind. I see this as an amazing buying opportunity and that's what I'm recommending to every one of my clients."

"For the average small-time investor out there, your recommendation is?"

"I have three recommendations. Buy! Buy! Buy! The oil industry is on sale. I'd also like to add a personal message to Mr. Hendry. If you have any more EExE you want to sell, give me a call."

Big Ed switched off the radio. Things were going exactly as planned. He made a few quick calculations. *If I were chicken shit like old Summers, I'd be buying back my EExE shares in the hope I could realize a gain of 32%. But that's only if the shares rebounded and I know they never will. By leveraging $12 billion into short contracts, I'll be committing, at worst, to sell $120 billion worth of EExE at the market price. When EExE's value drops to under $1 a share on Monday, I'll blow by Bill Gates so fast, I won't be able to see the look on his face.*

"Summers!"

"Yes Mr. Hendry."

"Have you unloaded the last $1.4 billion yet?"

"It's only been about an hour since we last talked. I'm in negotiations."

"Forget that. Call Roger Cochran. Something tells me he's lookin' to buy."

...

Big Ed scanned a real-time market report on his computer and at the clock attached to the page, 2:47 p.m.

So, Orville Tennesen has been busy dumping all his EExE stock and that's taken another huge toll on the share value. EExE's trading below $80 for the first time since . . . well, since forever. It certainly doesn't affect me, except for that last bit to Roger Cochran. The rest of my EExE shares went for much higher prices. I used the money to buy short positions, cashing them in as the price fell and bought bigger short contracts with the profits.

Big Ed closed the report. The corners of his mouth moved upward forming an expression no one could mistake for a smile.

The feeding frenzy was on. Feeding frenzy. That's a nice metaphor. A big fat cow tries to cross the Amazon River and runs smack dab into a school of piranha. Except today, the big fat cow is the oil & gas industry and the feeding frenzy is by a school of investment piranha – too stupid to know they are attacking a skeleton. Big Ed ate all the meat last week.

When the market clues in on the game on Monday, I'll be the only one standing. Sure Tennesen saved himself – a little. But he and the others will be weaker. And I, Big Ed, will be oh so much more powerful.

I love playing the markets when I set the rules and nobody else knows what the rules are. When I'm done, governments will be in shock. Presidents and Prime Ministers will be calling me for advice. Possibly, I'll return their calls.

If I gave him any wiggle room, that weenie Summers would convert my short contracts into cash now. If I did that today, I could give Bill Gates and Carlos Slim a run for their money but why? I can make them eat my financial dust on Monday. If EExE falls as low as $2, I'm the world's richest man by far, richer than Gates, richer than Carlos Slim, richer than all the Walton kids or the Koch brothers combined.

—

27

THE CODE

NATHAN THOUGHT BACK to that first night in Quantico when Reyanna planted the seeds of his plan.

The girl with extraordinary hearing outwardly presented a calm front. On another level she communicated only to Nathan in almost the identical way Bonnie and Nathan connected in their high school years. Reyanna stressed her mind and body to create tension and fear in short bursts.

These bursts caused mini blossoms of perspiration to erupt on her skin's surface, too little to cause dampness or be seen but enough to flavour the air for someone with a super sense of smell.

Nathan sensed Reyanna's tension instantly. It wasn't until he concentrated on the odours that he realized the scents followed a pattern.

Short short short, long long long, short short short.

It's Morse Code.

Dot dot dot, dash dash dash, dot dot dot. Dot dot dot, dash dash dash, dot dot dot. She's sending an S.O.S., a distress signal only to me.

He nodded ever so slightly and responded in kind by adjusting his breathing to three short breaths out, three long inhalations in and then three short exhalations out again. He repeated it several times to be sure.

When Nathan came before Seiji, he was ready for more ESP communication. He wasn't disappointed. The all-seeing agent sent a stresser signal in short bursts, which he repeated over and over.

Again it was Morse Code. This one was more complicated.

It spelled out a four-letter word, dot dot dash dot, dash dash dash, dash dash dash, dash dot dot. Nathan didn't know Morse Code. He memorized the pattern to look up later.

Seiji helped by getting Bonnie riled over her nationality. Nathan believed

147

there was no truth to Bonnie having a Korean heritage. The ploy worked to get Nathan back to his room to decipher the messages.

Behind closed doors, Nathan thought better of Googling Morse Code for fear any use of the Internet might be monitored. Instead, he tried to puzzle it out himself.

$$\bullet\bullet-\bullet, \; - - -, \; - - -, \; -\bullet\bullet.$$

If SOS is dot dot dot, dash dash dash, dot dot dot, that means dash dash dash is the letter O. The word Seiji was signaling had dash dash dash down twice as the two middle letters of the word.

Nathan took pen and paper and began playing a form of hangman – filling in the blank letters.

Starting alphabetically, AOO wasn't the start to any word that came to mind. Nathan concluded he could rule out all other vowels.

Next came 'B'. BOO_ book? boot? boon?

COO_ cook? . . . coot?

DOO_ doom? . . . door?

FOO_ food? . . . foot? . . . yes Food? FOOD! That had to be it.

The two messages together SOS FOOD – save our souls food.

It's a warning. Beware of the food.

. . .

Nathan wasted no time after he and DeRoach pulled away from the FBI offices.

"Who is Julian Menck?"

"Dr. Julian Menck?" DeRoach gave a wide-eyed stare, an amalgam of astonishment and repulsion, as he choked out the name.

"He was the original director of the ESP project. We fired him and expelled him from the unit, in fact from the FBI and all other law enforcement agencies because of his unethical practices."

"That's what you think. He's still pulling Special Agent Jordan's strings and those of Seiji and Reyanna. I'm not sure what power he has over them, but they are terrified. Seiji and Reyanna found a way to tip me off."

DeRoach wheeled to the curb with a screech and turned off the car. Nathan watched as the machinery within the assistant director's mind whirred. An elixir of hatred, fear, anxiety, sorrow, dread, and tense determination oozed from every pore.

"Well, they would be very afraid if he's got control over them again. We've been idiots. How could we have missed it." The emanations of fear and loathing continued to pour off his body.

"After 12 years, I can barely say his name without feeling sick to the pit of my stomach. He used experimental and very dangerous hormonal therapies to amplify their powers. As soon as we realized it and understood his therapies had life-altering and life-threatening consequences, we stopped the program, or so we thought."

...

Eighteen-year-old Rebecca Jordan blossomed from a pale and frail 13-year-old into a beautiful, sensuous woman, possessing what the French describe as, *je ne sais quoi.* When she walked through a room, she left a wake of drooling males. That included her current location, the normally stiff-collared environment of the FBI's Quantico offices.

Her appearance with Dr. Julian Menck, brought all work by males to a breathless, blank-minded halt.

Menck walked into FBI Deputy Director Jackson Garcia's office without an appointment, as usual. The deputy director despised everything about Menck, his sense of entitlement, his lack of respect, and especially that annoying, affected speech pattern, almost a reverse stutter where the final syllable is drawn out in a cough/throat-clearing utterance.

"A high school graduate?" Garcia barked, nearly spilling his coffee, while leaning over his desk and aiming an are-you-crazy glare at Menck.

"The FBI takes only the cream of university graduates. Many are lawyers or have advanced degrees."

"You won't find any of your other agents-ents who possess a high-end specialty like Rebecca-ca," Menck said, turning to her, his eyes opening wide, a prearranged signal to turn on the charms.

Garcia's next angry barrage was at the back of his throat, cocked and ready to fire, when a warm wave overwhelmed him. At 53, Garcia hadn't had an amorous thought in years, at least not that kind of amorous thought and at that level of intensity. It wasn't the kind of groin-centred sexual arousal sparked by the sight of a Playboy Playmate in the flesh. It was a full body and mind experience that caught Garcia with a fogged brain and at a loss for words for the first time in his storied FBI career.

"You were saying Deputy Director-tor?" Dr. Menck enunciated each word softly but purposely with his usual slow, annoying delivery. He reached into his jacket pocket, withdrew a tri-folded sheet of paper, flattened it on the desk and slid it in front of the numb-tongued Garcia.

"Your signature goes right here-ere."

...

Rebecca's first introductions were to Seiji Mishima and Kirk Bannister. The 18-year-old dubbed Seiji as Super-eyes and Kirk as the Vibe King.

Seiji, who'd been in the program more than 10 years, could see distant things better than through the best binoculars. He could see in the dark and in light that fell in the invisible bands of the spectrum. That was easy to understand.

Kirk's powers were more complicated. He had been in the ESP program for two years because of his ultra-amplified sense of touch, not just via his hands but through every part of his body.

"There's another micro tremour. And an aftershock and now another."

He could be quite annoying. Kirk felt at least 500 and perhaps as many as 2,000 micro tremours a day. It was his life mission to announce every single one of them.

When a real quake happened, one that no one else perceived but big enough to make the needle move a tick on the Richter scale, Kirk didn't announce it. Rebecca, Seiji and everyone else in the unit became aware when they heard Kirk making gagging sounds.

A moderate shake made Kirk throw up and shiver for an hour. If a true earthquake occurred, registering 5.0 or more, Kirk became queasy hours in advance and went into convulsions a few minutes before the shockwaves hit and maintained the fit more than an hour after the final vibrations. While a horrid affliction for Kirk, his ability drew Dr. Menck's interest as a means to predict earthquakes.

If seismic shocks were all Kirk detected, his abilities might have been manageable. The hormonal treatments kept increasing his powers to the point he had constant nausea, brought on whenever someone coughed, sneezed, slammed a door, or even walked with a heavy foot.

"The guy Kirk is constantly sick to his stomach. He's just skin and bones," Garcia told then-Special Agent-in-Charge Jimmy DeRoach. "I've ordered Menck to stop all hormonal treatments until we get a handle on what's happening to Kirk. I don't trust that double talking bastard. I need you to watch him. I think he'll do whatever he can to get around my orders."

The idea of having a watchdog incensed Menck. He designed his agenda to keep DeRoach in the dark. One day, when DeRoach was supposed to be on a day off, he surprised the doctor, needle poised over Kirk's arm.

Menck received a reprimand and a suspension. All three ESP agents had their hormonal treatments cut. All three went into their individual form of painful withdrawal.

For Rebecca, her constant periods and the excruciating cramping were back. She began to look anything but glamorous. Seiji experienced extreme headaches and nausea. Kirk had it the worst. His sensitivity to vibrations of all sorts, including sound, seemed to amplify.

He was constantly going into convulsions, rolling in his own sickness and suffering from blackouts.

Deputy Director Garcia had no choice but to bring Menck back. The doctor's return hinged on certain conditions. DeRoach was to be off his back. On the surface, things returned to normal, or at least as normal as things get when a mad scientist is in charge of the care of three people with extraordinary sensory perception.

In the doctor's absence, DeRoach pored over the lab, took samples of hormones and medications used in treatments, and hacked his computer.

DeRoach's efforts ended in frustration until Seiji came forward. He told DeRoach he wanted to speak out many times but fear of Menck's reprisals silenced him.

"Why tell me now?"

"It's the new therapy. He put Kirk on it two months ago. It will kill him or he'll kill himself."

"How do you know?"

"Kirk says he feels different and has dark thoughts each day about killing himself."

"But about the new therapy . . . ?"

"Dr. Menck mentioned nothing but I can tell the therapy is new because the colour and density of the injections is different and I read his notes."

"You read his notes?" DeRoach stared in astonishment. "I searched his computer and went through all files. I found nothing."

"He doesn't leave important data on the lab computers. When he writes notes, he keeps the paper with him."

"How did you read his notes?"

"It started with a few random words. Dr. Menck had a sheet of paper in the breast pocket of his lab coat. He walked toward me under a bright light. Some of the light entered his pocket and for an instant it acted like a projector with his pocket as the screen. I saw the outline of words written in black ink against the background of white. The words were 'Kirk', 'gene therapy,' 'Seiji's stem cells,' a bunch of medical terms I didn't understand and a few formulas."

DeRoach stood amazed. "You pieced the story together through occasional glances when Menck put notes in his breast pocket?"

"That was the start but it didn't tell me enough. The breakthrough came when I picked up on a second trick. He kept his notes and charts on a clipboard. I can't see through the clipboard, of course, but what I can do is see the reflected light from the sheet as it projects onto the opposite wall or the ceiling."

"You read his notes from light reflected by the ceiling?"

"It's diffused, distorted, faint and backward. It took a lot of concentration but, in time, I trained my brain to see it quickly. It's a little like those Magic Eye posters that were once the rage. They provided a stereographic picture that revealed itself if you trained your brain to see it.

"In my case, if the light was really bright, I could read the full top page and catch a word or two on sheets below."

"What is Menck really up to?"

"He wasn't satisfied with his hormonal treatments. They weren't amplifying our powers in the way or as much as he wanted. He also knew you were trying to stop him. He moved to stem cell replacement. He implanted them in Kirk. Kirk's body now self-generates Menck's designer hormones."

"So, cutting off Kirk's hormonal treatments . . ."

"Will do nothing," said Seiji. "There's no reversing what's been done to him."

"Menck's a monster. You're very brave for coming to me."

152

"Not brave, terrified."

"Terrified?"

"Menck's notes say he plans to start stem cell replacement on Reyanna and me next week."

DeRoach shook his head sadly. "I'm sorry the bureau got you into this. I'm sorry we didn't control Menck. Surely he knows it will kill you in the end. The side-effects are hideous no matter what good he thinks it might do for the world."

"It isn't about any of us and it had nothing to do with the good of the world."

"Then what . . . ?"

"Immortality – his immortality. He discovered that those with extraordinary sensory perception regenerate cells on a scale exponentially greater than other people. Reyanna's ear drums regenerated in less than a month. I have millions of times more light receptors than other humans. I also have millions, perhaps billions more light receiving neurons than an average person. In a regular person, these light receptors start going off line and the neurons get filled as they age.

"Kirk's nervous system keeps producing more nerve endings and Rebecca's endocrine system keeps renewing itself and expanding. Dr. Menck postulated that there are unique triggers in each ESP team member that, if understood and harnessed collectively, would produce a therapy that could preserve youth indefinitely."

"We've got to stop him before it's too late."

"Too late for Kirk but you may be able to save Reyanna and me. You see, I'm not so brave."

"Menck will pay for what he's done to Kirk, Reyanna, and you."

"Uh, you should know one other thing."

"What's that?"

"We aren't the only ones. I've seen dozens of other names on his notes, people who I've never heard of. He's using their stem cells, too. While, I can't be certain, it appears that there have been multiple casualties."

"Casualties?"

"People have died from his experiments."

—

153

28

BAD STUFF

DEROACH continued his story with Nathan hanging on every detail.

"The next day, Deputy Director Garcia and I placed Dr. Menck under arrest. The charges didn't hold because he wouldn't release the full hormone cocktail for each of the ESP agents until he was guaranteed he wouldn't be prosecuted. We had to let him go but that was supposed to be the end of his involvement with the ESP Team and the FBI."

"What about the others, the casualties?"

"Menck admitted nothing. We had no evidence, no clues to act on, just a random group

of common first names like John, Sue, and Lisa that Seiji remembered from the notes."

"And that's been it until I mentioned it now?"

DeRoach started to speak, stopped, hesitated and then spoke in a voice so soft that it didn't seem to be his. "I wish that were true."

The assistant director described how Kirk's mental state began to worsen rapidly. He screamed constantly. He ran at the walls as fast as he could. He sustained a broken wrist, dislocated shoulder, four displaced ribs, a broken collarbone and too many head injuries to list, all from the collisions.

"He said something about external pain making the internal pain more manageable. Strangely, all of Kirk's injuries no matter how severe they seemed, healed on their own and often in a day."

DeRoach closed his eyes but continued speaking, describing a memory movie playing in his head.

"Two months after we chucked Menck out of the program, Kirk attempted suicide. No, the term attempted is wrong. He got some phone and computer wires, wound them into a noose, tied them to the railing in the emergency stairwell and jumped off. The wires were about 10 feet long and the impact snapped his neck, nearly pulled his head clean off."

"And he didn't die?"

"That's the monstrosity. He did die, clinically. His heart stopped and his brain ceased activity. Then those damn hormones and the stem cell therapies kicked in. In a few hours, he came back to life. His neck was more than a foot long and twisted at a 45-degree angle. His jaw was crushed in at one side. The damage healed with new flesh and bone filling in the gaps in his neck and jaw. Conceptually, the neck and jaw functioned but he looked like something that walked out of your nightmares. Kirk was in constant pain, and the headaches and nausea, if possible, got even worse."

DeRoach paused. Nathan was thankful for the brief respite. This Frankenstein tale was so far removed from his world of food, wine, celebrity and travel, he could do nothing but listen in open-mouthed horror.

"After a week of this abomination, I accidentally on purpose left a loaded pistol where Kirk would find it when I left for the night. The next morning Rebecca and I found him in his room with three bullet holes in his head. Chunks of brain matter and blood were splattered all around.

"One wound had healed over leaving just an ugly, pulsating crater. The second was well on its way to healing and the third was fresh with blood and brains starting to congeal above the right eye socket. His right eyeball dangled against his cheek, like some kind of ghastly optic nerve yo-yo that bounced with every wheezy breath he took."

"Three head wounds?" On the surface, Nathan understood the answer but his brain refused to accept what it meant.

"Yeah. Over the course of the night, he shot himself in the head, died, regenerated, shot himself in the head again, died, regenerated, and then shot himself a third time, died, and was well on the way to healing."

DeRoach stopped, seemed to weigh whether he should continue. He fixed Nathan with a look that formed an unspoken bond between them. Nathan nodded and the AD, with a seriousness that made him look at least 10 years older, resumed his story.

"Jordan threw up. Once she did, I did, too. I'd seen some bad stuff in my career but this? Up to that moment I thought I was an atheist, but thoughts filled my head that this broke all the laws of God, never mind man's laws.

"That's when I decided, this had to end. I didn't care what happened to me. I remembered the display we put up after we busted the Black Sky Ring. I smashed into the display case and returned to Kirk's room with a huge machete. He saw me with his one good eye, smiled and stretched that appalling foot-long neck forward. I didn't think. I just swung with all I had and his head rolled off ending with his face up and smiling, his one good eye looking right at me as if to say, thank you."

Nathan let out his breath and was about to say he understood but DeRoach held out his hand. His story wasn't over.

"Rebecca was the first to see it. The blood spurt from his neck, doing rope tricks like twin lassos. Then it stopped, way too early. The stump began to congeal. Little polyps formed on it and then started stacking on one another like a Janga game from hell."

"Christ!" she said. "He's still regenerating."

"I ran to our forensic lab and grabbed a body bag and a gurney. Rebecca helped me put Kirk's body in it. We used a pillow case to hold his head and tied it to his belt and zipped up the bag. Then we put everything on the gurney. A few people saw us. We were covered in blood and God knows what else. I didn't care.

"The FBI has an incinerator at the back of the property where we destroy confiscated drugs and weapons. We put Kirk's body into the back of a Suburban and drove round to the incinerator. I used my badge to bully through the support staff who operated the oven. Rebecca and I tossed Kirk's body into the maw of the furnace. As the door swung shut, I swear I saw the legs start to kick. I hit the button and the flames roared like a squadron of jets taking off.

"For a minute, I heard crackles, hissing and popping noises as the furnace raced to its peak of 2,200-degrees Celsius, a temperature guaranteed to destroy anything. I still went back to the incinerator the next two days to take a look, just in case.

"When the incinerator finished its work, for the first time in an hour, I managed to breathe normally. Rebecca stood next to me, shaking uncontrollably. We looked at each other, embraced and we both started to cry with huge convulsive gasps and sobs. We stood like that for a very long time. The support staff just stared at us with their mouths open.

"We both should have been fired that day and charged but Deputy Director

Garcia intervened. He swore an oath that Kirk had died a week earlier by his own hand. He produced the photos and the original documentation of Kirk's death by hanging. Rebecca and I got reprimands and two-week suspensions for not seeking proper authorization before disposing of the body. We both needed the time off.

"I swore that if I ever laid eyes on Menck again, I would kill him. I meant it then and I still mean it today."

Nathan held back his questions until now. "Somehow, he's managed to sink his claws into Jordan again and, through her, Seiji and Reyanna. After what you just told me, why would Jordan go back to him?"

"It's easy to ask that question when you're not in her shoes. The therapies Menck used are worse than heroin in terms of their hold on Rebecca, Seiji and Reyanna. Without it, they experience immense pain all of the time and, in other ways I can't begin to understand, their bodies go into revolt, which they say is worse than the pain. Part of the deal was that Menck had to hand over all his research and medical stores so we could keep the three on minimum dosages until something better came along. I suspect he left a little something out. What we used clearly did not have the effectiveness of what he offered."

The grim AD explained that, at some point, Menck compromised Rebecca and got her to help him regain a hold on the others.

"When you came along, Seiji saw another Kirk in the making and recruited Reyanna to warn you."

"So what are we going to do now?"

"I'm afraid I'm going to have to arrest Rebecca and then use her to find Menck."

—

29

GINI MANEUVRES

BACK IN CHICAGO, Jason Sage paced anxiously as Mo tracked the latest stock reports.

"Big oil is down 20 per cent and EExE's down almost 35 as of 2 p.m. today. All the big boys know about negative gravity and it's a panicked sell-off. We should sell our shorts now," said Mo.

"Tomorrow – Friday – first thing in the morning when the markets open. The market moves of the ultra rich have gone public today. They are the only ones with the clout to dominate the market. The little guys won't be able to get a trade in for love or money.

Big money will own the market moves for the rest of today and tomorrow."

"What about the small guys who trade on their computers. Can't they get in?"

"Very unlikely. The people selling now are looking for big partners, single trades in the hundreds of millions, and a few in the billons of dollars. Little Freddy day-trader can't get a nibble unless he comes up with a few million minimum and only then as a preferred customer of one of the big financial services houses."

"So tell me again, how can we get attention for our measly $2.3 million?"

"Simple, our $2.3 million is leveraging, $23 million. That's a good enough chunk even for the biggest players. On top of that, we're going against the flow. All the big guys will be selling short and they'll want every last dollar of our short positions."

...

Friday, May 16, 9:05 a.m.

"That's it," Sage announced to the group. "We're all in. We've sold our short positions and made a $14 million profit."

"Sager! Sager! Sager!" chanted Mo and Alessa at their Chicago hideout with harmonizing voices and happy faces beamed in by Jazzy, Olga, and DD via Skype from Toronto.

"Now we proceed to stage 2."

"You're sure we want to do this?" Alessa cautioned. "I mean $14 million exceeds any dreams we ever had to put the world aright."

"A drop in the bucket, a mere drop in the bucket."

...

A sweaty Big Ed looked at the paperwork before him. He could have looked at it on the computer screen but having real paper in hand made it oh so much better. Thank you Roger Cochran for coming in for that last $1.1 billion. Nice to get a short position on that last bit.

Old Roger drove a hard bargain, $70 a share for EExE, which had been $143 a month and a half ago. He's patting himself on the back right now for getting me to drop that last $300 million from the price. He couldn't wait to leave my office. I thought he was going to pee himself because of the bargain he thinks he got. So, Big Ed has lost his marbles has he Roger? Let him think that, for today. We'll see who's laughing on Monday.

Big Ed glanced at the clock. It was 3:58 p.m. Chicago time and 4:58 New York time. In two minutes, the NYSE would be closed and that pretty well locked everything in until Monday, he thought.

Big Ed waited the two minutes before shouting: "Summers, get in here."
"Yessir."

"Summers, I think I'm going to give you a raise."

"Oh, thank you sir."

"How does $50 bucks a week sound. Ha Ha Ha Ha Ha."

Summers returned to his office and could still hear Big Ed's sick laugh 10 minutes later as he left for home.

That was it, Summers thought. This was my last day of work for that, that, *that man*. A civilized chap, even in the throes of intense hatred for everything Big Ed stood for, the worst name he could dredge up to call him was, *that man*.

159

Summers had engineered nasty deeds on behalf of that man over the years. A lot of people got hurt. Big Ed preyed on his CFO's weakness, bullied him to carry out his financial dirty work. He enjoyed seeing it tear at Summers' soul.

Summers was gifted at crafting the type of financial scenarios that could bait and swap at Big Ed's direction. Hundreds lost their life savings to what Big Ed explained was 'plain dumb luck.' If investigators probed deep enough, the web of lies and financial maneuvers would be exposed for what they are – crimes with lengthy jail time a certainty.

But no financial investigator or regulator came near Big Ed, partly because of Summers' skills and partly because Big Ed had so many in his pocket.

Once a plan was completed, Big Ed experienced the joy of the money and the ecstasy of being just that much smarter than everybody else. But he couldn't brag because that would be a 'Go-Right-To-Jail card.' Instead, he fed off Summers' revulsion.

"What's the point of wrecking people's lives if you can't see them suffer," Big Ed bragged one day.

"Too dangerous looking my victims in the face. Might piss 'em off enough to sic the securities cops on me. That's why I've got you. I can content myself with that wretched look on your skinny face. Next best thing to watching the suckers suffer."

Most times, Big Ed had pictures, which he would flash before his CFO.

"Look here. This one's great. She's an 86-year-old great grandmother whose nest-egg vanished, the result of her poor investment decision making," Big Ed said with a wink to Summers.

"That's a photo of 12-year-old Stephanie, left a paraplegic, after a car crash."

The courts awarded Stephanie $8 million for pain, suffering and medical bills. The money went into investments to take care of her perpetual care.

According to Big Ed, "Stephanie's parents weren't smart."

It wasn't that the great grandmother or Stephanie's parents weren't smart. Their undoing came because they were trusting – trusting of Big Ed. He took it slow to gain their trust and once they were hooked, he'd reel them in.

He had a great speech about the power of inflation. "It's the devil. It will cut your spending power in half every five years."

He warned them that the only way to outrun inflation and ensure there's enough money to keep Stephanie for all her days, would be to take on a little risk. Of course, the initial risks, the ones where they ventured a couple thousand dollars, worked out spectacularly well. The investments notched returns of 15%, 20%, 30% and more in a single month just as Big Ed predicted. After all, they had placed their money and their trust in a genius, a man who rose from nothing to become one of the richest men in the world.

"Now I'm working for you."

When the big client money started to flow, for some reason, the investments didn't have the same snap. It was time they put more, perhaps the entire portfolio, into something a little riskier that will provide the spectacular returns they expected. The worlds of the great grandmother and Stephanie's family soon came crashing down.

Summers suspected Big Ed was guilty of many more heinous crimes, perhaps even murder. Where did all those girls go and why did none come back? Summers thanked God that Big Ed only pressed him to set up the financial scams.

Summers couldn't run them, of course. He had no poker face at all, Big Ed complained.

"Sure, they lost money but it's only money. They don't physically get hurt. After all, don't people lose money on the stock market every day?"

Big Ed would act all innocent when he made such statements to Summers, the same man who designed the circuitous trading scheme. What was the point of feigning innocence with Summers? Summers created the convoluted system that meant all Big Ed's clients were ultimately trading shares with Big Ed. That made it easy for them to win when he wanted and to lose when he wanted.

But someone very close to Summers did get hurt and it changed his life forever.

...

Hélène Augustin was wonderful, a true Southern Belle with long dark curls and green, green eyes that a man could get lost in. When Summers spotted her at the Dallas Oil Men's annual convention, he looked away. She tried to strike up a conversation. His tongue remained frozen.

Hélène, the daughter of a small oil producer, asked questions on production ratios and delivery dates for the oil business. That got Summers talking.

'Ah, she's just picking my brains. Well, that's something I know about and

161

I certainly don't mind helping such a pretty girl.'

It wasn't production ratios that interested Hélène. She saw in Rick Summers the type of down-to-earth guy her father had been before he struck it moderately rich with a gusher on the back 40. She remembered her father as a loving dad who spent endless hours telling her stories and letting her ride on his knee in the combine during the harvest.

Then came the oil and the money. It transformed Cameron Augustin from loving husband and father to just another one of the back slapping, tall-tale swopping, rich, divorced braggarts who hung out at the Dallas Oil Men's Club.

Never much of one with the ladies, Summers found himself literally swept off his feet when Hélène made all the moves to start their courtship.

"Your shyness attracted me to you. But you would never make a move so it was all up to me," she later confessed to him in her silky Louisiana drawl.

Their talk soon turned to marriage. That's when Big Ed inserted himself into Summers' relationship. It took no time for the fast-talking Chicagoan to set his hooks wrist-deep into Cameron Augustin.

EExE, the resource company, has its corporate headquarters in Texas, virtually a mandatory location for a major American gas and oil company. Big Ed's private office and the headquarters of EExE Holdings, the mothership for Big Ed's assets, however, was in his hometown, Chicago. As EExE's chairman, Big Ed split his time between the two cities, something he did not relish.

The Dallas area was home to too many undeserving nouveau riche. There were too many cocky millionaires. Self-made men, they bragged. Big Ed scoffed at the notion. The source of their wealth was dumb luck – inheriting a farm parked above a prehistoric jungle where the flora, fauna and dinosaurs composted into a giant pool of oil.

Big Ed, on the other hand, considered himself to be a true self-made man. Luck never entered into it. His fortune was built one gold brick at a time from what he took from others. He fancied himself a modern-day Genghis Khan who created his empire through a thousand financial conquests over those self-made pretenders, each victory made all the sweeter by the lessons he dealt.

One of the braggarts that Big Ed believed was sorely in need of a lesson was Hélène Augustin's father. The loud mouth talked to Big Ed like he was an equal.

'Taking candy from a baby – even easier than that,' Big Ed mused. The clincher was an invitation from the chair of EExE to a private one-on-one lunch in one of the Club's private rooms. Augustin eagerly accepted.

"I've got this property. The assays look really good. We've been holding back some of the information to allow our friends to get in ahead of the rush. You interested?"

Augustin's eyes were wide open. Just a bit more of a nudge to make his wallet do the same.

"I've got a position left that will likely triple in value within 60 days for, say $3 mill?"

Augustin shifted nervously in his seat and welcomed the interruption of the waiter who dropped their lunches before them just as Big Ed leaned in for an answer.

Big Ed shook out his linen napkin and tucked it into his collar to drape his shirt and tie from the plentiful juices of the po'boy sandwich. He'd never do anything so crude in Chicago but this was Dallas and, as intended, it sent an unmistakable, 'just-one-of-the-good-ole-boys' signal to Augustin.

"Best soft-shell crab po'boy in Dallas."

Augustin was worth about $10 million, enough to shoulder his way into the Club but not enough to play in the big leagues. He'd have to move money around, take some losses to get the funds. An investment of $3 million was peanuts to Big Ed. Turning him down would not only be an embarrassment, an admission of relative poverty, but it would forever close the door to all the opportunities the billionaire could introduce.

Big Ed leaned in again with his hand extended. "So, are you in?"

Augustin gulped dryly. Steeling his body, he thrust his hand forward and gave Big Ed's hand a shake. "I'm in."

"Smart man. Would it be convenient to get your cheque on Monday?"

Like a man about to take his first parachute jump, thrill overcoming fear, Augustin gave a slow nod.

"Tremendous. Now let's get back to our lunch before it gets cold."

Big Ed picked up the sandwich and took a massive bite. He liked the taste but loved the crunch of his teeth crushing the soft-shelled bodies whole.

Now that Augustin was hooked for $3 million and felt he was in with the big boys, his financial death warrant was as good as signed. He might get a quick $1 million boost, on paper, as an enticement to hand over more of his wealth. In no time at all, Cameron Augustin was in deep, too deep.

It was easy with Big Ed's wealth. Augustin was like all of the others. Big

Ed used his financial might to force dividends and share prices down when the mark had notes or key payments due. Then he offered to bail the mark out with loans that had certain conditions, conditions that would become impossible to fulfill.

It was the old donkey and carrot trick. When the donkey stepped forward, the financial carrot remained just out of reach.

When Augustin struck it rich, he cut his roots from farming, Louisiana, and his wife. He picked up the glad-handing ways of Dallas' oil-rich crowd. After Big Ed helped his riches disappear, his new buddies, the luscious young women who fought to be at his side, and the Dallas glam-life vanished. All he had left, he believed, was his trusty Beretta 20-gauge shotgun and the knowledge to use it.

He had more than that. He had a daughter who loved him and who never forgave those who played her father for the fool. She saw Summers as a part of it.

"I had nothing to do with it." At the funeral Summers reached desperately to hold his fiancé's hand but Hélène shook it off. "Mr. Hendry did not inform me he was talking to your father."

"But you know the kind of man Hendry is. You should have warned me, warned my father. You could have done something to stop him."

The truth is, Summers had no ability to stop Big Ed. Hendry would just as easily pull the trigger on him as anybody else if he had a mind to. He also realized, very early on, that he possessed too much information for Hendry to ever let him leave alive.

The funeral was the last time Summers saw Hélène. He wrote six letters. Each came back unopened. He didn't try to see her in person. What was the point? Hélène would never tolerate Hendry in their life and Hendry would never allow Summers to leave.

Then 20 years passed. Where did those years go, Summers thought as he silently wept, a photo of Hélène at his side.

...

Big Ed now sat on nearly $300 billion in short positions for EExE and other oil and gas companies.

Not bad, Big Ed said to himself. *If I cashed in Friday at those prices, I'd have a super-tidy profit of $270 billion give or take a few hundred million bucks. On Monday, when my people release the information about negative gravity, I can buy those shares for almost nothing and the entire $300 billion will be mine.*

Forget about Bill Gates. Hell, I'll be richer than all but a handful of countries.

...

A surge of sickness welled within her as Jordan stared in shock and fear at Davis' laptop.

"Oh God!"

The Ginis posted yet another video in their e-mailbox. This time it featured Nathan, tied to a chair next to Plank.

"Don't worry. We won't be sending you into space like your girlfriend. You're far too valuable to us."

Jordan recognized the voice and the crazed tone as belonging to the very scary Olga Kalata.

Jordan choked back the nasty bile creeping up her throat. This was, indeed, a horrible day for her ESP Team, for the FBI, and most especially for Nathan. The dramatic drop in the price of oil and gas shares had the world's major stock markets reeling. The House, the Senate and the news media turned up the heat on the President.

Jordan imagined a torrent of angry blasts down the chain of command all converging on the office of FBI Deputy Director Jackson Garcia.

DeRoach was in Garcia's office, getting reamed, she thought. And then this. We recruit Bonnie and Nathan. Because of it, Bonnie's dead and Nathan is being held captive. When DeRoach returned to his office, Jordan was waiting for him.

"Jim. This is really, really bad. I don't know how it happened. The Ginis have Nathan. They put another video into their email account. They had him trussed up next to Plank."

"Are they . . ."

"I don't know, but a woman, it was that crazy bitch Olga Kalata, she was saying something about not sending Nathan into space because he was too valuable, whatever that means."

"Christ. I'm sorry Rebecca. I know you really liked Nathan," he said, approaching her and giving her his version of a fatherly hug.

"Why did you let him go, Jim? At least why wouldn't you let me put a tail on him like I asked, for his own protection, if nothing else."

"He's a Canadian, living in Canada. We can't be doing that with nationals of other countries and especially in their own country. I notified Supt. Beauchemin and he was supposed to take it from there."

Jordan threw up her hands, gave him a WTF grimace and stormed from his office. DeRoach was a super smart cop and he never let bureaucracy stand in his way. That's why she liked him. But he dropped the ball on this one. Why was he allowing bureaucracy guide him?

And what was that hug all about? We haven't hugged since Kirk died. I was just a teenager then and, considering the circumstances, I really needed a hug, but now? Besides, he was kind of sloppy with his hands, letting his fingers run through my hair. If I didn't know Jim so well, I'd swear he was coming on to me.

That thought vanished. Her head ached. Her chest went hollow. A nest of vipers writhed within her, all with dull fangs trying to chew their way out.

How could we have failed Nathan so badly. If something happens to him . . .

It wasn't love or anything Jordan could define. Perhaps, it was a kinship, a shared experience among those who possess extraordinary abilities. Yes, that was it. Mutual support of each other as individuals with special abilities. She wept.

What a wonderful person I am. I've betrayed all of my brothers and sisters on the team and now Nathan. And why? Because I am a coward.

When I leave work in an hour, I know I will betray them all, yet again. I will see Dr. Menck and I will tell him that Nathan has been captured. He will be angry beyond measure, not because of any concern for Nathan. No, he'll be angry because he lost another lab rat.

—

30

CELEBRATION PLANS

THE NEXT DAY, Big Ed turned on the TV. It was 11:59 a.m.

"Flying saucers! Flying cars! Flying everything! That's the news coming up next on our noon report," an unseen announcer reeled off excitedly.

The WAM-TV logo came on screen accompanied by the familiar musical intro and an unseen voice: "It's WAM-TV Noon News. When you want the news, WAM, we've got it, featuring Sylvester Ballantyne."

The show title disappeared, replaced by a tight angle on the news anchor.

"It's Saturday, May 17. I'm Sylvester Ballantyne with a startling report at the top of the news at noon. The world is abuzz about unconfirmed reports that a Canadian scientist has discovered the key to unlocking gravity. We have Johanna Johnston reporting from the University of Toronto in Toronto, Canada."

"Thanks Sylvester. I'm here in front of the University of Toronto's Physics Building where professor Dr. Gustav Plank is believed to have found the formula to create what he calls, negative gravity. Up to now, negative gravity or anti-gravity was considered the stuff of science fiction.

"Now we're hearing that Dr. Plank, who was under contract with the university until May 31, has done it. As exciting as this negative gravity story is, there's a plot twist. Dr. Plank is nowhere to be found. Colleagues say he mysteriously vanished about one month ago. No one has seen him since and no one from the university's administration is returning our calls.

"None of the university's staff would go on the record but off the record two university employees confirmed that investigators from the Canadian Security Intelligence Service, SEE-SIS for short, had been on the scene over the past month to look into a reported break-in at Dr. Plank's lab and to uncover the physicist's whereabouts. Our sources have also confirmed that Dr. Plank had, indeed, isolated negative gravity, which they say will have a more profound effect on mankind than the invention of the wheel.

"This is Johanna Johnston reporting. Back to you Sylvester."

"Thanks Johanna. Now we go to our financial markets reporter Chen Wu on Wall Street.

Chen are you there?"

"Yes I am Sylvester. As you can see the New York Stock Exchange is right behind me. It's pretty quiet today because it's Saturday. It was anything but all week because of the spectacular and, at the time, inexplicable meltdown in the energy sector. The suspicion is that leaks about an anti-gravity technology contributed to the free-fall in oil and gas stocks all last week.

"To explain why, I have economist, engineer and former astronaut, Dr. Jerome Arts with me. Dr. Arts, why all the excitement about negative gravity?"

"If it's true that this Dr. Plank has isolated negative gravity, it's a complete game-changer for how we view and live in our world.

"Things that we saw as impossible are now possible and things that we saw as valuable no longer have value."

"Dr. Arts can you give me an example of what was valuable but is no longer valuable?"

"I think we've already seen some signs in this building behind us. The oil and gas sector was killed in market trading. Why? Because a primary use for petroleum is transportation. When you have cars, trains, airplanes and ships that weigh nothing or very little, it doesn't take much fuel to move them around.

"Auto manufacturers spend billions trying to knock off a few pounds from their vehicles. The result is cars are smaller and more expensive because lighter materials cost more. We can return to the huge boats of yesteryear and get 500 miles a gallon. Hell, if the overall weight of a car is neutral, meaning it weighs just enough so it doesn't float away, you could use solar or pedal power and never need gas at all."

"Dr. Arts, you also mentioned that things we thought were impossible are now possible. Can you explain further?"

"Well Chen, something I'd personally be interested in is a flight suit – not the kind that I wore as an astronaut, but the kind Iron Man wears in comic books. The kind that lets him fly like a supersonic bird. If you weigh next to nothing, the same propellers that lift pizza size drones can eliminate your boring commute and fly you – Superman style – across the city to work. Vacations will never be the same. Buy yourself an inflatable cabin; snap on a few anti-grav plates; put on your flight suit and take your vacation on top of the Rocky Mountains, in a cloud, anywhere."

"Wow, that is fantastic."

"It's just the tip of the technological iceberg. Forget about transportation on Earth. Boring! This is how we will travel to the stars."

"You mean using anti-gravity to shoot rockets off the planet?" "Nothing so ho-hum. Gravity is the result of a large object like the Earth distorting space and time. If we can control gravity, we are in effect manipulating time and space. Remember the warp drive in Star Trek?"

"Uh, I think so."

"Einstein believed you can't travel faster than light but he also talked about gravity folding space. Other scientists postulated that you can get to distant parts of the galaxy quicker if you take a short-cut by folding space as you fold a piece of paper. Rather than going from one edge of the paper to the other, you hop across where the edges meet. Distance becomes irrelevant." "So the whole world is about to change?"

"Anything's possible. The only real question is – is negative gravity real?"

Big Ed switched off the TV.

Hey, the news got out a couple days early but who cares? I guess Roger Cochran will care. I expect Roger won't be having the best weekend.

He was so happy he pranced around like an eight year old on a sugar high, albeit, a 225-pound eight-year-old. He needed to celebrate, really celebrate.

Unfortunately, I can't call Honeymoon. He always got me the best girls. He brought me Cleopatra and that worked out spectacularly well. Too bad about Honeymoon, but if there's one thing I can't tolerate, it's incompetence. How can you be incompetent as a pimp? You just smack the girls around until they do what you want. How do you lose a 14-year-old girl who's nearly catatonic, injured and has no friends or money? Pure incompetence.

When you deal with Big Ed, incompetence is never tolerated. The pimp wasn't a problem for long. No one missed Honeymoon, not even his girls. Dr. Bob and Nurse Jane, that was a little more complex, but they had to pay the price, too. Nobody disappoints Big Ed and lives to tell about it. Now where was I? Oh yes, I need to celebrate, something special.

He reached for his phone and dialed.

"Hello Frenchie, Big Ed here. I want to do some celebrating. I want you to find me someone really special. She has to be pretty, of course, Muslim, big brown eyes, and 14," he said, greedy fingers sliding along the length of his silver letter opener. "And she has to be a virgin. Absolutely no tattoos or marks on her body – well, maybe just a tiny scar."

—

31

THE BIRTHRIGHT

JORDAN'S WORDS rode on quick shallow breaths that even over the phone made no disguise of the sheer terror that Menck instilled in her.

"No, no further leads. I've been calling our associates at CSIS and they have come up empty as well. The Ginis and Nathan have disappeared."

"That is unfortunate-ate. Unfortunate possibly for your Nathan-an but definitely for you-ou." Pure menace laced each of his words.

"DeRoach interfered. I tried. I really tried but he refused to let me near Nathan before he put him on the jet to Toronto."

Her stammered reply was a weak excuse. Menck had to understand that she had done everything she could. If he remained angry, she'd suffer another reprisal. Just the prospect created a cool trickle of sweat down her back.

"My sweet Rebecca-ca, you know that is not an acceptable answer for me-me."

He slammed down the phone without further comment and sat back trying to hold his anger at a slow simmer.

Why after 57 years of fighting for every inch of progress does the battle never get any easier?

He had overcome every obstacle placed in his path and every idiot who inadvertently and, occasionally, purposely tracked mud all over his shiny, perfect plan.

...

Menck expected to be special by birthright. He had been pre-selected to receive every physical and mental advantage and, through political promises, a decided social edge. All of it had been stolen from him two months before his designated birth date.

The expected day of Julian Menck's birth, as printed on a special certificate provided by Deutschen Sportausschuss, the organization that directed the sports movement in East Germany, was July 19, 1957. Instead, his mother, the former Frieda Schneider, went into labour eight weeks early. She delivered Julian Menck the following day, Friday, May 24, 1957.

Menck weighed two pounds, two ounces at birth, not good for any baby but an exceptional disappointment to Frieda, her husband of exactly seven months, Dieter Menck, and the East German sporting committee that had arranged the couple's marriage.

Eight months earlier, Frieda and Dieter hadn't met. They knew only that the other was an elite athlete, Dieter a decathlete, and Frieda a swimmer.

The sports organization coordinated the East German government's investments that combined sports and medicine. On the surface, it made sense. Fit citizens are healthier citizens

For elite athletes, the program went much further. Scientifically designed diets, training, coaching programs and the secret use of steroids paid immediate dividends. Eastern Bloc nations broke most of the world weightlifting records at the 1952 Olympics in Helsinki.

Past their best-before-dates as athletes, Frieda and Dieter got a call from a Deutschen Sportausschuss administrator in October, 1956. A state computer had selected them as ideal genetic mates. They were given the honour to continue their contribution to the nation's pride by producing children destined to be superior in mind and body.

Premature birth notwithstanding, program administrators believed that with proper nourishment and a precise exercise regime, Julian Menck might still reach his potential.

The scientists determined within a month he would never catch up. The early birth and possibly internal bleeding in his brain caused the boy to develop hypotonia, a condition commonly referred to as rag doll or floppy baby syndrome.

Far from having the makings of a world-class athlete, young Julian Menck could scarcely hold up his head. As the years passed, he found he had mobility impairments, little flexibility, and not much of an appetite. Hypotonia also affected his speech and breathing leaving him with a pronounced stutter.

Surrounded by elite athletes and scientists, Menck knew his shortcomings too well. His mother further reinforced the message with frequent complaints how he had ruined her life.

Menck's parents wanted as little to do with him as possible. They had been promised a home of their own in Leipzig, access to good food without lining up, and a modest, but adequate pension to ensure that he had everything he needed to reach his potential. Once the sports medicine administration realized there were no gold medals in Menck's future, the home, the food and the pension were off the table.

Frieda and Dieter argued incessantly, caught in a marriage that was not only loveless but one where there never had been love. They were caring for a child they never wanted, and one whose maladies drained all their money and energy.

It was after another evening of screaming that Frieda left the house during a blinding snowstorm and jumped off a bridge. Dieter went off the deep end, too, but sunk no further than the bottom of a bottle of schnapps.

Menck bounced around from one institution to another as a ward of the sports administration. Through it all, he discovered the organization hadn't been completely wrong about him. As young as age eight, Menck focused on ways to overcome his physical limitations.

He had a keen mind and helped the physicians and researchers at the institutions with their computer models. At 16, he rose to a level of trust and respect that allowed him to assist in the research.

With unfettered access to labs and computers, Menck set about using them for his personal advantage. He fashioned computer-training systems to increase his strength and to control his stuttering. He saw in the steroids and hormonal treatments for athletes a means to a cure by increasing muscle mass and removing the last of his speech impediment.

About six months after his 18th birthday, Menck self-administered a hormonal cocktail.

The concoction left him in a coma for 40 days. When he awoke, he had an average person's muscular control and his stuttering was gone. Starting words was no longer a problem but the final part of multi-syllable words often disappeared.

While the scientists appreciated Menck's brilliance, other support staff despised him. His modified speech pattern gave them new ways to mock the upstart youth and his sense of entitlement.

"You are just rab_. A collec_ of stup_ peop_," a lab assistant said within Menck's earshot amid laughter from fellow technicians.

It didn't bother Menck. *Lesser minds, lesser beings.*

Over the years, he trained himself to complete words properly except those that finished a phrase or sentence. More practice gave him a strategy that worked, imperfectly. If he pushed hard on the final syllable, he produced the sound – twice – repeating itself like a creaky echo.

The scientists recognized the odd young man's genius and dedication. They supported his admission to university and were rewarded with the knowledge he graduated at the top of his medical class and went on to specialize in hormonal studies.

…

Menck cursed Jordan's incompetence, DeRoach's interference and a group of kids playing terrorist. After all of his struggles, their petty concerns, morals and stupid lives conspired to thwart him.

What's this Nathan Sherlock's life compared to what I am so close to achieving? His silly existence is spent cooking frivolous meals that have no more permanence than the next digestive cycle. Through me, his contribution to mankind can be everlasting.

Like he did with Kirk, Reyanna, Seiji and the others, Menck needed to understand how Nathan's olfactory neurons mimic stem cells in their ability to regenerate on demand.

He is not afflicted by his powers as are the others. He will provide the puzzle pieces I need not just to replace dead brain and nervous system cells but to grow billions of new ones on demand.

I will possess the Holy Grail that directs the body's immune system to destroy all disease without medicine, correct genetic flaws and turn off the mechanism that causes cells and therefore people to age. As always, I will transform myself first. I will become a god in body as well as mind.

Menck was so steeped in thought that at the conscious level he didn't register the crash of his hotel room door splintering open. The sound puddled in his brain and then bubbled to the surface a second later as a memory replay.

The doctor looked to the source of the commotion. A grim DeRoach stood framed in the shattered door casing. He held a foot-long, stainless-steel Taurus .44 magnum revolver.

Menck started to speak: "Ah, DeR . . ."

BANG

For a millisecond, Dr. Julian Menck's face expressed annoyance. He did not countenance interruptions when he spoke. His protest and the grey matter that held the half-formed salutation, now dribbled behind him from a red/taupe Jackson Pollock spatter on the wall.

The 246-grain bullet hit Menck with deer-killing power. Seasoned sports hunters know, despite its exhaust ports and the revolver's 3-1/2 pounds of inertia, that much firepower at the business end exerts a hell of a kick.

A gunman experienced with the magnum's power holds elbows loose to absorb the recoil. In this case, too many years behind a desk and the fearsome emotions coursing through DeRoach overrode his training on lighter firearms.

The explosive whiplash jabbed hot needles into his wrists. Still, he welcomed the sting. After parking his vengeance for 12 years, DeRoach embraced the pain happily.

"I don't know about you Menck," DeRoach said with a satisfied sneer over the still smoking magnum, "but you certainly made my day."

...

The big wall clock's hands rotated ever so slowly. It was just before 5 p.m.

In just five hours, I'll bring the entertainment.

That was Frenchie's promise and Frenchie always delivers as promised.

He had the girl but she required a bit of tutoring before she was a suitable date for Big Ed.

To fulfill his special client's requirements, Frenchie had to go beyond his harem and find fresh meat, not an easy task, especially in broad daylight. Where's the best place to find a Muslim girl? Obviously at a mosque.

"Where the hell is there a mosque around here," Frenchie asked his girls.

"There's one six blocks over, just past my corner," said Cheryl, a gum-snapping frizzy blond with a raccoon-eye smear, a match in class and colour for the well worn black fishnet stockings swaddling her skinny legs.

"Sometimes I take my Johns there. We use the parking lot out behind to make acquaintances."

"What about girls, young girls. See any of 'em around there?"

"Yeah, lots of them. They have some kinda school there. I think they teach kids how to speak Arab. They run it Saturday mornings. If we hurry, we can get there before they get out. Park across the street. You can do your window shopping from there."

Frenchie liked Cheryl. She was his most reliable girl, never came back without the cash, and never held anything back. One time when he was doing her after she finished her shift, in a moment of rare tenderness brought about after she stuffed $600 down the front of his pants, he went to peck her neck. Right behind her ear, there was a big wad of gum.

"Hey, you got gum by your ear."

"Oh yeah. I wondered where I put it. I just popped two fresh sticks into my mouth when this John comes up to me and wants a BJ. I wasn't going to waste that gum. It costs two bucks a pack these days."

The girl knows where her bread is buttered.

He relied on Cheryl for the most difficult jobs and he definitely needed her assistance today.

Frenchie positioned his van across and just down the street as Cheryl directed. Several girls went by but all of them in groups or in the company of an adult. Then he saw her. She was alone and the right age. He grabbed his super-duper Vortex Razor HD field glasses for a better look.

A good pair of binoculars is a wise investment for somebody in Frenchie's business. It possessed the clarity he needed to see great distances in less than ideal lighting situations, which is to say, business as usual for a pimp keeping watch on his girls and on the look-out for cops.

A pair of spyglasses of that quality looks downward on a grand in a store. In Frenchie's world, the price was $100 and 20 minutes with one of his girls.

The new girl was, indeed, a pretty little thing, so innocent looking. Like the rest, she wore that head whatchamacallit? – a hijab? – as she left the mosque and walked solo down the street. He called Cheryl to take a position a half block away.

When the girl approached the spot, Cheryl waved her over and asked for directions, arranging her with her back to the street. Frenchie pulled up in his van. Cheryl pushed the girl into the open side door. Frenchie was right on her, slamming his fist into her face and knocking her cold.

When she awoke, she found herself bound and gagged. Frenchie delivered specific instructions on her expected behavior. He made her repeat his instructions with a ruler on the knuckles or a heel on the toes for each mistake. Frenchie ended with the words: "And if you treat my friend right, you'll walk away from all of this alive. If you don't . . ."

Of course, Frenchie didn't intend for the girl to leave alive. If Big Ed didn't do it, he'd finish the job.

...

Big Ed was about as restless as he had ever been. The time was coming up to 6 p.m. The girl wouldn't arrive for another four hours.

I want to celebrate. I need to celebrate. Might as well watch the news and see those idiots running around looking for Dr. Plank.

De dee de dee de dee de dee.

The techno music intro for the evening news played as the colourful WAM-TV logo faded to reveal the image of a handsome 40-year-old, immaculately coiffed man at the news desk.

"This is WAM Chicago's Evening News, with Scott Sandleberry," an unseen voice announced. The logo vanished.

"This is Scott Sandleberry and this is the evening news for Saturday, May 17, 2014."

"We have some startling new developments just in about the hunt for the anti-gravity technology and for the scientist who discovered it."

Big Ed raised an eyebrow.

...

In a modest bungalow on the South Side of Chicago, Sage, Alessa and Mo gathered around a TV set for the six o'clock news, exchanging smiles of anticipation.

Their colleagues in Toronto had performed everything perfectly. Dr. Plank had been doing and was prepared to do anything that they asked of him. The appearance of that girl Bonnie had been a complete shock. While he wasn't in complete agreement with the way they handled it, Sage didn't have a better plan.

Olga was the right team leader. She was tough and when she made up her mind, she acted and acted without wavering. This wasn't the play that the group had started with but it's worked out even better, Sage thought.

—

32

LOST & FOUND

FOUR HOURS EARLIER, Nathan Sherlock shuffle-stepped southward through an obstacle course of '$5-Any-4-Ts-or-Shorts' racks and the multilingual hagglers that clogged the sidewalk on Spadina Avenue. At Baldwin Street, he made a right turn into Toronto's veritable palace of pungency – Kensington Market.

Stopping next to a large black oak tree, Nathan surveyed the panorama of scents to check off the final items on his list before crossing the street toward a well weathered door tucked behind a handful of café tables,

The entrance lay between Taste of Thai and Ja Eats!, two compact eateries of the Thai and Jamaican varieties, separated by a row of potted grey owl junipers.

As the email instructed, Nathan applied a bit of shoulder power as he turned the knob, adorned by specks of paint and the imprints of inner-city living. The sticky door opened with a squawk. Squeezing by two battered, coaster bicycles and four of Toronto's prescribed blue, plastic, garbage bins, each with its own unique perfume, Nathan made his way up a narrow, creaky staircase to the second storey. He extended knuckles toward the first door and delivered a series of hard, rapid knocks.

"Who is it?" came a woman's voice from inside.

"It's Nathan. I believe you were expecting me."

The door flew open and before Nathan could move, Bonnie jumped into his arms.

"We did it. They did it. We all did it," she cheered, pointing to Jazzy Irianto, Delroy DeSoto, Olga Kalata, and Dr. Gustav Plank.

The Toronto contingent of the Gini conspirators rushed to meet Nathan, giving him hugs and high fives.

Olga, always the detail person, rushed around him and shut the door.

"We're not at the finish line, yet," she cautioned. "Let's start with the introductions. We pretty well know you because you're famous. Besides you're all Bonnie talked about for two days . . . I'm Olga."

"Yeah, the scary one." Nathan's face lit up with a huge and knowing smile.

"Well, yeah I've been given that reputation." Olga gave a mock-apologetic look and a half shrug before adding, "This is Jazzy, our very own physicist."

"Almost physicist. I'm a fan of yours. I watched your Wine and Dine series religiously," she gushed.

"I'm a fan of your videos, too," Nathan replied.

"And then there's DD. That stands for Doctor Deception when it comes to fake videos."

"At your service." DD made a regal bow with his hand leading the way with a flourish.

"Amazing work. You should come by to see me. Perhaps you could pep up my show," Nathan said.

"Here's the infamous genius Dr. Gustav Plank." Olga gestured to the rail-thin man in the thick glasses.

"A pleasure to meet you." Plank held out his hand as an awkward grin filled his face.

"Likewise." Nathan returned the smile and shook his hand. "How have you been holding up these past few weeks?"

"That, I suppose, is a matter of relativity. In basic terms, my career as an academic is over. However, through this escapade, I learned that I was viewed in a much more positive light by the scientific community and among my colleagues than I could have imagined."

"And how did you come by this knowledge?" Nathan asked.

"Olga and Jasmine showed me the email correspondence between the dean of science and CSIS. Dr. Coleman alluded to my possibly being unstable but he described me as 'a brilliant scientist whose intellect will lead to great discoveries.' He said that it came as no surprise to him that of all the physicists at the university, that it was I, who unlocked the secret of negative gravity."

"That really shocked me. I had no idea that Dr. Coleman held me in such high regard or, for that matter, any regard."

"We've got to introduce you to our other team members, Jason Sage, Mo Hatcher and Alessa Reese. They're in Chicago. They've just finished putting the final touches on our financial work and are standing by right now," Olga said.

DD hit speaker mode on his cell phone.

"Hey Sager! Got Nathan Sherlock here. He wants to say howdy. He also wants to know how we started this whole thing."

...

In early 2013, still feeling the warm glow of the group's corn commodities success, Sage and company felt they were unstoppable. They had accumulated $2.3 million after expenses, all of it legally. Using the money for a second round of manipulating the Chicago Mercantile Exchange wouldn't work because of new safeguards and traders now on the alert.

Alessa snapped her fingers. "We should distribute it back to the Occupy Movement."

Olga shook her head. "There's no real structure to the movement and we sure don't want to pay taxes on the $2.3 mill. We have to make sure it goes to recognized charities, something involved in Third Word social enterprises or an animal welfare group."

Sage mulled over all of the suggestions and then addressed the group. "Let's make a decision not to make a decision until we have better information. I'll get an accountant to make sure the taxman's onside. Mo, Alessa, Jazzy, poke around on the Internet and see if there are any social enterprises, causes or other places we can put the money that will do the most good for the greatest number of people."

Several months later, Mo called the group together.

"I think I found something."

Mo explained that he intercepted a series of emails from the dean of science at the University of Toronto directed to the Canadian Security Intelligence Services, CSIS, a Canadian agency that investigates terrorism threats. The emails carried a decidedly worried message. A professor Coleman wanted CSIS to hush up and close down the research of one of his colleagues. He characterized the physicist as 'potentially uncontrollable.'

"Academic freedom prohibits me from ordering him to stop. I would be censured for even trying. CSIS must put a stop to this. I believe the individual in charge is unstable and the consequences, if he continues, could be catastrophic."

Sage studied the email and then looked quizzically at Mo. "I'm curious what that's all about but what does that have to do with us?"

"Well, I poked around a bit into the university's email system and found some correspondence between Drs. Coleman and Plank. Plank says that he has discovered a way to produce gravitons with a negative charge."

"Huh?"

"I'll let Jazzy take over from here."

"Thanks Mo. Let me put it in every day words. You know that anti-gravity stuff in all those sci-fi books and movies? Well, Plank says he's done it. He's found a way to reverse gravity and it can be done cheaply."

DD was missing the thread, too. "Okay, so we get flying cars and maybe a flying skateboard, like in Back To The Future. Really cool but what's the big deal?"

Jazzy signaled that she was about to provide the answer. "Just what you said. Think about it. If cars float, skateboards float on their own, no energy required, just reversed gravity, what does that do to the energy market?"

"Holy G-Force Batman! Oil prices will plummet," gasped Sage.

Mo egged the others on to pull the pieces of the puzzle together. "And when that happens . . . ?"

Alessa snapped her fingers and with a huge smile made a declaration. "The rich get less rich, and the poorest of the poor get a reasonable standard of living."

"I've got the rallying call: Rise Up!" DD sang as he performed a happy dance with open hands waving rhythmically in the air.

Sage took control of the meeting. He outlined a plan that must take effect once Jazzy cracked the code and created some negative gravity samples. The group would release the tiny floating particles of freedom to people who thought like them in every country across the globe. The samples would be the catalyst for change. In an instant, the drudgery and enslavement gravity imposed on the poor, since man lived in caves, would end.

Jazzy stared hard at each person in the group. There was no mistaking what they were committing to. "It may cost us everything, but we really, really, really have to do this."

The prospect of igniting world-shifting events caused Sage's mind to explode with the possibilities and generated a hunger to make it happen. He was confident the entire group was with him. Whatever the personal and, possibly, criminal consequences, they would release negative gravity to the world. He just needed to say it aloud.

"Julian Assange and his family received death threats because he released embarrassing information that might impact on the rich and powerful. When we release negative gravity, there are no 'mights' about it. It will take huge slices of wealth from some of the world's richest and most powerful people. They will not accept that meekly.

"If they can stop us, they will. They will use any and every means, legal, illegal, violent and lethal. We will be on our own. The authorities will not help us. In fact, many of them will be the agents of the rich who will hunt us down. If any of you have doubts, now is the time to walk away."

All eyes were on Sage. No one said a word. No one left. Sage had his answer.

After a few more days of research and poring over emails from Plank to his boss, Jazzy and Mo raised the possibility that Dr. Coleman may have been right. Negative gravity could be used to unleash great evil on the world, perhaps even lead to its destruction.

Jazzy, disappointment written across her face, spoke first.

"From what I'm reading, it appears negative gravitons readily pass their charge on to materials with similar atomic properties. It's too easy. It's an amazing power, but as much as I believe in the phrase, Power To The People, not everyone can be trusted with such incredible power."

Once she outlined the potential for negative gravity to be misused by terrorists, the mentally unstable, or amateurs, the entire group deflated.

"Dr. Coleman was most worried about amateurs whose tinkering might cause what he called 'an irreversible cascading effect' where accidentally everything has its gravity polarity switched to negative. All life on Earth would come to an end."

Alessa gave a huge sigh and nodded her head in agreement. "It's the perfect answer but we can't be responsible for such potentially horrific consequences."

Olga jumped to her feet. She stared at Sage, excitement lighting her eyes. "Jason, we had $2.3 million and the possibility of many times more than that. Did you ever consider using that money to burn $2.3 million in cornfields?"

"Of course not. You know that."

"But did THEY?"

"No, that's why they ... That's it! Olga, you're a genius. We do everything to get negative gravity, perhaps destroy Plank's notes so they know we have it and then we threaten to release it to the world."

Alessa caught the logic. "Only we don't. It's only a threat. We demand a ransom of some sort, not for us, but a change in legislation or extra funds for programs that alleviate the suffering of the poor."

DD joined the conversation, adding a note of caution. "Just remember that when we do that, however noble the cause, we are breaking the law. If we get caught, I they won't go lightly on us."

"Only if we're caught," Olga added. "Only if we're caught."

—

33

DEAD END

"COFFEE BREAK'S OVER," Sage addressed Jazzy on April 7, the final day the full group assembled in Chicago. "Time for you to produce a little levity."

"Geez, is he gonna keep this up from now on?" DD gave his best impression of a torture victim.

Jazzy's face bore a different expression. "No levity – the laughing or the physical kind. It's all dead ends."

A review of the first block of data pointed to solutions and certain conditions that were to be set in the next series, she explained. When she investigated the following data set, there was nothing there except a lot of nonsense to anyone who knew anything about higher-end physics.

Sage gave a pained look. The effort to date took nearly a month with the entire team working around the clock to hack into Plank's computer. After all of this, could they really end up with nothing? Had the scientist outfoxed would-be hackers? He needed to clarify his understanding. Was he missing something?

"So we have a beginning that looks promising and an end with tangible results but all the how-to in the middle is missing?"

"That's about it." Jazzy gave a wide-eyed look of surrender accompanied with a massive shrug.

Sage tapped his fingers on a desk, trying to make sense of it.

"So, did Plank set all of this up purposely as a red herring for people like us who might try to hack his research, sort of a security measure?"

Jazzy shook her head. "I don't know. It seems like a pretty elaborate, time-consuming thing to do when he could have just put up another off-the-shelf firewall or simply shut down all connections to his computer."

"So where does that leave us?"

"Absolutely, nowhere. We have nothing."

"Any ideas, Mo? Anybody?" Sage looked from face to face.

"Well there is something curious. While I was still downloading the files and setting up to erase them and our tracks, I went back in to see if I had missed anything. There was an extra file that I thought I forgot to copy. I clicked on it and downloaded it. I hadn't looked at it until just now. Apparently, that file came from Plank. He was up at midnight when we did the hack and just watched the last part of it happening. He couldn't stop it. Instead, he placed a note to us in the same folder that the files were in. Here it is."

Alessa nudged in next to Mo for a closer look at the screen. "A note to us from Plank?"

"Yes, look right here. He wants to meet us. He says he has something really important to discuss."

Alessa stuck her nose right up the screen and then looked at the others.

"I don't get it."

"It's got to be a trap." Sage had gone from forlorn to worried.

Mo shook his head.

"I don't think so. I hadn't quite erased our trail at that time. He had a moment when he might have traced us and alerted authorities. With his help, they may have had time to find our location. But he didn't do that."

Sage considered Mo's comments for a moment and then threw his hands in the air.

"I have no idea what's happening. Okay, I say we check it out but we have to be really careful. We go ahead with everything as planned but with our antennas up. Jazzy, when you're in Toronto, I need you to speak to Plank but find a plausible excuse."

"What excuse?"

"Pretend you're a physics student and hit on him. Get close to him on the pretext you're studying the weak nuclear force and need his opinion on a paper. Something like that. Even geniuses revert to their lizard brain when it comes to a beautiful girl."

"Hey Sage, were you just complimenting me?"

"Just a fact," Mo said.

Jazzy blushed.

Pulling Sage off to the side, Alessa whispered, "I think sometimes he just tries too hard."

Over the next several minutes, everyone discussed final details and got ready to go their separate ways. Mo and Jazzy locked eyes across the room. Mo approached her and grasped her hand.

"I'll miss you girl," Mo said, his eyes locked on hers.

"I'll miss you too. You're my best friend."

"Just your best friend?"

"My very best friend," Jazzy replied, planting a kiss on Mo's cheek.

Mo bristled at her remark. She realized, however well meaning she intended it, it cut him deeply.

"There is no one else," she said softly, gazing intently at him with her beautiful, dark brown eyes. "But what you want, I can't give you, not just yet. Perhaps, in time. You have to be patient with me."

Mo sighed and nodded gently. It was the same old story. He thought that when she left her studies in Canada and joined him at the Wall Street Occupy protest almost three years ago, she was coming to be with him. But, clearly, it was the cause that attracted her and he was very much a secondary consideration. He watched, with every emotion in his being askew, as the woman he'd love till his last breath walked out the door.

...

The following day, Tuesday, April 8, Jasmine Irianto and Delroy DeSoto took their positions at the University of Toronto's physics building.

DD waited in a lounge next to the corridor that Plank would have to use when he left his office.

"He's leaving now, heading down the main staircase to the front entrance," DD reported via his cell phone.

"I've got it from here," said Jazzy.

As Plank left the building, Jazzy walked straight to him.

"Hi, Professor Plank? My name's Samantha. I'm glad I bumped into you. I'm a new postgrad physics student and I was told you are the one to speak to. My paper's on the absorption properties of W and Z bosons. You're an expert on the weak nuclear interaction, so I was wondering if I could buy you dinner sometime and perhaps you could point me in the right direction."

"You have my data," Plank said in a low accusing growl. It was not a question.

Startled by his response, Jazzy came back quickly. "Whoa, all my research is my original research. You aren't researching bosons."

"Look young lady, I wasn't born yesterday. In fact, in the 40 years that I've been on this planet, no member of the opposite sex, even one tenth as pretty as you, has even glanced my way. Now, I leave some bread crumbs for the thieves to follow and suddenly this gorgeous girl hits on me and wants to go for dinner? I think not."

"What's this data you mentioned?"

"You know very well. It's my negative gravity research. What do you plan to do with it? Please don't release it. It's not worth anything to anyone but me. It would ruin me. I don't have much money. I've just been let go from my job. I really can't pay you much.

Will you take $10,000?"

Jazzy was stunned. She needed time to think, to get more information from him.

"We need to go somewhere private to talk."

The two walked to the St. George subway station and took the southbound train to College Street. From there they hopped aboard an eastbound streetcar, where DD, who was trailing them, made his presence known.

"This is ... uh ... Bob. He's working with me," Jazzy said to a worried-looking Plank.

The trio disembarked at Jarvis and walked a block to Allan's Gardens to a series of greenhouses that form a year-round tropical oasis in the heart of Toronto. As Jazzy expected, the greenhouses had few visitors. The lush foliage blocked prying eyes and provided private areas where they could speak.

"Samantha, Bob, why are we here?" Plank stammered, his serious yet mysterious demeanour juxtaposed to the explosion of beautiful scents and colours from orchids, begonias and the hundreds of flowering trees around them.

All of that, and the use of the phony names, struck Jazzy as funny and she started a nervous giggle while responding: "To speak privately."

Her apparent amusement made Plank even more agitated.

"Okay, look. I can mortgage my house. If I did that, I could get you $30,000."

DD and Jazzy looked at each other, both completely baffled.

"We need to talk this over with someone else," said DD, who then hit a speed dial on his cell phone. "Hi, uh, Mr. uh, Mr. S. It's ... uh ... Bob here. No Bob. Listen it's Bob for now. I'm here with ... uh ..."

"Samantha," Jazzy added.

"Yeah, I'm here with Samantha and we're talking to Dr. Plank and his offer on the table is $30,000 to get back his research."

"Uh, no . . . Uh, no . . . Uh, no . . . No, that wouldn't be it . . . I can't really say. Tell you what. I'll put him on speakerphone and you ask him yourself."

"Hi, Dr. Plank. This is . . . uh . . . Mr. S. I would like to hear directly from you just what you are proposing."

"Please, you can't release my research to the university. I've been writing letters, causing them trouble and the Dean has it in for me. If you give them my notes, I'll be disgraced. They'll trash my reputation. My career will be over. I'll never be able to get a job anywhere."

"Right. Okay. We hear you. Just stay there. I need to talk to Jaz . . . er Samantha and Bob privately for a moment."

DD turned off the speakerphone and walked with Jazzy to the other end of the greenhouse. Both DD and Jazzy leaned an ear into the phone.

"Give me a second. I've got get Alessa and Mo with me and I've connected with Olga. I need them to hear this. What the F is going on? What is he talking about?"

"Dunno. He's acting like, like he's the criminal, offering us money," said DD.

"What?" said Olga.

No one spoke for a few seconds. The silence broke when someone's fingers snapped. It was Jazzy.

"I think I may know what's going on. He was being fired, right? And his weak force work was pure research, not something many universities and research centres want to pick up on when money's tight. It's certainly nothing a private lab would want."

"So . . . ," said Sage wearily.

"Let me walk you through it," said Jazzy with a much calmer voice. "Some of the stuff we downloaded was this correspondence with the university about Plank losing his job."

"Yeah, I remember that," said DD. "I remember it was a March 2 confirmation email to the notice of his dismissal as of May 31."

"And when did he unveil for the first time that he was working on and had cracked negative gravity?"

"He first hints of it about a week later, March 10, and sets up the video demonstration on March 12th that we grabbed when we hacked his system.

189

He gave another demonstration to his dean, a Prof. Coleman on April 1 but it didn't have any effect on his termination."

"That's it for sure," Jazzy said in her eureka voice.

"What's it?" asked Sage.

"All the research we downloaded dead-ends. Remember me telling you that the initial data points to solutions and certain environments that must be created in the next series and the next series leads nowhere?"

"Sort of but that's all scientific gobbly gook to me."

"Well, I didn't think about it at the time but when you're doing coding and entering scientific notes, it becomes second nature to put in the date and time as a means of identifying specific parts of your work. It's good science and it makes it easier to double-check your stuff with backup notes, your calendar and track entries by date in your computer."

"Okay, I get that."

"And I presumed that the initial part of the work was correct and the end pieces were correct because it all worked. The middle was missing, I presumed, because Plank was taking certain security measures."

"Right."

"Wrong!"

"Wrong?"

"Right!"

"Now you've got me totally confused," said Sage.

"Precisely and that was exactly what Plank hoped to do – get people confused, especially people who only got a cursory glance at his work. He never intended that anyone would be able to download the whole thing and analyze it at their leisure."

"Because . . . ?"

"Because it's all bull. The initial data is just standard stuff. Many experiments start out the same way. In fact, he may have just copied and pasted it from somewhere else."

"So you're telling us that Plank did not discover a way to generate negative gravity."

"That's correct."

"It's all BS?"

"Correct."

—

34

THE CON

"Shit. Why would he do that?"

"TO SAVE HIS JOB. What really gives it away are the time stamps. I remembered thinking they were weird but I was so engrossed in the big picture, I didn't give it much thought at the time. Most of it is dated March 12 or later. There were no dates prior to that. How do you spend years developing research and entering the information and then dating it on the day or after the day that you do your first demonstration? The answer is, you don't."

"This is all pretty elaborate just to save his job, don't you think?" DD said.

"It's actually not so original. There are a lot of instances where researchers have exaggerated findings and even falsified research results to prolong research grants or their term of work," Jazzy said.

"It was suggested to me that I exercise my creativity so that I would be able to get research money to the end of my PhD studies. But nobody who I ever heard of has ever done anything as bold as this. Nobody has ever lied so blatantly."

"What about what we saw on the video?" Mo said.

"Smoke and mirrors. A lot of magicians use the principles of physics to make things look like magic. The old card levitation trick is done with static electricity and I'll bet that's what he used here. The neat thing is, in a lab, you have all kinds of exotic and powerful equipment that you can use to create the exact environment you want. And the isolation glove box plays perfectly, just like a magician's box."

"How did he expect to get away with it? Eventually, he'd have to admit there was no negative gravity technology?" said Sage.

"He wasn't thinking that far ahead. He wanted to get his contract renewed and he'd worry about the rest later."

"Wouldn't that be the big embarrassment he wants to avoid by paying us off?" said Sage.

"How many times have we heard some researcher somewhere has found the cure for cancer?"

"Lots," said Sage.

"Same thing here. He would drop hints over time that it wasn't quite what he had hoped and eventually it would fizzle out. Besides, we downloaded a very promising but incomplete paper that might create a name for Plank a year or so from now. I'll bet he was counting on that to keep his job."

"A paper on negative gravity?" asked Mo.

"No within his field, the weak nuclear force. It's too specialized for this crowd to understand but it might open the door to a whole realm of research, using the force as a detection system, maybe a power source. It would take decades of additional research to incorporate his ideas into a functioning product."

There was a long silence until DD broke it.

"So, we've just been wasting our time and risking jail for hacking a university computer, not to mention spending a pile of cash, just because some guy's running a scam to save his job?"

"That's about it," said Jazzy.

"Crap. Double crap. Well, it was my idea to pursue this, so I'll wear it. Boy, do I ever feel stupid," said Sage.

"Don't feel bad, bro. You're not the only one. I see that the FBI's anti-terrorism unit and some others I can't yet identify also took the bait," said Mo.

"I've caught some chatter about the highest levels in several governments receiving initial alerts. And I'm not quite positive about this, but it looks like some big corporations may be getting a heads up from somewhere."

"Yeah, well stupidity loves company. I think . . ."

"Now wait a minute," said Olga. "Who besides us knows this is BS?"

"Well, Plank but . . ." Sage stopped speaking mid-sentence. "Olga, again you're a genius."

"Hey you guys in Toronto, Sager's got the same gleam in his eye he had the day he figured out how to play the corn commodity scam," said Alessa.

"We're the only ones who know it's BS, aren't we?" said Sage.

"I suspect we are," Jazzy replied.

"Tell you what. The game may not be over. In fact, it may just be beginning. DD, can you and Olga get into Plank's lab unseen and mess it up? Make it look like a burglary and a kidnapping. Make sure that when you leave clues that none of them lead back to us. Jazzy, as part of our agreement with Plank to keep our mouths shut and to help him afterward, he has to go into hiding with us to maintain suspicion that he's been kidnapped."

Turning to Mo and Alessa in Chicago and with the Toronto team leaning into DD's cell phone, Sage made an announcement.

"It's time for us to commit the imperfect crime."

...

Olga's curiosity needed feeding. She pressed Nathan for answers.

"Bonnie's given us a bit of information about how you figured out we were running a scam with this negative gravity threat. Tell us the rest."

"I believe Bonnie has explained a little about my special abilities. We needn't revisit that. The rest is rather long and complicated, but here goes."

It was the second time in two days that Nathan provided the same details. He delivered his first explanation when DeRoach drove him to the airstrip on Thursday. He needed the FBI man's help for the rest of the plan to work.

Nathan had no choice but to trust him. He was the only one who could make the rest of the plan fall into place.

"What you do with the Menck information is up to you, but I need you to promise me that you will follow my instructions to the letter when it comes to the Ginis and anything about the Ginis."

"I'm not sure . . ."

"You've pretty well told me you committed murder, or at least a mercy kill-ing. I know you're willing to stretch the law as long as it's the right thing to do. All I'm asking is that you do not move on the Ginis or reveal anything about what they're up to for at least 48 hours. Hold off until Saturday evening when all the pieces will be in place. I will call you and CSIS Supt. Beauchemin no later than at 5 p.m. Saturday Toronto time. If you'll do one more thing, I guarantee I will get the Ginis to voluntarily to turn themselves over to CSIS."

"You're willing to hold off even after they killed Bonnie?"

"Hold onto that thought for a second. First, I need you to give me your word."

"Since we don't have a clue as to the whereabouts of the Ginis, I guess it couldn't hurt. Now, if they release negative gravity and start shooting more people into the stars, this deal is off."

"Agreed. You may have your own means to find Dr. Menck. If not, I could trigger events to force Jordan to see Menck."

"And just what would make Jordan show up at Menck's door?"

"Another video, this time showing my capture by the Ginis. That would allow you to track her to the not-so-good doctor's location."

"How are you going to upload a video onto the Ginis' email site without tipping them off."

"Not a problem. I'll hand myself over to them and they'll upload the video themselves."

"You can't be serious. They're terrorists. They killed Bonnie."

"Not really."

"They kidnapped Plank."

"Not really."

"And I suppose they didn't really highjack negative gravity – the technology that makes the atom bomb look like a slingshot?"

"In a word, no. The Ginis aren't terrorists. They aren't kidnappers. They aren't killers. They are, however, consummate con artists."

Nathan reminded DeRoach of the havoc the group caused in the corn commodities market.

"They fooled everybody and now they're doing it again, except with the potential for a much greater impact. Negative gravity doesn't exist – or at least neither Plank nor any other Earthling has ever managed to prove it exists. Through sheer subterfuge and without making a single public demand, the Ginis have convinced powerful people that Plank has discovered negative gravity and it will destroy the value of the world's energy companies.

"As a result of this inside knowledge, some of the wealthiest and most powerful people in the world have removed their investments from oil & gas. That has left these shares available to average folk and pension funds at bargain prices. Usually inside information wins out. In this case, the insiders inside information will backfire on them.

"When it's revealed that negative gravity was a hoax, oil & gas share values will rebound and with them, by the numbers I've seen the market reporting today, that will effectively transfer about $1 trillion from the world's ultra-rich to a lot of average people and, in some cases, to Third World development funds.

"The Gini's goal is to take some of the wealth of the world's richest people and transfer it to the poor. If we keep quiet about this until Saturday, I believe it will be mission accomplished."

"And Bonnie?"

Nathan explained that Bonnie's apparent death launch was DD's masterful work with CGI.

"Perhaps he does deserve that Oscar."

"How did you know negative gravity was bull?"

"It was obvious from the first moment I walked into the FBI lab that Plank was a fraud. I deduced that the Ginis discovered the deception and kept it going. My first clue was the scent of ozone inside of Plank's isolation glove box."

Nathan explained that ozone is a natural byproduct when an electrical discharge hits oxygen. The discharge could be something as small as static electricity. Plank, like others in charge of a lab, took steps to prevent static electricity buildup because of the potential for an explosion or skewed test results.

"The question is, because there were pronounced levels of ozone in the isolation glove box, what could the source of the static electricity be? The obvious answer is, it was a source specifically designed to create static electricity. And for what purpose would one want to create static electricity? The answer again was obvious – to fake negative gravity. To make things float in the air. To make objects appear to defy gravity. It was a simple magician's trick, not a scientific miracle."

"Wait a second. If you discovered the Ginis weren't a threat and that negative gravity wasn't a danger, why didn't you tell that to us on Sunday when you first got here?"

"For starters, we didn't know who we could trust. Bonnie, in particular, was a strong supporter of the Occupy Movement. I was less so. I guess when the establishment is paying you millions of dollars a year, it becomes tough to protest against yourself.

"Bonnie convinced me to keep my mouth shut until we learned more. Besides, before we went to the lab, Reyanna and Seiji told me they were pretty well being held here against their will."

"I don't think they'd say that."

"They were definitely afraid to speak out. Otherwise, why would they use such elaborate means to get a message to me secretly."

"Okay, I get that. But back to the lab and you knowing negative gravity was a scam. You can't have deduced all of that simply because you smelled ozone," DeRoach said.

"No there were many other clues."

Nathan recounted his list.

Clue #1: Cotton lab coats, special foot gear and cotton towels were de rigueur in Plank's lab because cotton and the special footwear all prevent static buildup. The small carpets in the lab were grounded to prevent static.

"I could smell the other devices had an anti-static spray applied. Extraordinary steps were taken to eliminate static electricity in the lab generally. Why? To prevent it from interfering with the specific static electricity properties inside the isolation glove box."

Clue #2: Plank used aluminum as his preferred medium to demonstrate negative gravity because metals conduct electricity. While one piece of aluminum can be attracted to an object that holds a static charge, that piece of aluminum will not attract a second piece of aluminum because it conducts and, therefore, cannot hold a static charge. Scientists would dismiss any notion that static electricity was used to fake negative gravity because the medium was metal.

"Like all the best magicians, Plank carried out classic misdirection. He didn't use aluminum or any metal. He performed his illusion by using a plastic that to the eye appeared to be aluminum. I came across this aluminum look-alike previously in the construction of food displays and TV studio sets and recognized its odour in the isolation box."

Clue #3: How could the Ginis move from a non-violent and brilliant scheme that broke no laws during their corn scam to a horrific criminal act and the bluntest of blunt actions – a kidnapping. Nathan refused to believe people that smart could be so dumb.

"Peel back the veneer and wasn't the Ginis' modus operandi really the setup and execution of a great con?"

Clue #4: The Ginis left signs of Plank's kidnapping in his lab when the video shows him leaving voluntarily with Jazzy, never to return.

"Why fake a kidnapping in the lab? Clearly, in this case they over-thought their plan."

Clue #5: How could people so incredibly clever at covering their electronic trail and eliminating all traces of their computer hacking, their physical presence, fingerprints, DNA, and even their financial trail be so astoundingly stupid when it came to communicating with other members of their group through something as simple as a shared email account?

"Flynn even mocked them for sharing a Gmail account just like the key players in a couple of thriller novels. His only excuse for their carelessness was the notion that the Ginis didn't read thriller novels," said Nathan.

Clue #6: Videos of the Ginis committing criminal acts left in the Gmail account where Canadian and American counter-terrorism agents could easily find them.

"Think about it. While Rebecca and Flynn were dancing over the evidence we just found, who in their right mind would leave something that damning where it could be discovered? The answer is, they wanted it to be discovered and the FBI and CSIS played right into their hands."

Clue #7: The supposed members of this terrorist cell were scrupulous about keeping their identities secret and then suddenly they weren't. They allowed themselves to be seen.

"Jasmine Irianto was captured on two different security cameras with Plank. One member visible.

"Even though they cleaned the car and lab of their DNA, they couldn't be positive they could get it all even if Seiji and I hadn't been on the job. To use DD, the one team member who has a sibling with a criminal record and could be tracked through his DNA was careless, too careless. That's two members visible.

"Bonnie and I, obviously, were already on to them when Olga Kalata was caught on video tossing Bonnie into space. But for anyone else, that should have been Clue #8.

That's three members of the team visible. Why would they be so careless about their identities unless, in the end, it didn't matter."

"Now, you got to tell me about that one – about Bonnie still being alive," DeRoach said with growing impatience.

"Okay but let me finish with Olga Kalata. Here she is caught on the video, her face clearly visible as she launches Bonnie to her doom. Olga Kalata is someone who had been a minor celebrity as a top U.S. college gymnast. She was interviewed on national TV many times as a teenager. It meant that she, too, didn't worry about being caught after the fact. That could only be if they had committed no crime. It was all way too easy. They were laying bread crumbs and we followed where they led us."

"And about Bonnie?"

"Yes, yes, about Bonnie."

—

35

AN OLD SCHOOL TRICK

IT WAS A MATTER OF GETTING ACCESS to Seiji to get more information. Secondly, I needed a good excuse to leave Quantico before the Ginis' capture, Nathan said.

"It wasn't about the Ginis, but about the internal threat to me and to Seiji, Reyanna and Jordan. Bonnie and I figured we needed something startling. Another Gini video was the obvious answer but we feared Davis might examine the video and discover it was a fabrication. We needed to have Seiji's assessment on its veracity and quickly. No one would question Seiji's assessment.

"The video had to have a direct bearing on me so I could demand to have an audience with Seiji. And I had to have a way to tell Seiji that we wanted him to lie, say the video was the real thing.

"What is more dramatic than murder? And what would upset me more than anything?

Bonnie's murder would give me the perfect excuse to demand a meeting with Seiji."

"Whew, that it did, for certain. We were all pretty shaken."

"My biggest worry was my acting. I had to fake shock and anguish. I'm glad neither Jordan nor Flynn have the abilities that Seiji, Reyanna and I possess to weed out lies or the game would have been over before it started."

"Still, you had to be amazed when you saw that video. I mean, it looked like the real thing."

"I was surprised how well they executed the production. It looked like it was videotaped by somebody scared out of her wits holding a shaky cell phone. I might have believed it if some of the words spoken by the killer hadn't been written by me."

"You-you wrote the killer's script?" DeRoach stammered.

"Not all of it, just a couple of the lines so I'd know it was an act. All this international CSIS-FBI cloak and dagger stuff rubbed off and we worked out our pass codes. I was pretty sure that negative gravity was a scam, but I needed Bonnie to tell me she was okay and everything was happening as planned. I especially didn't want to be caught in a con of my own making if negative gravity turned out to be real."

Nathan explained that the original idea for launching a body into space came from Jordan on that first day in Quantico.

"Remember what she said?"

"The possibilities for its use and misuse are endless. For instance, the mob reverses the gravity of the lead plates in a diving belt. They wrap the belt around someone, living or dead. The solution to the problem is out of this world, literally."

Bonnie's Space Odyssey video was a ploy to meet with Seiji again. This time Nathan was ready for two-way communication.

"Special Agent Jordan was with you the entire time. How were you able to communicate so effectively with him?"

"It's an old school trick. Kids use it all the time to cheat on exams."

"And that is . . . ?"

Nathan rolled up his left sleeve and showed DeRoach the tiny lettering he had written on his forearm that provided Seiji with specific instructions.

"And he was able to use those instructions to communicate back to you?"

"Absolutely using our form of ESP. The lettering is pretty small. I'll explain. I wrote a set of instructions and questions on the back of my left forearm and the alphabet on the inside of my forearm."

Seiji, follow these instructions exactly.
1. When you see the video, lie. Tell us it is real.
2. Create a diversion so people won't focus on what I'm doing.
3. Answer the questions below.
4. Once we complete communications, create an issue to get me out of there.
Here are the questions:
1. Is something in the food keeping you captive? Y / N

2. Who is:	Good?	Bad?	A Pawn?	Don't Know
a. Jordan	G	B	P	DK
b. Flynn	G	B	P	DK
c. Beauchemin	G	B	P	DK
d. DeRoach	G	B	P	DK
e. Other	G	B	P	DK

3. If other, spell the name.

"When I came before Seiji, I stepped forward and positioned Jordan to my right so my body blocked her view of my left arm. I carefully bunched up my sleeve and pointed to the top line on my forearm."

When you see the video, lie. Tell us it is real.

Aloud, I said: 'I need you to tell me, is it real or is it some kind of CGI fakery?'

"Seiji understood my instructions and responded accordingly."

'I'm afraid it's definitely real. Sorry Nathan, I know she was your friend.'

"I then did my best to act like I was coming apart and fell to my knees with my face hidden in my hands. What I was actually doing was pointing to the first question."

Is something in the food keeping you captive? Y / N

"When I fingered the Y, my nose detected a sudden on-rush of emotion from Seiji. So I knew the food's controlling him, too. I moved my index finger to the next question."

2. Who is	Good?	Bad?	A Pawn?	Don't Know
a. Jordan	G	B	P	DK
b. Flynn	G	B	P	DK
c. Beauchemin	G	B	P	DK
d. DeRoach	G	B	P	DK
e. Other	G	B	P	DK

"Along the line with Jordan's name, when my finger touched on the 'P', a scent pulsed through the air. So she's a pawn.

"For Flynn, the signal came over the DK – Don't Know. Beauchemin also registered a DK. However, when my digit slid across DeRoach, your name, the wave hit on 'G'. I realized you are a guy I could trust.

"When I fingered the 'B' for bad on the line for *Other*, I hadn't quite been prepared for the intensity of the emotion from Seiji. It was literally the smell of fear."

...

The final question, triggered by Seiji's fear-driven scent, was to spell out the name of *the Other*.

As Seiji said something about Bonnie being a North Korean sleeper agent and got everybody rattled, I flipped my forearm over and ran a finger over the alphabet.

Abcdefghij – pulse – J

Abcdefghijklmnopqrstu – pulse – U

Abcdefghijkl – pulse – L

Abcdefghi – pulse – I

A – pulse – A

Abcdefghijklmn – pulse – N

Abcdefghijklmnopqrstuvwxy_ –_ (space)

Abcdefghijklm – pulse – M

Abcde – pulse – E

Abcdefghijklmn – pulse – N

Abc – pulse – C

Abcdefghijk – pulse – K

No more pulses.

"I assembled the letters in my mind and discovered that the name of our mystery villain was JULIAN MENCK. I also learned that Special Agent Jordan was a pawn and not to be trusted but that I could trust and confide in you.

The last part was to be able to get out of Seiji's chamber fast. Seiji helped there with that yarn about Bonnie being a North Korean sleeper agent. Again, it was a real whopper but Jordan and Flynn bought it hook, line and sinker. So here we are."

Once Nathan provided the full explanation, DeRoach shook his head.

"You and the others are even more astounding than I thought. Unfortunately, I think Jordan may go down on this one. I'll put a bug on her. If she meets with Menck, I will find him and settle our accounts."

Nathan nodded. "And I'm heading to Toronto. I've got some Ginis to put in a bottle."

...

"So that pretty well sums up everything," Nathan told the Ginis.

Jazzy still looked a bit puzzled. "There's one more question. How did you and Bonnie find us? We made it impossible through phone or computer tracking and our money trail led nowhere. Bonnie said we'd have to wait for you to explain."

"I have a computer database where I inventory all the scents that I come across. I enter the information through an app I created to make it easy to do. As you know, I have an eidetic memory of sorts for odours. I never forget something I've smelled. The trouble is, I don't always remember where I came across the odour, and sometimes when you are dealing with multiple odours that I've detected in a variety of places, it's impossible for me to figure out on my own the single place where I detected all of the scents at the same time.

"In this case, what I detected in Dr. Plank's car was the combined perfumes of ginger fried grouper, Thai three-flavoured nam prik pao sauce and Jamaican Escovitch Fish, exuding aromas of scotch bonnet peppers, vinegar, and pimento berries.

"Combine all of that with a black oak tree, grey owl junipers, scents from a lot of different cars, and roofing tar and what does the computer say?"

asked Nathan.

"A second storey flat on Baldwin Avenue above two restaurants that is next to a parking garage and has access to a flat tarred roof that people can access and walk on – likely a makeshift patio," said Bonnie.

"A quick look on Google Earth along Baldwin revealed a parking garage next to restaurants with apartments above, one of which had a walkout second-storey patio. Voila, there's the lair of the Ginis."

"One more question," asked Jazzy. "Why are you calling us the Ginis?"

Bonnie looked at Nathan. They both shrugged. "Isn't your group called the Gini Conspiracy?"

"The what?" Olga said.

"The Gini Conspiracy. That's the name the FBI uses for you."

"We know what the Gini Coefficient is and try to use it as a yardstick but we've never called ourselves the Gini Conspiracy or Gini anything," Olga said.

"I kind of thought it was catchy. So what do you call yourselves?"

Alessa's voice came over the speakerphone. "I don't know we've ever thought of having a name. We just kind of thought we were just a bunch of friends with a strong social commitment."

"I think Friends is taken. Why not the Gini Conspiracy? It sounds mysteeeeriooous," Bonnie said in her best B-film horror voice.

"I wish you'd stop calling us that," said DD. "I was hoping for a cooler name like the Super Studs."

Olga rolled her eyes and shook her head with feigned disdain. "You wish. We should just be known by our deeds. Forget a name."

"Hey, how about the Deed Dudes." The words had scarcely left her lips when Bonnie realized she had just placed a big target on her backside.

"She's known us for less than a day and she's already trying to take over. Besides, Deed Dudes – DD – is just lame for a group and it clashes with my name."

Time to switch topics, thought Bonnie. "Anyway, there is something that you can do for Nathan and me. It fits in perfectly with your Gini goals."

—

[36]

THE FLEA

AS DEROACH AWAITED Nathan's jet to depart for Toronto on Thursday, he pulled a small black cube from his jacket pocket. A flip of the plastic lid revealed a new-issue GXP45-9004 geo-positional locator or, in the veteran FBI operative's technical parlance, the Flea. The device was a fraction of the size and weight of any 'bug' DeRoach had ever seen.

The Flea measured a bit bigger than its namesake, but no larger than a medium-sized red ant. In his hand, it seemed to have no weight. When removed from its tiny sheath, the Flea transmitted its location with pinpoint accuracy. The signals lasted up to 48 hours.

Another feature, and the one that inspired DeRoach's pet name, was the powerful adhesive on its tail. It stuck inconspicuously to anything, like a real flea to a single hair. When 48 hours passed, the Flea's programming released it from its sticky tail to tumble to the ground. A moment later, its nano-tech battery provided a pulse that fused the shell and its circuitry into an unrecognizable black sliver of plastic litter.

The Flea dutifully reported Jordan's movements after work – routine stuff – a supermarket and then home. After dinner hour, she headed toward Washington D.C., not an uncommon destination for a good-looking, unmarried woman in search of some fun, entertainment and perhaps companionship.

When Jordan arrived in Washington, her actions caused DeRoach to invest his full attention. The Flea tracked her making four successive right turns, coming to the originating point and zigzagging along another set of streets to her first stop.

She exhibited classic FBI training to spot and shake a tail. The map-

205

ping software identified her stop as the parking garage of the Arlington Residence Hotel.

Less than a minute later she was on the move again. DeRoach compared the data points where she stopped her car and where she resumed driving again. The Flea was accurate within 10 feet. The two points did not match. They were more than 50 feet apart.

If I'm reading this right, she switched cars to throw off anyone following her. She's smart enough to shed her clothing and, with it, tracking devices on her clothing or the vehicle, DeRoach concluded. The Flea remained on the job, tenaciously hanging by a single, long blonde hair, somewhere close to the base of her skull. It was well out of sight and, with luck, not on a main route for comb or brush.

Jordan drove to an address on O Street. DeRoach looked it up. La Casa, the ritzy private hotel and power broker meeting place.

That's it for sure. Motel 6 just doesn't fit Menck's imperious view of himself.

DeRoach couldn't move in yet. He needed to wait until Sunday when he'd be able to bypass the skeleton crew attending the ESP team.

...

Back in Toronto, it was Nathan's turn to ask the questions. "Okay, we showed you ours. Now you show us yours. How did you come up with this whacky anti-gravity con to begin with?"

"That would be Jason. He's got this really devious mind," Jazzy said.

"Sage was pissed when he found out negative gravity didn't exist but then Olga asked the question, what if people believed it existed. From there, Sage designed how we could play the markets.

"I was over my head in all of this," said Plank. "I only wanted the Dean to extend my contract another year. With an extension, perhaps I could have published, made a small discovery in my field during that year and kept my job. I never intended anyone outside of our department to learn about it."

Plank then related how he admitted in a phone conversation with Sage that his negative gravity research was a hoax.

Sage was well into his plan and needed Plank's cooperation. "But you did leave us, what did you call them? Ah, yes, breadcrumbs. It certainly worked on us. Maybe we can make it work on everybody else."

DD jumped into the story. "That's when Jason devised a series of breadcrumbs that the FBI, NSA, and the super rich would pick up on."

Breadcrumb #1 was to stage Plank's office and lab to look like a break-in and kidnapping. Breadcrumb #2 was to make Plank disappear and to leave indications that it was a kidnapping. Breadcrumb #3 was the condition of Plank's house; newspaper not cut off; no bags packed; food left out.

"The piéce de resistance, of course, were the Super Breadcrumbs Videos #4, #5 and especially #6," Jazzy said with a sly smile. "We borrowed that idea from Dr. Plank, too. He was the one who got everybody worked up with his anti-gravity videos."

Video Breadcrumb #4: With Plank's assistance, DD used what appeared to be his cell phone to create a very fuzzy, very shaky, real-life video of various materials flying off an unseen person's hand and then soaring into space – a pin, a safety pin and, finally, a penny. The video was in fact shot with a studio quality camera and then doctored through computer generated imaging and then reprocessed through a cell phone processor to make it virtually indistinguishable from a badly shot, jumpy, cheap burner phone video.

Video Breadcrumb #5: For the second video, DD used his skills as film director / makeup artist / chief bottle washer to make Plank look worse for wear and terrified while trussed to a chair.

Then he coached a hooded Olga how to strut, shake her fist and wave an M-16 replica like she meant it.

...

"We have Dr. Plank and we have the technology . . ."

"Cut, cut. It's important we do this in a single take from beginning to end. You need to say it like you mean it. Each part of that sentence has to be emphasized. You have to sound crazy, that you're ready to allow the Earth to blow up and you don't really care. Be mean. Scream. Be Charlie Sheen," DD instructed in his director-as-tyrant impression of Cecil B. DeMille.

"Okay, okay. I got it this time."

"Okay, take six, roll tape . . ."

"WE HAVE DR. PLANK and WE HAVE THE TECHNOLOGY," Olga roared in a half rant, half snarl, her right arm coiled around a replica M16 and an angry left fist punching the air to accentuate every high point.

"We will send samples of materials that possess negative gravity to our

friends all around the world UNLESS YOU FOLLOW OUR INSTRUC-
TIONS EXACTLY."

She growled out the words as she strutted toward the camera until her
black hooded face was so close to the lens that it obliterated everything except
two fearsome eyes.

Absolutely perfect, DD thought to himself.

...

"I did the CGI and filtered it through a cell phone processor to make the
video ready for prime time. Mo set up a Gmail account and we dropped all
the fake messages and videos into it. We figured it wouldn't take the FBI, NSA
and some rich guys long to come across it and get the idea they were one step
ahead of us."

"Yeah, we used burner phones and travelled around town to different hot
spots to upload the videos to the Gmail account. Right after that, Bonnie
arrived and things got really wild," said Olga, reaching around Bonnie's shoulders to give her a squeeze.

It all came together as Sage had planned, almost. As much as he liked
being in control, he realized controlling the uncontrollable, especially at long
distance was impossible. When Bonnie first arrived, she was a wildcard that
made him nervous. The last video erased his doubts.

...

"So tell me about this new girl Bonnie that Olga's talking about."

"Yeah Bonnie. That girl's a hoot. You gotta meet her," Jazzy said.

"Wait, wait. Explain this to me. Who is she? Olga says she's not a problem."

"Indeed, not a problem at all. We think she'll be a big part of the solution.
Wait till you see the video we're going to post with her in it. Once you see it,
give us a call and we'll explain everything. The video was her idea. It'll knock
your socks off."

A few minutes later, Sage, Mo and Alessa called back.

Mo spoke first expressing amazement and admiration.

"Holy shit! If I didn't know better, that would have scared the crap out of
me. Olga, you can sure play a scary bad guy."

"And that girl Bonnie's definitely the one if there's another remake of Lost

In Space," Alessa said. "Pretty amazing work DD. Too bad only the anti-terrorism people and a few of super greedy will see it. So, who's this Bonnie?"

"That would be me."

Bonnie's cheery voice piped in while the others were trying to formulate their complex answer.

"It's a really, really long story but I'll try to give you the short version. My best friend and boss Nathan Sherlock has this astounding ability to smell better than a bloodhound. The FBI's international anti-terrorism something or other grabbed us to try to track you down and recover Plank and negative gravity . . ."

"Whoa, wait a minute. You're with the FBI?"

"Hey Sager, give her a second to explain. She's on our side," Olga said.

"And if she's lying, I'll just toss her into space. I know a new Aikido move that Bonnie taught me. Did you see me use it on DD – ryo kata something."

"Ryo kata dori," Bonnie added. "Where was I . . . oh yeah. Anyway, Nathan figured out Plank was pulling off a scam for some reason and you were on to him. Once Plank realized you saw through his con, he had to go along with whatever your plans were. Nathan and I were awe-struck by what you did with the corn commodities."

"Uh, wow. I understand what you just said but I'm amazed that I do. You summed up our work over the past two years in about six seconds. Anyway, carry on."

Bonnie picked up on the story. "The FBI's anti-terrorism unit recruits us and tells us all this scary shit about the Ginis – uh, you guys. All the clues seemed to be pointing one way but Nathan's nose was telling him a different story. He suspected it was Corn Commodities Part II, the Gravity Scam.

"If it works, lots of fuss and bother and rich people taking it in the wallet but there's no crime. Plank's in on it; so, there's no kidnapping. You haven't issued a ransom; so, there's been no fraud. If a bunch of super rich guys start playing the market using information that's been obtained illegally and they get burned, whose fault is that? Nathan and I decided, we'd just let it happen."

"That's the way we look at it," said Olga.

"Despite what the world thinks right now, Olga and I are destined to be besties," Bonnie said, adding a nudge and wink to Olga who returned it in kind.

"Yeah but it was fun having Sager jumping up and down trying to figure out who Bonnie was and what she was up to," Olga added.

"I couldn't believe what she was suggesting, making a movie where Olga pitches her into space. It was just wild," DD said. "It was just so nuts that I had to do it, had to do my best work. I don't mean to brag but it was so cool that when I first saw it run real-time, it gave me the chills, even though I built it frame by frame with my computer and filtered it through a cell phone processor."

When there was a pause in the conversation, Bonnie cleared her throat, a signal that she had something important to say.

"You may have this covered but Nathan and I did some thinking. We believe the best thing to do now is turn yourselves in because you didn't do anything and have nothing to hide."

There was a long pause while the two teams exchanged startled glances in Toronto and Chicago.

"Nathan and I are Canadian and aren't up on American law but the way we see it, the FBI can't touch you either. They made it clear to us that you never issued a ransom or did anything other than post stuff in your own Gmail account. If they try to touch you, it's sort of like charging you for what you're thinking. Doesn't your Constitution protect you against that kind of mind-police stuff?"

"Well, the 4th Amendment provides privacy for people and their possessions against unreasonable searches," Sage said. "I think Gmail falls into that. You've heard of the 5th Amendment in all those TV police series. You know, 'I plead the 5th, I refuse to say anything that might incriminate me.' That ought to cover the rest."

"Bottom line," Olga said. "We committed no crime."

"A good lawyer should be able to use all of that to tie any would-be prosecution case into knots," DD added.

Bonnie picked up the ball again. "And just to put a little icing on the cake, Nathan offered this suggestion. DD, you're a filmmaker. Alessa, you're an actress. You're putting together a movie about some crazy anti-gravity technology and you hired the just-fired Plank, a physicist, to be your scientific advisor for the movie because he thought he was on to anti-gravity but it fizzled.

"DD is shooting in Toronto and wanted Alessa to review it in Chicago. They posted it on Gmail. That way they could both see the videos and discuss them. The movie is being made in the Blair Witch style, hence were made to look like portions were shot with cell phones."

"They'll see through that in a second," Jazzy said.

"So, can they prove it didn't happen that way? We can certainly prove it didn't happen the other way."

"That's incredible. You and your friend Nathan pretty well had the whole thing figured," said Sage.

"He had some help from some equally gifted people. But that's something I'll get into later."

"And you're not going to tell the FBI or other authorities the real story?" asked Sage.

"No, why should we. We'll just plead ignorance."

"What about your role in the video about being launched into space," Mo said.

"Don't worry. I have a cover story for that, too."

—

NEWS CONFERENCE

IN DOWNTOWN CHICAGO, Big Ed grabbed the $22,000 bottle of House of Rémy Martin's Cognac Louis XIII, Rare Cask 42.6 and poured himself a double into a Waterford Elysian snifter. His eyes locked firmly on his television screen.

Across the city, in a rented South Side bungalow, Alessa, Mo and Sage watched the same TV newscast, but with Buds as their beverage of choice.

The TV anchor appeared on the screen to explain what would transpire next.

"We are joining a live broadcast from Toronto. The Canadian Security Intelligence Service, pronounced See-Sis, is holding a news conference. We're told CSIS investigators have discovered the location of Dr. Gustav Plank, the scientist who reputedly has unlocked the secret of negative gravity.

"We join the news conference in progress."

A well dressed and coiffed man took centre stage to address the assembly.

"Thank you for coming at such short notice. My name is Superintendent Richard Beauchemin of the Canadian Security Intelligence Service. As many of you know, my agency has been tasked with Canada's security against all terrorist threats foreign and domestic. In recent days, there have been rumours of the potential for a major threat against the citizens and the economies of the U.S. and Canada. CSIS has been engaged in uncovering the facts behind this perceived threat.

"I am happy to report that CSIS, in cooperation with the FBI, has uncovered these facts. We will share them with you during the course of this news conference."

"Superintendent Beauchemin is Dr. Plank all right? Has he been injured?" a reporter shouted.

"No, no, no. There has been a big misunderstanding. Dr. Plank is mystified by all of the publicity. He has been working on a secret project over the past month and was not aware of the controversy about his studies into negative gravity."

"So he was not kidnapped?" a second reporter asked.

"I have been assured by Dr. Plank he has been staying quite voluntarily with friends who have been involved in a sensitive project. They were so engrossed in their work, they were not aware anyone was looking for him."

"And what about negative gravity? Is he prepared to release his research?" a third reporter said.

"I believe at this time, I should invite Dr. Plank and his colleagues to join me for a fuller discussion of everything that has transpired."

Dr. Gustav Plank, Delroy DeSoto, Olga Kalata, and Jasmine Irianto walk onto the stage and take seats flanking Supt. Beauchemin. A large buzz courses across the room.

"Normally, CSIS would not take such an extraordinary measure. There has been so much publicity impacting the stock exchanges around the world, the Service has been compelled to step in. It is in the best interests of all to put the facts on the table."

"Dr. Plank! Dr. Plank! Dr. Plank!" a dozen reporters shouted at once.

"Please, we need order. We will deal with your questions one at a time," Supt. Beauchemin said.

"Yes, the gentleman in the tweed jacket in the front row."

"Trevor Keeler, CBC News. This question is for Dr. Plank. What is the status of your research into negative gravity. Has it progressed as far as we have heard?"

"I'm not certain what you have heard, Trevor. I have released no information about my work into negative gravity."

"Supplementary question. Is it true that your negative gravity process can be used to eliminate the need for oil and gas as an energy source?"

"That is false. My work is very preliminary and my latest research indicates that some early promising results were false positives. It is a disappointment to me."

Big Ed's massive mouth hung open. His gaping eyes stared in disbelief at the group on the TV stage.

Voices combined into a roar as all reporters shouted questions simultaneously.

"Please, please. I need everyone to settle down. One question at a time. Ah yes, the woman in the second row in the navy jacket."

"Constance Sinclair, Globe and Mail. Am I to take from your last answer that you are now saying that you have not, I repeat, not been able to create negative gravity – that you have not been able to orient an object so that it is repelled by the Earth's gravity?"

"Quite right. The theory of negative gravity remains but no one, including myself, has been able to generate a negative gravity field."

In Chicago, Big Ed dropped his glass of cognac.

Pandemonium erupted. The reporters screamed questions. Cameras flashed like the finale of a hundred fireworks displays.

In their house on the South Side of Chicago, Sage, Mo, and Alessa rammed their cans of Bud together in a sudsy toast.

Within one hour of the telecast, all major stock exchanges around the world issued statements they had suspended trading in oil and gas shares until further notice.

...

At the end of the telecast, Supt. Beauchemin drove Jasmine Irianto, Olga Kalata, Delroy DeSoto and Dr. Gustav Plank to the Toronto offices of CSIS.

"We did as you asked, included you in a special news conference," Beauchemin said. "Now to complete the bargain, you must answer all of our questions. Do you agree this was our understanding?"

"We do," DD said.

"Yes, I am quite happy to cooperate in any way that I can," Dr. Plank added.

Just then Flynn, eyes wild and face glowing pink, stomped into the interview room.

"Ah yes, I would like to introduce you to CSIS Intelligence Officer Frank Flynn who has returned from the FBI's anti-terrorism unit in Quantico, Virginia this minute. He has been in charge of our investigation into the activities of the Gini Conspiracy,"

"The Genie what?" DD said.

"The Gini Conspiracy. You guys," Flynn snapped, beaming a venomous glare all around.

"The only thing we've been conspiring to do is make a movie. We had no idea anybody was lookin' for us."

"What a bunch of hogwash. We have evidence you murdered Bonnie Nakagowa and kidnapped Nathan Sherlock and Dr. Plank."

"Uhhh. I was never kidnapped," Plank said. "As my friend DD indicated, we were just making a movie."

"And about Nakagowa and Sherlock?"

"Extras," DD said. "We didn't even have to pay them scale. Nathan is fine and so is Bonnie."

"We saw Bonnie murdered by her," Flynn said, stabbing a finger in Olga's direction.

"You are mistaken. It was just special effects. How many times do you have to be told, we're making a movie."

Olga made the statement, her look of pure innocence infuriating Flynn.

I want to smash her in the face so bad, he thought. He checked himself when he realized he had stomped up to her with both fists clenched.

Supt. Beauchemin took control before Flynn did something that would cause both of them endless paperwork.

"Ah, Officer Flynn, we have you at an unfair advantage. Perhaps you and I should excuse ourselves for a moment to get you caught up."

Beauchemin motioned, at first politely and then with full bureaucratic sternness, repeated swipes of his index finger toward the doorway. As he reached for the door, there was a knock.

"Ah, I believe that would be Mr. Sherlock and Ms Nakagowa now. Officer Flynn, please let them in."

When the door opened, Nathan's eyes and nose assessed Flynn's state. The chef's arms and shoulders rose into a shrug.

"It's all been a mistake. They were just making a movie. All the videos and emails were just script notes and storyboard videos. It was all part of the movie."

"Bullshit! Bullshit! Bullshit!" It was the only word that came to the flabbergasted CSIS operative's mind.

"Well that's our story and we're sticking to it." Bonnie accompanied the remark with a wink to Olga whose tiny frame had earlier been backed into a corner by Flynn's aggressive stance.

Flynn's pink face stepped up to crimson. His hands itched to strangle someone. "You, you. How can you just stand there and lie your face off. I can bring in Davis and Jordan to back me up."

Supt. Beauchemin raised a hand to end his underling's rant and explained in his satiny, French-dusted voice how everything had come together.

"Excuse me Officer Flynn. I conversed with Mr. Sherlock and FBI Assistant Director DeRoach about two hours ago. It was through these gentlemen that we came to an agreement. We hold a news conference in return for these ladies and gentlemen turning themselves in voluntarily. Isn't that what we wanted all along?"

Flynn turned to the thin, older man.

"What about you Dr. Plank. Are you all right? Have they harmed you? Are they making you say this?"

"Harmed me? Who would harm me? I was just staying with some friends who were making a movie."

"But what about the negative gravity pulser?"

"Negative gravity pulser?"

"Yes the negative gravity pulser."

"Oh, you mean the gizmo in the movie. My research touched on the possibility of isolating negative gravitons. However, I hit a wall and cut my losses. While it's theoretically possible, I don't think any tools on Earth would be able to replicate the force."

"But . . . but . . . but we saw the demonstration . . . We saw the film footage, your notes . . . You were a hostage . . . You were tied up."

"Well yes, when one loses one's position, one needs another job. I had cause to mention to my esteemed friend Delroy that I had studied negative gravity. He suggested that it might make a good action film about negative gravity being invented and that, I, as the inventor would be abducted. It sounded like great fun. They paid me to be a scientific consultant. They also hired me as an actor – to play myself. Both parts paid well, even better than being a professor."

It was time for Bonnie to keep her mouth shut and wipe the smirk from her face, but she couldn't resist winding Flynn up even more.

"Again, all part of the movie. When Dr. Plank couldn't create the negative gravity machine, Sage and his buddies thought it would be a great premise for a movie. They started shooting some scenes to use as the mock-ups when they pitch it to the Hollywood money men."

"And you being hurled into space. Why didn't you call us and let us know that it was baloney?"

Flynn delivered what he considered his 'ah-ha' I got you and waited for Bonnie's attempt to wiggle out of it.

She didn't wiggle. She fired back. "Well, I kinda always wanted to be in a movie. Delroy told me that his Chicago partners were going to be pitching it on Monday and he needed to get the raw impact of my space blast off to get them to loosen their purse strings. If the video got out prematurely and people saw it, the impact would fizzle and deal might be lost."

Bonnie, on tip-toes, went nose-to-nose with Flynn, giving him her evil eye close-up. "Besides, I didn't see you worrying about Nathan or me. We didn't have any choice but to go with you. I wouldn't be pointing fingers about who kidnapped who."

As usual, Nathan found himself trying to dial down the emotions. "When I found DD, Olga, and Jazzy, they agreed to turn themselves in to clear the confusion. I called Assistant Director DeRoach and Supt. Beauchemin and, well, here we are, no harm, no foul."

"No harm, no foul? Are you kidding me? It looks like some people lost more than $1 trillion on the stock market in the past week. I'd say that's a harm." A trickle of foamy spit trickled down Flynn's lower lip as he stood with mouth and eyes in angry wide shapes.

The practised calm state Nathan projected, shattered. Outrage and amazement rolled over the CSIS officer's premise.

"Are you saying that the people who grabbed several trillions of dollars from average folks over the past few years through the world-wide bank crisis and the surge in the price of gasoline and heating oil ended up losing a small percentage of their wealth?

"Are you saying that the market swing may have provided, in relative terms, a miniscule rebate to those same folks, who will pay taxes on the money they get? If that's what you are saying, I will change my words. Much good, much justice."

The game was on and Jazzy had no intention of sitting on the sidelines.

"Oil and gas shares fell by an average of 25% for three days and will now climb back. If someone owned those shares and held them for four days, they lost zero dollars. However, if somebody on the inside tipped them off, which, by the way, is insider trading, a federal crime, then golly gee willikers, maybe they rolled in their own poop. Getting' my drift, or do I have to rub your nose right in the shit."

Bonnie leaned into Olga's ear. "I like your chutzpah, but as ballsy broads go, Jazzy's giving you a run for the money."

If possible, Flynn went redder in the face and used a plush chair to try to sink from view.

—

INTO THE DARK

BIG ED'S MONSTER headache morphed upward to Category 5 where his dark thoughts swirled like evil, hurricane driven winds. He had to think. He had to think. The lights made the pain worse. He walked to the wall and threw the main switch.

At last, darkness. He walked with practiced steps back to his desk and fell into his oversized leather chair. Try as he may, he could make no sense of it.

How had everything gone so wrong. My information was perfect. It came right from the source. I had it all confirmed. Cleopatra was a scientific researcher. She had personally tested negative gravity and it worked.

What if I hadn't double-crossed her? Could that possibly have made a difference? Of course not. She couldn't have known. She was expecting a huge payoff, as much as $200 million. That kind of money blinds them all. Nobody kisses that kind of opportunity away. She must have been wrong but how could she have been so wrong?

One way or another Cleopatra screwed me. Nobody fucks with me like that and gets away with it. I'll take her out.

Then he realized he didn't have the time or money to hire a hitman. His mind whirled earthward. Not since he was 18, before he drugged his parents and set fire to their home, had he been this broke and powerless.

Big Ed started to do some quick calculations and then stopped. His head hurt too much. Besides, what was the use?

It didn't take any calculating to know he lost all of his money and billions more. He had nearly $300 billion in short positions, 75% on EExE and the other 25% on other oil and gas companies' shares he was obligated to provide, shares that would now cost him $400 billion to $500 billion to buy.

The margins on the $300 billion amounted to just under $30 billion. When the markets open on Monday and prices start heading upward even modestly, he'd be hopelessly underwater.

The entire $30 billion margin – far more than his net worth had been – will evaporate. It won't matter if negative gravity is actually true.

If for just one day, hell, for one minute, the market believes there is no such thing as negative gravity, I'm broke. Every penny gone and tens, maybe, hundreds of billions in the hole.

There was no Plan B. Not for him. The closest thing he had to friends were enemies like Orville Tennesen. These *frien-emies* did business with him and deferred to him because they respected or, perhaps, feared his ruthlessness.

He could hear the long knives unsheathing. And there were a lot of them.

Sure, he owned a few properties and had a few million tucked into accounts around the world, but guys like Tennesen were monitoring his finances even now. If he tried to access a penny, they'd know about it and would hunt him down. They'd tie up every account, every asset in the courts. They'd want Big Ed to grovel in the mud.

Once he was down, all those he outwitted would delight in piling on every public indignity, every particle of nastiness their sick minds had learned from him.

Thoughts of poverty and humiliation rolled like waves across Big Ed's mind until it made him sick. He swiveled his chair to the side and made no effort to reach for his wastebasket before vomiting the $200 steak dinner and making a $2,000 puddle of cognac on the 19th Century Kashan carpet.

Big Ed opened his desk drawer. He felt around in the dark. The first object was the video camera. Next to it, he felt the smooth precision of his pearl-handled Colt 45.

No matter that it was a Saturday evening, if Big Ed required it, Summers would be seated at his desk in the anteroom. But Summers was at home. He had turned off his cell phone.

He wanted no more of Big Ed's blustering demands, his enslavement finally at an end regardless of what the ultimate cost would be. He steadily prepared for a move far, far away from Big Ed to a new life, however short that may be.

Summers had not turned on a radio nor the TV. He had not been on the Internet. He had not heard the news. And as he quietly packed his bags at home, he definitely did not hear the loud BANG from Big Ed's office.

...

It was a great night for Frenchie. Big Ed was going to be so happy. The girl was perfect, exactly as he had described. He knew the story about Cleopatra and Honeymoon's error. He would not make the same mistake. He'd make the girl available as long as Big Ed wanted her but not a second longer, just like Delores.

He approached the office building. As Big Ed instructed, the door was unlocked with no one on security. No need for caution. On a Saturday night the lobby was deserted. With an exaggerated swagger, Frenchie walked to the elevator with the whimpering girl in tow. He entered a four-digit code before pressing the button for the 9th floor.

They rode the plush, walnut trimmed elevator to the appointed level where the doors opened into a hallway with dark walnut paneling, plaster cast cove molding, and a bunch of those modern paintings hanging on the walls. Frenchie always thought they looked weird but obviously cost a bundle.

Pulling the girl along, like a dog on a leash, Frenchie walked through a doorway marked EExE Holdings into a dimly lit office. He ignored a large desk in the anteroom with the nameplate R. A. Summers, CFO, and headed straight to double doors with large gold letters that spelled out, E.V. Hendry, Chairman.

Frenchie knocked. No answer. He knocked once more. Again no answer. He tried the handle. The door swung open. Frenchie took six steps into the darkened room. In the gloom, he could make out only shapes. He felt around for a lamp on the desk.

It was wet and sticky.

Frenchie felt along the walls. At last his fingers fell across a switch. He flicked it on. The light revealed what he had seen only as an outline.

Big Ed was dead. His body looked almost comfortable, face up in a fully reclined leather executive chair. His dead eyes looked to the ceiling with the back of his head poised over his desk. The business end of a pearl-handled Colt 45 remained unnaturally deep in his mouth, its tip poking through the chasm marking the bullet's exit. A blackish-red goo formed viscous icicles that connected the hole to the blood-covered desk. The pimp realized he was covered in his client's gore. His bloody fingerprints were everywhere.

Panic-stricken, he ran from Big Ed's office, not knowing or caring what became of the girl. Frenchie was a man on the run. Police had his fingerprints on file. In time they would hunt him down.

—

39

SOUND SOLUTION

DEROACH'S EYES FIXED on his companion. "You can still back out. I can return you to Quantico before you get in any deeper," he whispered.

He stared at the iPad as words formed.

"No, I absolutely have to do this."

The girl next to him was calm, her slight frame, encased in what appeared to be a white Formula One driver's suit and helmet. Her outfit contrasted sharply with the over-sized black seats of the Suburban.

He nodded and gave a soft, "Let's go."

Reyanna scanned the street for the slight whirring and the even quieter but, for her, telltale hum of surveillance cameras. She found a blind spot to park the Suburban and plopped a fedora over her helmet and a trenchcoat over her silent suit to make them less conspicuous.

"Wait two seconds, one second. Now go fast," Reyanna messaged as her super hearing echo-located everyone on the street, their direction of travel and where they faced by the sound of their breathing. Exact timing of movements and the zigzag route that Reyanna continuously updated to avoid the cameras and line of sight of passersby, effectively rendered them invisible on their approach to La Casa's side door.

"There are two people in the hallway. One is moving away from this doorway and the other appears to be entering a room," Reyanna messaged. "All clear. Let's go."

Five more strategic pauses and one deke into a closet later, the two stood outside of Menck's room.

"He's on the phone, talking to Rebecca."

"Let me know when he hangs up. Then I'm going to break down the door."

Reyanna signaled the call had ended and prepared for the loud crash to follow. Normally, she avoided noise of all varieties because of its profound physical and mental effect on her. In this case, she dropped the trenchcoat and fedora, peeled off her helmet and unzipped the top of her silent suit, an athletic bra her torso's only cover.

DeRoach heaved his mighty body at the ornate mahogany door and it flung open with . . . nothing, no sound at all entering the hallway. Reyanna's unique power amplified noises within her so she could hear and interpret the most minute sounds. That was only half of her abilities. The flip side was her body's capacity to act like a sonic magnet to attract and absorb sound.

When DeRoach broke into the room, both he and Menck heard the crash. Reyanna, standing outside the doorway, acted as a sound barrier, plucking sonic waves from the air like blueberries from a bush. A moment later, as expected, Reyanna absorbed an even louder noise – the revolver's huge bang.

DeRoach felt terrible about the magnum. He preferred a weapon with a smaller sonic calling card. It was the only non-registered, non-traceable firearm he could access without resorting to buying a handgun on the street.

The revolver was among weapons confiscated years earlier when the FBI took down a major crimes theft ring. A few untracked weapons found there way to selected agents, just in case.

The effort took its toll on Reyanna. DeRoach rushed to her, helping to zip her suit and snap on her helmet. He squashed the fedora on her head and wrapped the trenchcoat around her. Fighting the pain, Reyanna guided the duo invisibly through the hotel and back to the black SUV before she blacked out.

DeRoach returned Reyanna to her egg where she'd spend the next week or two in agony.

In the back lot, rugged FBI man used his sleeve to give the Taurus .44 magnum a last polish. He wasn't worried about fingerprints. He wanted one last look at the finely crafted revolver. The firearm was a work of art. Its stainless steel body gleamed as he put it on the incinerator pad as gently as a jeweler placing a tiara in a display case.

The Assistant Director pressed the incinerator's 'on button.' Super hot tongues of flame licked at the weapon. In three minutes, the revolver was an unrecognizable blob of metal. In six, a fiery river. In nine, just one more constituent in a melting pot destined for a recycling centre.

Early the next morning, DeRoach surveyed the office he had occupied for the past 12 years and sighed at how much he had accumulated. Too much stuff, he muttered. On top of one large cabinet, lay the three dusty file boxes of unsolved crimes he had worked on years earlier. Even after taking on the anti-terrorism portfolio, he still hoped that one day he'd get back to them, solve them.

That wasn't going to happen now. The original files still resided in the FBI vaults. There was no harm trashing them now. He loaded them on the incinerator-bound dolly.

The bottom cabinet contained all the files he had collected on Menck. He piled those on the dolly, too.

Three certificates of commendation for 'Valor Beyond the Call of Duty' occupied centre stage on the wall behind him. They wouldn't command much in the way of bragging rights once he was drummed out of the Bureau, or worse.

Still, he had no regrets.

He left no fingerprints or DNA at the scene. Reyanna ensured no one saw them and there were no videos to place them there. The Taurus magnum and the generic bullets were untraceable and no longer existed. He wore gloves when he loaded the revolver.

DeRoach understood how the police work a case better than anyone. A smart investigator will puzzle out the evidence and conclude DeRoach is the killer.

It was well documented that he loathed Menck and several people heard DeRoach threatened to kill him. As a former high-security federal employee, Menck's DNA is in the FBI's database. Soon after Menck's body is bagged and tagged, a pathologist will probe the huge hole in the head and take DNA and blood samples. It won't take long to establish a link to him, DeRoach reasoned.

Garcia can't save him this time. He won't have an alibi. He can't use Reyanna for that without implicating her. He will lie through his teeth to deny any involvement by her. But in his own defence, DeRoach decided not to fight. Menck deserved to be killed. He had to be killed.

I won't deny it. I wouldn't give the slime ball the satisfaction, even after death.

—

40

WHAT'S A TRILLION?

THE OIL AND GAS markets remained frozen on Monday and Tuesday but after quick negotiations, they resumed controlled trading on the Wednesday under the watchful eye of security regulators.

The financial pages and television business reports related the carnage.

"Somebody has to be arrested," rant meister Van Hammersley screamed over the right-wing Coyote Cable News Channel.

"The oil markets lost $1.3 trillion and a lot of that was pure waste, going to Third World countries. We know they're all dictators. None of that money will help anybody."

Sage switched channels.

"In today's world, what's a trillion? The market will recover and quickly," said economist / commentator Brad Smith, on Business News Today. "The oil industry has not been harmed. The only losers were rich investors who, with one notable exception, could afford it."

Sage hit the remote's off button.

"We'll make sure prices are normalized before we start unloading the shares."

"What do you think our shares will be worth?" Mo asked.

"At least $25 million, maybe as much as $30 million."

"Wow, we can really kick ass with that much," said Mo.

"Compared to the wealth out there, we're still tossing pebbles into the ocean."

DD scrunched his face in disagreement. "We accomplished what the

Occupy Movement set out to do – rebalance the world's wealth. I'm proud of that."

Sage gave a resigned sigh. "I don't want to rain on our celebrations but $1.3 trillion isn't going to change the world."

"No but it made a pretty big dent," Mo said.

"A temporary setback."

"You are nuts. How many people in the history of the world have done as much as we did in restoring balance between the rich and the poor?" said DD.

"That's the point," Sage said as a slight smile flickered then disappeared. "Everything we did, the $1.3 trillion transfer from the one per cent to the 99 per cent is just a hiccup."

DD's mouth and eyes opened wide. "A $1.3 trillion transfer of wealth is a hiccup?"

"Sage is right," said Olga. "I just got off a call to an economist with the Global Initiative Think Tank. He's sending me an Oxfam report that tracked the growing spread between rich and poor. The richest one per cent gets wealthier by $4 trillion a year at the expense of everyone else. In 2016, the wealth of that one per cent is expected to be greater than that of the other 99 percent."

"Yikes," Mo said. "If that's true, $1.3 trillion delays the world's richest from owning all of the planet's wealth by three, maybe four months. Now you've got me bummed out."

"As much as we did a great thing, nothing changed," said Sage. "It will take a revolution in everyone's thinking to have a true impact. I think it's hopeless."

As always, Alessa brought a broader perspective.

"Jason Sage, if you walked on water, you'd complain your sandals leak. We showed the world that it's not hopeless. If a scruffy bunch like us could do what we did, what can be accomplished by the millions and millions of others who think like us?"

DD's toothy smile returned. "And we are connected to a lot of people who want a fairer world. With $25-$30 million in the kitty, we can help them make things happen."

...

Over the next five trading days Sage and Mo unloaded all of the oil & gas shares at normalized prices.

After Sage converted the investment portfolio into cash, he called for the group to assemble in Chicago.

He explained how the $2.3 million they gained from the corn commodities was used to prime the pump. The leveraging and trading of short positions during the price decline and then swopping out for options, just before the oil & gas shares roared back, brought the group's investments to $29.4 million after expenses once the markets settled and the freeze on trading resumed.

Mission accomplished but a mission without a clear objective for the use of the money. It was clear; they never believed it would happen.

"What do we do with it?" asked Alessa.

Jazzy put on a bright smile. "This is a good problem. We collected the initial funds from crowd funding, $1 million. We should put that back in the kitty and offer it up for any worthwhile cause. Let's add another $1 million to it."

Alessa made the simple mental calculation. "That leaves us with $27.4 million."

Sage stood, raised his hands and made a surprise announcement. "Actually, it's $32.4 million. For our 'noble work,' we received another $5 million from a mystery source."

"Who's our mystery source?" asked Mo.

"If I could tell you, it wouldn't be a mystery. It was sent to us anonymously, sort of.

There was just a notation with the cashier's cheque drawn on a bank in the Bahamas that it was a gift from Cleopatra."

Puzzled, DD glanced around at everyone. "Cleopatra? Anybody know a Cleopatra?"

"Hey, I heard that name before," said Jazzy. "When I asked Dr. Plank how he was doing, he was ecstatic. He got his old job back at U of T. Dean Coleman told him that an anonymous donor identified only as Cleopatra donated $5 million to the university on the condition that Dr. Plank's contract be extended permanently.

...

By the end of the week, DeRoach tired of waiting for the inevitable call. He figured he might as well see how the investigation into Menck's death had progressed, better to prepare himself.

There was no surprise that the discovery of a body with custom air conditioning in the head hadn't been splashed across the news pages. La Casa was the favourite hideaway of many of Washington's power brokers. It wouldn't do to generate attention for a private meeting place frequented by Senators, Supreme Court Justices, members of the White House Cabinet and run-of-the-mill multi-millionaires.

More worrisome than the absence of news coverage was the absolute lack of any mention of the discovery of a body at La Casa in top-tier law enforcement circles. Against his better judgment, DeRoach drove to La Casa and started asking questions. The official word was, no one knew what he was talking about. The unofficial word, available for a coffee and two rolled up $100 bills at a secluded eatery across town, was the following:

A maid discovered the bloody remains of a Mr. Gunter. As per instructions regarding Mr. Gunter and the $800 a day room he occupied for the past five years, Jonathan Harrison, the Director of La Casa was to report anything out of the ordinary immediately to a Mr. Fellowes.

The Director placed the call. Within minutes, two men in dark glasses, black suits, and trenchcoats arrived flashing government credentials. A half hour later, attendants arrived in an unmarked ambulance and bagged and removed the body.

"Do not contact the police about this unfortunate business. We are the police and will take it from here," they told Mr. Harrison.

"Would you like to question the staff?"

"That will be unnecessary," the men in black responded.

After all of the government people had gone, La Casa's staff set to the grim task of cleaning the room. When the maids entered, they found the chamber had been thoroughly cleaned and repaired, no blood, no splattered brain matter, not even dust balls. The shattered door casing and holes in the walls had been expertly and invisibly restored.

"Do you have the number Mr. Harrison was to call?"

"Perhaps," the La Casa employee said, glancing at the $200 on the table.

DeRoach reached into his pocket for another $100 bill, which he exchanged for a tiny slip of paper.

...

"Hi, Agent DeRoach? It's Nate. I'm in Europe. I'm on a promotional tour for Let's Eat."

"Really good to hear from you. Everything's been straightened out between CSIS and the Ginis. They basically are off the hook after a couple days of interrogation and paperwork."

"Yes. Thanks to you. And is the FBI okay with the Ginis?"

"Absolutely. We won't be pressing charges or putting any black marks against any of their names. After all, they helped us a lot. Even if they didn't know it, they helped us stop Menck. As we explained after their corn commodity actions, cops, even federal cops, are just working stiffs. If social justice happens and no law is broken, we're more likely to be in the cheering section."

"And Menck?"

"Let's just say he won't be a problem any more for anyone. I'm a little mystified by that myself, but all's well that ends well, I guess."

"What about Rebecca, Seiji and Reyanna?"

"Things are settled down as much as they can be settled down, considering. Rebecca's under suspension. Jury's still out on whether she'll lose her job although I doubt that's the most important thing on her mind right now. She's on a new therapy as are Seiji and Reyanna."

There was a long pause. Nathan didn't interrupt the FBI Agent as he struggled to find the right words, the right approach.

"None of them are doing that well. We are keeping them sedated. They all have tremendous headaches 24/7 and they're constantly physically ill. It's not just the hormonal therapies' physical effects. It's the psychological addiction as well. Hormones trigger emotions. Out of whack hormones trigger wild emotions. It's worse than being hooked on crack and heroin at the same time. They're addicted to the therapies that Menck put them on and, frankly, we aren't close to an answer."

"That's where I can make a recommendation." Nathan could tell from the silence that followed that he had DeRoach's full attention.

"If you like the idea, you have the Ginis to thank because they came up with it. It may not work but I believe it's absolutely worth a try. You'll need to get the highest levels of the FBI to press the Canadian Government. Supt. Beauchemin is doing the same to get CSIS to make the same request at its end."

...

"Hey Mo, where'd Jazzy go? We haven't seen her in ages." Olga mindlessly made the remark as a conversation starter while peering over the latest copy of Animal Advocacy Quarterly. Instantly, she regretted it when she saw a dark shadow cross Mo's face.

"She called me two days ago and said she was working out a bunch of things, getting her life back together and needed some time to finish things off."

"Is she thinking of returning to her PhD studies?"

"Yeah, I think that's part of it but . . . I really don't know what's going on."

On the other side of the Chicago loft apartment that now serves as the world headquarters of the GINI Foundation, Alessa Reese and Jason Sage snuggled on an overstuffed couch and exchanged a meaningful glance.

"Why is she doing this? It's tearing the guy's heart out," Sage whispered in Alessa's ear.

"I don't know. I asked her a couple of times and all she'd say is, 'It's complicated'."

. . .

In an upscale hotel room in downtown Chicago, Jazzy looked at her Blackberry and noted her three tasks for the day. First up was Dr. Plank. Now that he had a tenured professorship at the University of Toronto, he had offered to act as supervisor to help her complete her PhD thesis.

"Miss Jasmine, we've come to know and respect each other. If you would do me the honour and allow me to be your supervisor, I promise my utmost attention to make you and your thesis a priority. And, as I am so painfully aware, to protect you from any and all bureaucratic interference."

"How can I refuse an offer like that? I need to make a few arrangements. What if I start up my work with you in, say, a month?"

"Perfect. Absolutely, perfect my dear."

"Professor, I do have one more question. You sound upbeat but aren't you a little uncomfortable with being back on the job? Is Dr. Coleman giving you a hard time because you were forced on him?"

"Quite the contrary. Dr. Coleman congratulated me upon my return and then apologized for not explaining my termination notice. It turns out, the termination notice was a bureaucratic thing. Dr. Coleman did not intend to fire me but he had to comply with the rules set between the faculty association and the university. It states that if a faculty member is to be laid off, that person must receive notice of the termination a minimum of 90 days in advance. Apparently, the university's federal grant was delayed because of red tape. To stave off catastrophe if the money failed to arrive, the university was forced to issue termination notices. Twenty per cent of the faculty received the notices. The school newspaper explained it all in a story but I am not a reader of that paper. I have always been a solitary person. I did not know the game."

"There was never an intention to fire you?"

"Dr. Coleman told me that he fully intended to withdraw my termination notice until I announced that I had discovered a way to reverse the polarity of gravity. He was so frightened of the potential for cataclysmic consequences, the only way to stop me was to continue with my firing."

"So, we weren't the only ones playing a scam," said Jazzy.

"I would venture that everyone involved, including CSIS and the FBI, was operating some sort of gambit."

"Let's hope our future scientific investigations at the university are just that – scientific investigations – no make-believe technology, no cons, just plain science."

"I am all for that. So Miss Jasmine, I will see you in one month's time?"

"I'm looking forward to it."

"Auf Wiederhören."

"Goodbye to you, too."

Jazzy clicked off her phone and hit the speed dial for call number two.

Ring . . . ring . . . ring

"Hello."

"Hi mom. It's Iri."

Iri was the pet name Jazzy's foster mother had given her those many years ago when they first met. It was a shortened version of Jazzy's last name, Irianto.

When Jazzy's future mom got stuck on the pronunciation, the girl looked at her and offered: "Just call me Iri as in, well, eerie. I'm a pretty strange girl."

The private nickname stuck.

"Iri dearie, when am I going to see you?"

"Sorry I missed Mother's Day. I was really caught up in a bunch of stuff, really good stuff. I'll explain it when I see you next week. I'll stay over for a few days. I think you'll be proud of me. Oh, and I'm moving back to Toronto so we'll be close. I've taken an offer to work with a physics prof to complete my thesis."

"Whoa. Slow down. You're going a mile a minute. Let's start with the part about moving back to Toronto. Who's this professor and which university? U of T?"

"Yes, U of T. I'll explain about the professor when I explain what I've been up to. It's all part of the same thing."

"Well hearing that you're moving back to Toronto is the best Mother's Day present any mom could ask for. And don't apologize for missing Mother's Day. I know I have no one to blame but myself. I pretty well trained you to be a social activist like me from day one. I do have one personal question for you. If you come back to Toronto, what about that boy you liked, Morris?"

Jazzy took a deep breath and replied, "That's something he and I are going to have to discuss. Got to go. Bye, love you."

Jazzy ended the connection and waited to gather her thoughts for her third call.

She hit 'M' on the speed dial. The call was answered before the end of the first ring.

"Hi Mo."

"Jazzy! Where are you? Where have you been?"

"We've been cooped up as a group for months. I just needed a few days by myself to clean up some stuff and make a few arrangements, resume a normal life again."

"You're quitting the group?"

"Of course not. After all we've been through, I don't think any of us will ever 'quit the group,' especially now that we're the keepers of the Gini Foundation. It's just that we all don't have to be together all of the time. We don't have to live together, to work together, to fight for social justice together. We now have the means to lead normal lives while we keep doing the social justice thing."

"Not living together as a group or not living together, as in, you and me?"

"That's not what I mean. Look, I've accepted an offer from Dr. Plank for him to supervise my PhD thesis. I'm moving back to Toronto. We need to discuss things. Let's not do this over the phone. We need to talk face-to-face but I still need more time to complete everything I'm doing. Can we get together, just the two of us in a week and discuss things?"

"Sure, just name the time and place."
"Good. I'll call to let you know."
Click
Good? Or really, really bad, thought Mo.

—

41

THE INMATE

A WEEK LATER, at the Toronto Central Detention Centre, two guards escorted inmate No. 21223-9677 down the long corridor through a series of four steel doors that opened en route to the visitor's room. One of the guards directed the strikingly tall, gaunt prisoner to a table where he came face-to-face with FBI Assistant Director Jimmy DeRoach.

"We've got all the paperwork for the Commissioner of Correction's Order cleared with both of our governments. If you agree, as you have indicated you would, you will be released into the custody of the FBI, specifically into my custody. The order says we are obtaining your temporary release for compassionate reasons, to perform a community service, and for rehabilitative purposes."

The FBI emissary withdrew a series of documents and slid one marked 'Agenda' in front of the prisoner. "We will travel to Quantico, Virginia and, for a period of four days, you will work with three specific subjects."

He shuffled the papers again and pushed a second sheet of paper marked 'Necessities' toward the man.

"All of your necessities, including your special dietary needs, have been arranged. If there's something you need that's not on the list, let me know now."

DeRoach waited for the inmate to look at the sheet and then gathered the remaining papers and placed them in reading position before him.

"Once you have completed your mission, I will return you to this facility. The only thing you will receive in return is an acknowledgement of the help you have provided to the FBI and the recommendation from us and CSIS that this be a consideration during your trial for second degree murder and, if you are convicted, consideration prior to sentencing. It's all in this document. If you accept all of these conditions, please sign here."

He flipped to the final page and pointed to a line at the bottom. "We will be able to leave within the hour."

DeRoach slid a pen to the prisoner, whose penetrating yellow eyes quickly scanned the document. With grand looping flourishes, he signed his name, Dragul Mangorian.

...

The inmate, Dragul Mangorian, was at the centre of the sensational vampire hunt and arrest by Toronto police seven months earlier. The 6-feet, 6 being with the paper-white skin, three-inch fangs, and who feeds on human blood, was depicted in screaming headlines around the world as a 'real vampire.'

Mangorian is charged with the second-degree murder in the death of his lawyer, Al Hamblyn. If convicted, he could receive a life sentence, which considering his long life expectancy, could be more than 100 years. He is also charged with assault causing bodily harm to nine persons, who he admitted in a police statement that he fed on.

Pre-trial statements and filings from the Crown Attorney and the defence reveal that Mangorian is not a typical human being. Both sides agree that the accused is believed to be the sole surviving member of a sub-species of Homo Sapiens, which Mangorian explained translates into human languages roughly as Homo Sanguinus. The name comes from the Sanguinus' need to consume blood to sustain themselves with human blood being the meal of choice.

Gregory Mazpera, the lawyer who inherited the case after the death of his predecessor, submitted in his statement of defence that Mangorian's intent in all nine assaults was to take blood, but not enough to cause permanent injury to his victims.

Hamblyn died because Mangorian, himself, was dying from internal bleeding and blood loss, the result of a severe beating by police after he was rendered unconscious during his capture, the defence statement alleges.

"I was shackled, hand, foot and neck and I was dying. I asked for blood. I told them I needed blood or I would die, but the police just laughed," according to a statement by Mangorian that was submitted into evidence.

"When my lawyer arrived, I could not control myself. It was a matter of survival. When I had the opportunity and Hamblyn expressed his wish to die, instinct took over and I drained him to the last drop, an act I profoundly regret and which will haunt me forever."

Mazpera also submitted statements from three of the alleged assault victims who thanked Mangorian for taking their blood and, in the process, linked minds with them. Through the mind link, Mangorian had the ability to relieve two of severe mental illness and the third of a 10-year-battle against drug addiction.

Since the day of his capture, the story generated headlines around the world. It was that ability, to link with a victim's mind, ending addictions and dispelling mental demons that the Ginis pinpointed as holding promise for the ESP team members.

...

Over the course of the four days, Mangorian spent time with Seiji, Reyanna and Rebecca.

He took their blood and spent hours with each of them transferring positive images into their minds to help them through their mental anguish and addictions. At the end of the fourth day, Rebecca walked into DeRoach's office and declared herself fit to work.

"I think Seiji is almost back to where he was 10 years ago and Reyanna is no worse than when she first arrived."

"But you are not cured," DeRoach said.

"Menck's therapies changed our cellular makeup. That's beyond Mangorian's abilities to reverse. It's just that we aren't in constant pain and the mental urge is gone. There are still physical pangs that, in time, I believe we will overcome. In the meantime, I'd like to get back to work," she said.

"It's not my call. You betrayed us at the most basic level. And, as you indicated, you are not cured."

Rebecca Jordan had been an FBI agent her entire life as an adult. While not unexpected, DeRoach's words hit her like a kick to the stomach.

"I understand, Jim. I'll get my things and be gone before the end of the day."

"Rebecca, no need to rush things. I'm taking Mangorian back to Canada tomorrow. I want you to stay here until I return. I'll take your case upstairs. They recognize that you're an incredibly valuable asset. If we're creative, I'm sure we can work something out."

DeRoach returned Mangorian to the Toronto Central Detention Centre the next day.

"I want to thank you, both as an FBI agent and as a human being. Rebecca, Seiji, and Reyanna are my friends and with your help, they now have a fighting chance. Are you going to be all right here?"

"Yes, yes of course."

Those fearsome yellow eyes colour-shifted toward a friendlier fireplace orange, making a mash of DeRoach's emotions.

"I feel quite at home here. Before my arrest I lived in Toronto's sewers for 10 years. Now I have a bed. I receive blood rations every day."

"Will you be safe?"

Any warmth DeRoach had switched off as Mangorian broke into a deep, creepy laugh.

"Safe? Absolutely. The inmates respect me and many treat me as their leader. It seems silly to me but deadly serious to them because they want protection from the more violent elements in prison.

"A few want to join my circle because of their mistaken belief that I have the power to transform them into powerful, immortal beings, which is a stupid myth based on wholly laughable vampire novels and movies.

"To curry my favour or to find peace within themselves, many inmates have volunteered to donate their blood to me, which makes my life in prison almost pleasurable. Of course, this is strictly against prison policy but the prison superintendent and guards have turned a blind eye to it. Privately, they admit that my feeding has had a significant calming effect on the prison population."

The calm recitation shook DeRoach and got his mind churning.

I can't begin to understand the weirdness of this. All I know is he helped me and I'm in his debt.

DeRoach extended his hand and Mangorian took it and gave it the awkward shake of someone who had never done it before. The hand was cold with the texture of snakeskin.

"I don't know what your full story is, why you killed your lawyer. I do know you did a good thing this week. You saved the lives of three very special people. You ever need anything that's within my power to give, just get a message to me. I will come day or night."

"My pleasure entirely," Mangorian said.

—

42

ALL THAT'S JAZZ

GLOBE & MAIL, Report on Business, Monday, May 19, 2014.

Former billionaire E.V. Hendry dead, at 61

E.V. 'Big Ed' Hendry, formerly one of the world's richest men, is dead of an apparent suicide. It appears he took his own life after he lost his multi-billion dollar business empire. Hendry's death follows a bizarre series of trades that cost him all of his vast fortune. Analysts are unable to explain why Hendry had relied so much on rumours that there had been a breakthrough in negative gravity, which, if true, would have rendered his oil and gas shares worthless. His ill-advised sell-off had a swaying effect on all shares in the oil & gas industry. It's believed that more than $1.3 trillion in value was transferred from major oil and gas business holdings to pension funds and third world investment funds.

In a related story, police found a 14-year-old girl alive and well in the offices of EExE Holdings, where Mr. Hendry's body was found inside of his personal office. The girl, who isn't being identified because she is a minor, had been abducted earlier in the day.

Witnesses reported seeing a man about 6-feet, 2 inches tall with curly brown hair and a moustache in a blue velveteen suit driving away with the girl in a white cargo van.

Police have issued a warrant for the arrest of Val "Frenchie" Greene.

Former business associates of Mr. Hendry told The News . . .

A hard knocking on her hotel room door interrupted Jasmine's reading of the Internet news clip.

"Hey Jazzy, it's me, Mo."

She walked to the door, opened it and held it while an apprehensive Morris Hatcher shuffled in.

"Have a seat," she said, motioning to the only chair in the room.

Mo looked at Jazzy with a condemned man's eyes and then at the lonely chair. He realized this was it. The only woman he had ever loved was going to tell him he had no chance, that it was over before it began. He tried to find some inner toughness. If he had the remotest chance of salvaging this car wreck of a relationship, he wouldn't do it by falling apart and begging her on bended knee, tears streaming to give him a chance.

He remembered back to the first time they had met – virtually – in an online discussion.

Some Tea Party dolt was ragging on about being a Libertarian, a self-sufficient soul unlike the lazy 99% who live off the genius and hard work of the rich.

"Do you have a flush toilet? Do you get garbage pickup? Do you get police protection?" asked Jazzy. "Self-sufficient my ass. You so-called Libertarians are self-serving, self-righteous, selfish S.O.B.s who take, take, take and then whine about anyone else who gets government service. There's only one group of true Libertarians I know of. They call themselves Amish."

"Wow girl. Very impressed. You should run for President."

"Can't. I'm Canadian."

"Then run for President of Canada."

"Sheesch, you Americans have to learn something about the world beyond your borders."

"I'm very open to you teaching me."

They exchanged contact information and maintained an email relationship, which progressed into Skype video calls. When he first saw Jazzy on Skype, her beauty shocked him.

Beautiful, incredibly smart, and she has the same worldview as me, he thought.

Mo pressed for a face-to-face meeting but Jazzy appeared reluctant.

"Look I'm not a stalker or anything. We've been talking for almost a year. You ought to know me by now."

In the first week of September, 2011 fellow activist and film-maker Delroy DeSoto prepared for a trip to Toronto for the premier of Land Of Destiny, a documentary film about a town torn between high cancer rates among workers and the likely shutdown of industry. Mo offered to share the driving and the gas.

Jazzy left her studies at Western University and made the two-hour drive to Toronto. She and Mo stayed at her mother's house but in separate rooms for the three days.

Every moment with Jazzy felt wondrous. Their thoughts, their moods, their ideas synched better in person than long-distance. And she was so incredibly beautiful. Mo ached for more. Intimacy, however, remained elusive despite his every effort to move it in that direction.

Jazzy's over-the-top, social-activist mom liked Mo. She even appeared to encourage the relationship. Whenever they started to click as a couple, it triggered something else in Jazzy. She'd insist her mother or DD join them.

By the time their Toronto liaison ended, their relationship's direction appeared as straight forward as a pinball's trajectory. Mo felt like a player in that kids' game, Red Light / Green Light. Soon as he sensed a positive signal and made a move, on flashed the red light. Jazzy changed the subject or manipulated someone to chaperone.

The following week, Jason Sage pressed his friends to gather at Zuccotti Park with the Occupy Movement.

"You've inspired me to put school on hold and join Toronto's Occupy Movement," Jazzy said in a Skype call.

"Come to New York, Wall Street. That's where we'll have the most impact. It's the financial capital of the world."

Jazzy agreed. In Chicago, Mo's hopes soared.

Finally, finally my green light.

Almost three years later, Mo still waited for the light to turn green but in his heart he feared it was about to turn permanently red.

"What's up?" He rubbed at an eye that nerves set a twitching.

"I wanted to give you something." She walked up to him and leaned over his chair as close to him as they had ever been. She stared into his eyes as long seconds ticked. Mo's hands grew thick with sweat.

"Sure, what is it?"

"This," Jazzy said, placing her arms around his neck and kissing him deeply.

Astonished but not about to object, Mo rose from his chair and responded in kind.

After about a minute, Jazzy said, "Mo, I've loved you for years, just as you've loved me but it couldn't be, not with you, not with anyone."

"What's changed?"

"Everything. Absolutely everything. First you need to know some things about me."

And then she told her story.

It started with the pendulum of politics in Sumatra swinging between life and death with religion, politics, the military, activists and labour groups all vying for power. The family fled during the night, undertaking a harrowing voyage that eventually brought them to the United States.

Her father, a physician in Sumatra, drove a taxi in Chicago, but he didn't complain. The Iriantos had planted roots and were beginning a bright, new life. That all came to a terrifying end when a drunk driver smashed into the family car, killing her parents, her two sisters and leaving her with both physical and mental injuries that caused her to withdraw deeply into herself.

The small and poor Sumatran community had few resources to take in a child with such horrific problems. She ended up in foster care with a couple who were uncaring and abusive.

She fled, and fell into the company of unsavoury characters who further abused her mentally and physically. That's when the gods finally smiled upon her and brought her to the woman who would become her loving foster mother.

"There's more, much more to tell but that's enough for now."

With that, Jazzy slowly untied her robe, letting it fall to the ground. She had nothing underneath.

"I wanted you to see me, all of me. If you still want me, I am yours."

Mo's eyes drank her in, all of her. Happy, sweet, miraculous emotions performed pirouettes in his mind and body. He felt so light he could fly.

He caressed her, touched her raven hair, stroked her exquisite high cheek bones and then ran a hand down her neck to two firm, rounded breasts that were perfect in every respect except for three half-inch wide, ragged rivulets of flesh that tracked from just below the collarbone across her breasts and ran down to her belly.

Mo touched each scar lovingly, tenderly and then lowered his neck and kissed each one from top to bottom.

"You are incredible in every way. I love you Jazzy. I love everything about you."

...

To Jazzy, it was a foregone conclusion that Big Ed would double-cross Cleopatra. She counted on it. Big Ed never suspected Cleopatra might double-cross him. He was so obsessed with money that he could never conceive of the idea that money would not, could not be the sole motivation for everyone else.

The $10 million placed in her numbered account in the Bahamas and invested by Big Ed in EExE shares had swelled to more than $14 million when prices rebounded. She anonymously donated $5 million to her Chicago friends to direct and another $5 million to the University of Toronto as the incentive to rehire Dr. Plank.

Her third anonymous donation, $1 million, went to the Parkdale Community Law Clinic, the not-for-profit organization that her mother, Sally Wiseman, ran. Perhaps her mother would take life easier and hire some help.

Fat chance.

Jazzy smiled at the thought. Sally would take the money, hire some law students and possibly a young lawyer or two, but take it easy? No way, she'll just up the caseload.

That left $3 million, well $2.5 million, after she and Mo throw a huge outdoor wedding and barbeque with an open invitation to Parkdale's homeless to attend, have a memorable honeymoon – ugh – wedding vacation and put a down payment on a modest home in Toronto's over-hot real estate market. And then? A family and a house full of kids, all raised to become social activists.

There was one other thing to check on. Through Sage and Nathan, she provided details to DeRoach about the remarkable powers of Dragul Mangorian to penetrate the mysterious mechanism that is the mind.

Jazzy knew of Mangorian because he helped her those many years ago. She was deep within a shell after Big Ed disfigured her. She had fled from danger but the greatest threat came from herself. Strange how one can fear death at the hand of another and then carry out the same sentence by your own hand. That was to be her fate.

She spent her first night in Toronto under what she now knows as the Bloor-Danforth Viaduct half-cowering in fear and half-contemplating climbing to street level and hurtling her body onto the highway a hundred feet below.

A wraith, who she later learned was Dragul Mangorian, emerged from the mists. He spoke calming words and touched her cheek.

Her memory of that strange encounter faded until recent events. Newspaper reports of Mangorian's arrest and interviews with his victims triggered flashbacks. She remembered him tenderly coaxing his fangs into her neck. He took a little blood from her. In return, he sucked out her demons. She considered it more than a fair trade.

When she learned of Mangorian's arrest, it did not surprise her that three of the so-called victims thanked him in their statements. She suspected that most or all of those he supposedly assaulted would give similar testimony at the trial. After all, it was no small feat bringing order to the chaotic day-time nightmares that trapped her within her own mind.

On the murder charge, she had mixed feelings. Al Hamblyn was very close to her mother. In fact, Jazzy called him Uncle Al and his former wife was her Aunt Rosalie.

—

43

AN OLD ACQUAINTANCE

BACK AT QUANTICO, Assistant Director Jimmy DeRoach fingered the small slip of paper.

He paid an extra $100 for the scrawling on that 2-inch by 2-inch sticky note but had serious, and sensible, misgivings about trying the number.

Leave well enough alone. Nothing's to be gained . . . nothing?

DeRoach had no regrets, check that, less than no regrets passing a bullet through Menck's brain.

He and Belle had never been able to have kids. When he came to the program and especially after Belle's death from an aneurysm eight years ago, he regarded Seiji, Kirk, and Rebecca as the children he never had. It was his responsibility to look after them. He would die for them.

When Miranda and Felipe Cortez reached out for help, DeRoach met with them. He gave his word he would care for Reyanna as they would. He repeated that promise in each of their monthly calls.

It gnawed at him that in recent years many of his assurances were sugar-coated or out right lies. Today, his conscience ran with a greater lightness. It might soar if he had more answers.

He looked at the paper again.

Area code 202 is Washington D.C. The rest of the numbers looked fictitious.. The movie industry uses that kind of make-believe number when an on-screen friend dials 10 digits to reach Rachel McAdams or Taylor Kitsch.

In Hollywood's bygone days, random but real numbers resulted in brainless fans and pranksters interrupting the quiet evening of middleclass families with giggled demands to speak to the film star.

DeRoach leafed through a variety of government directories. No agency listing had anything that remotely resembled the number.

A month passed. No police reports about Menck's death circulated. No fingers pointed at him. He thought it extraordinary to exist in this nothing-out-of-the-ordinary state.

He forced himself to get his mind back on the job.

Rebecca received a two-month suspension with restricted duties thereafter until DeRoach decided otherwise. He'd have to get started on the paperwork.

Reyanna and Seiji rebounded well. Neither had a seizure or physical sickness in weeks. Headaches, while still a byproduct when they used their powers, tended to be less severe and lasted no more than a day.

The FBI man never found much fun in writing reports but this one just might bring a smile to his face and to Deputy Director Garcia.

DeRoach gave a happy sigh as he looked at his calendar. He had a scheduled call to Reyanna's parents tomorrow.

Life, more or less, was back to normal. He could keep sailing forward straight on to retirement. He didn't need to tempt fate, poke around where he didn't need to. He went to toss the slip of paper into the trash but what was the point? That number – 202 555-1111 ext. 1111 – was burned into his brain.

Curiosity clawed at him.

More than that, DeRoach never liked leaving loose ends. The people who removed Menck's body have an agenda. That agenda may yet threaten his kids.

What the hell, it's just a number.

The veteran FBI man gave in. If it backfired, all repercussions affected only him. No Belle, no children to share his shame.

If drummed from the FBI without a pension, he'd be okay. His savings would cover his few needs. If he were imprisoned, physically he could take care of himself as long as it mattered. Most of all, he could accept his fate – going from honoured FBI agent to inmate – because he did the right thing.

But he wasn't an idiot. He'd take precautions. He bought an anonymous burner phone and borrowed a friend's private vehicle to drive outside of DC to make the call. He stopped in a restaurant parking lot in Laurel, Maryland.

His finger hit the 2 and then a 0 and then another 2.

He paused, sucked in air, held it, and commanded his index to punch 555. He moved his finger over the 1 and hit the key four times.

"If you know the extension of the person you are calling, please dial it now."

The automated voice came on without the line ringing.

DeRoach raised his eyebrows. He had convinced himself the number wasn't real. He blew out his breath, long and steady. He considered not continuing.

The line remained silent. There was no repetition of the message, no added information, and no familiar query: "Are you still there?"

A second gulp of air filled his lungs as his finger stabbed at the final four digits, 1111.

This time he heard the phone ring.

Bzzzz bzzzz bzzzz

The line picked up.

He heard a male voice speak in a strange and annoying pattern.

"Hello Assistant Director DeRoach-oach. What took you so long to call-all?"

—

44

HOME AGAIN

DURING NATHAN AND BONNIE's absence, their bookkeeper Mrs. Cruz left the fan mail and invitations in pile 'B' and financial and legal papers demanding a signature in the 'A' pile.

For three weeks Bonnie pounded through the documents, fired off tweets, posted Nate The Nose news on Instagram and answered inane and occasionally obscene fan questions:

"If Nate was on death row. What would he order as a last meal?"

Depends who's doing the cooking.

"What smells better, a Mars bar or Three Musketeers?"

The Mars bar. Definitely the Mars bar.

"Can I smell if a girl's horny for me?"

That one went into the circular no-response bin.

The more interesting duties demanded the presence of Nathan and his nose. Let's Eat, dispatched him on a three-week European promotional tour, which included dinners with minor royalty and film stars.

"Wish you were in Europe, too?" asked Mrs. Cruz.

"Not really. I'd be returning to a pile of work. Now it's done."

Nathan sent a text to Bonnie to expect him on June 5. Let's Eat's private jet will land at Billy Bishop Airport. He'll take a cab from there.

As Nathan approached his office's Bloor West address, he detected a familiar musk. Warmth, comfort, and happiness washed over him. He examined his reflection in the elevator door's silver finish and practiced reducing the stupid smile on his face by a degree or two before summoning the lift.

When he opened his office door, he realized there was no point trying to hold back. Bonnie looked and smelled spectacular. She wore a similar grin that threatened to erupt into laughter, joyous crying, a scream, something.

They embraced. It was warmer and longer than the usual hug between best friends.

"How was Paris, Rome . . ."

"The usual – great food, great wine and over-stuffed personalities. But I want to talk about our fun before that."

"I don't think we can call that fun but it sure was . . . uh, interesting."

Nathan looked deeply into Bonnie's eyes.

"I'm proud of you, proud of what we accomplished. It was the best thing we've ever done. Maybe the best thing I'll ever do. We did it together – as always."

And, we made some great friends." Bonnie was exultant, gripping Nathan's hands tightly and hoping for him to up the response. She smiled and waited for him to make the next move.

"It was you – your sense of justice that made it happen," said Nathan. "I'm not sure what I would have done if I were left to puzzle it out on my own. Sometimes I feel co-opted by the money and the fame. I don't always think straight. You are my conscience."

Hmmm, conscience – a promotion from sidekick and business partner but . . .

She leaned in, hoping for him to up his response physically but he didn't move. Something else was on his mind.

"Do you think what I'm doing, this celebrity food thing is wrong?"

"Wrong?"

"Yeah. All that stock market stuff, the social media, that crazy Dr. Menck. It was all about excesses. More money, more power, more beauty, immortality. For what purpose? It's all about greed and narcissism."

"And so?"

"Isn't that what I'm promoting? It's no longer good enough to have a burger, fries and a beer. I'm helping food become an obsession. People have to make more money to buy that prime cut, import cheeses from around the world, and spend more than some people in the Third World make in a year on a single bottle of wine. Isn't this all insanity?"

Bonnie gave him a motherly hug then looked him in the eye.

"Yes and no. The great thing about food and wine is, there are limits. No one can eat more than they can eat and, alcoholics aside, drink more than they can drink. You are promoting a quality of life that may be excessive to some but has its limits."

"With all the flooding, hurricanes, tornadoes, droughts that have been happening, how can people not see our excesses are killing the planet? Sometimes I feel our cause is hopeless," he said.

"Not hopeless, just screwed up. The majority doesn't see the answer yet. People like the Ginis are opening people's eyes."

"But not before things start to get really ugly between the rich and the poor."

Bonnie made fists and banged them against her head. "You are a ray of sunshine. To think I figured I'd be happy to see you."

"And I wanted to celebrate being back with you."

"Remind me never to leave you in charge of the celebrations."

"It's a deal."

"Then let's start now. You owe me a dinner – one you make yourself. And use that super nose of yours for a spectacular wine pairing."

"Okay, I'll head to St. Lawrence Market for the ingredients. What are you thinking? Seafood? Vegetarian? Asian? French? Italian?"

"As long as it's not Star Trek replicator grub, you can surprise me."

"I just need to grab my tricorder – er – iPad for some ideas. Crap. It's still packed away. Bonnie, let me borrow yours."

Nathan began a search on the iPad.

"I'll go to . . . Oh, Bonnie you have an email. It's a Jib Jab card. I love them. Mind if I open it?"

"Knock yourself out."

The Flash animated card opened and showed a group of dancing pixies singing Happy Birthday to Bonnie with the cut-out face of the same man duplicated on the shoulders of each member of the elfin quintet. The dance ends with the puckish dancers holding a banner that said:

Happy Birthday

love John.

"It's your birthday?"

"Same day every year."

"I'm really sorry. I forgot. But who's this John guy?"

"Oh, he was my district editor when I worked for the Peterborough Daily Express."

"But that was almost five years ago."

"Is there an expiry date for friendship?"

"No, I mean, that's a long time to wait to send you a birthday card."

"He sends me a birthday card every year and we try to go out for drinks on my birthday and his."

"Why?" Nathan nervously blurted out what he intended to say only in his head.

"Because people send each other birthday cards and they go out on birthdays. It's sort of a tradition among us non-super powered folks."

"I meant to ask if you were close."

"Close? How close could I be to anyone? I'm working with you around the clock, seven days a week. That's not counting when we're not locked up seven stories below FBI headquarters. When do I have time for a boyfriend?"

"He's – he's your boyfriend?"

"BHRRR . . . MMRRTTH." Bonnie gave an unintelligible curse in exasperation.

How is it possible that someone as smart and perceptive as Nathan could be so dense.

"No, not a boyfriend just a boy who's a friend."

Everything had seemed so clear as Bonnie waited for Nathan's return. He had given her plenty of signals that their relationship might be moving to the next level.

Then he becomes this complete dumbass. Do I really need to get involved with a guy who just doesn't get it? Will I have to do all the lifting forever?

Bonnie fell silent. She figured whatever came out wouldn't help.

Nathan looked at her – finally getting a clearer signal either though his nose or the fog in his brain that he had done something wrong.

"I just want . . ."

Knock. Knock. Knock.

The two looked to the door.

"Come in," said Bonnie.

The door remained closed but the edge of an ivory-coloured envelope poked from under it.

Nathan opened the door. No one was there. He bent for the envelope and gave it a sniff on the way up.

"Curious!" Nathan said with emphasis and a nose scrunch as he tore the note open.

Nathan's over-reaction amused Bonnie. "Who sent it? What's it say?"

"Really weird. All it says is: 'The game's afoot. Prof. Jim Moriarty'."

"Sounds like a job for Sherlock Holmes. He must have the Sherlocks on his Rolodex mixed up. Give it a sniff and we'll know which joker really sent it."

"That's what I meant when I said curious!"

"What do you mean?"

"It has no scent."

"Perhaps this Prof. Moriarty wore gloves."

"No, I mean there's no scent. I can't smell the paper, the glue on the envelope or even the ink on the paper. There's absolutely no scent at all."

– END –

SOME OF NATHAN'S FAVOURITE RECIPES

COURTESY JILL WILCOX

Holubtsi
(Ukrainian Cabbage Rolls)

A traditional dish of cabbage leaves stuffed with a savoury mixture of beef, pork and rice. Bake in the oven with tomato sauce and dill. Serve with sour cream and a garnish of fresh chopped dill. (Serves 8-10)

Ingredients
1 large cooking onion, diced
2-4 cloves garlic, minced
3/4 lb. lean ground beef
1/2 lb. ground pork
2 c. diced mushrooms
1-1/4 c. long grain rice
1 tbsp. paprika
salt and pepper to taste
1 large green cabbage
8c. tomato juice or tomato puree

Directions

1. Remove the core from the cabbage and immerse head in boiling water long enough to wilt leaves (about 5 minutes). Remove from water and drain.
2. Remove large leaves and cut out large vein from the centre of each leaf with a triangular cut.
3. Place about 1/2 c. (125 ml) meat mixture on each cabbage leaf.
4. Start to roll up the cabbage leaf, tucking in the sides half way up.
5. Repeat procedure until all meat mixture is used. Set rolls aside.
6. Removing any remaining core from the cabbage. Chop the remainder of the cabbage. Place on the bottom of a large roasting pan.
7. Place cabbage rolls on top.
8. Sprinkle fresh dill over the top. Pour tomato juice to completely cover the cabbage rolls. Season with salt and pepper and some additional paprika. Cover with foil.
9. Cook in a preheated 350 F. oven for 2-1/2 to 3 hours.
10. Serve with sour cream. Garnished with fresh dill.
    Wine suggestions – Christie Pollard, Sommelier in training
    Pair the cabbage rolls with a dry German Riesling or a German wheat beer (both classic pairings with this dish).

Another option would be a New Zealand Sauvignon Blanc from the Marlborough region (the grassy notes in the wine should match well with all that dill).

Spanish Chicken with Green Beans
(Serves 2)

Ingredients
2 bone-in, skin on chicken breasts
1 tbsp. (15 ml) olive oil
2 tsp. (10 ml) smoked paprika
1 small Spanish onion, peeled and sliced thinly
1 tbsp. (15 ml) tomato paste
3/4 lb. (500 g) green beans
1 /2 cup chicken stock
*1 tsp. (10 ml) sherry vinegar
2 tbsp. (25ml) slivered almonds
1 tbsp. (15 ml) chopped parsley

Directions
1. Heat oven to 425F. (205C)
2. Season chicken with salt and pepper.
3. Heat olive oil in a skillet over medium high heat. Cook the chicken skin-side down until well browned.
4. Turn chicken over and sprinkle with half of the paprika. Transfer to a small baking dish and bake in the oven for 20-25 minutes or until the juices run clear when pierced with a fork. Remove from oven and tent with foil.
5. While the chicken is cooking, add onions to the skillet and cook until soft. Stir in tomato paste and remaining paprika cook until incorporated. Add beans and broth. Cover and cook until green beans are bright green and just barely tender. Remove lid and simmer until slightly reduced. Stir in the sherry vinegar.
6. Place the chicken on a plate and spoon green beans and sauce over top.
7. Garnish with the almonds and parsley.

ABOUT THE AUTHOR
JOHN MATSUI

John Matsui lives in London, Ontario with his wife and love of his life, Judy. He invites all comments from readers and invites you to post a comment at www.johnmatsui.com.

Gravity Games is John Matsui's second novel. His first is a horror / courtroom thriller titled *Late Bite* that introduces Dragul Mangorian, a vampire who goes on trial.

Mangorian appears in *Gravity Games*.

The sequel to *Late Bite*, *Lycanthrope Rising*, will be available in the spring of 2016.

ABOUT JILL WILCOX
FOOD DESCRIPTIONS AND RECIPE
CONTRIBUTOR

Jill Wilcox is a food writer and food entrepreneur. She is the owner of Jill's Table in London, Ontario, which promotes itself as A Feast of Kitchen Essentials. Jill is a food writer for the London Free Press and has published two cookbooks, Jill's Essentials Cookbook and Jill's Starters Cookbook.

Jill conducts culinary tours to the Languedoc-Roussillon region of France. The history, markets and food keep her returning year after year. Check http://www.jillstable.ca/travel for upcoming tours. For more information visit Maison Beaufort Tours.

Try some of Jill's favourite recipes by visiting:

http://www.jillstable.ca/learn/recipes/